THE
BAKER STREET
LETTERS

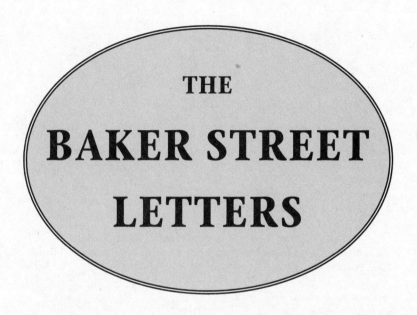

THE
BAKER STREET
LETTERS

MICHAEL ROBERTSON

Minotaur Books

A Thomas Dunne Book
New York

M ROBERTSON

This is a work of fiction. All of the characters, organizations, and events portrayed in this novel are either products of the author's imagination or are used fictitiously.

A THOMAS DUNNE BOOK FOR MINORAUR BOOKS.
An imprint of St. Martin's Publishing Group.

www.thomasdunnebooks.com
www.minotaurbooks.com

The Library of Congress has cataloged the following hardcover edition as follows:

Robertson, Michael, 1951–
    The Baker Street letters / Michael Robertson.—1st ed.
        p. cm.
    "A Thomas Dunne book for Minotaur Books"—T.p. verso.
    ISBN 978-0-312-53812-5
    1. Brothers—Fiction. 2. Letter writing—Fiction. 3. Holmes, Sherlock (Fictitious character)—Fiction. 4. London (England)—Fiction. 5. Los Angeles (Calif.)—Fiction. I. Title.
  PS3618.O31726B35 2009
  813'.6—dc22

                                                                2008045668

ISBN 978-0-312-65064-3

10   9   8   7   6   5   4   3

ACKNOWLEDGMENTS

For the publication of this book, I'm grateful to my editor, Marcia Markland, and my literary agent, Rebecca Oliver, and to the Maui Writers Conference, which introduced me to them both.

My thanks also to Diana Szu, Elizabeth Curione, Sona Vogel, Elizabeth Catalano, and David Rotstein at Thomas Dunne Books/St. Martin's Press, and to Richie Kern (for representing the television rights) and Laura Bonner (for the audio) at the Endeavor Agency.

And thank you, Barbara and Michele.

THE
BAKER STREET
LETTERS

PROLOGUE

Los Angeles, 1997

He only wanted just one cigarette.

He knew he shouldn't, and not just because both of his ex-wives used to say so or because his doctor still said so.

He knew he shouldn't because the company rules for sandhogs on the new subway dig said so.

But the rules hadn't been pulling twelve-hour shifts.

And the hot permits for acetylene torches had already been granted, so he knew there wasn't any flammable gas.

And he really only needed just one.

So he moved farther into the tunnel, beyond the shining fresh concrete, away from the flammable plastic liners, and out of sight of the foreman. He sat on a muck hauler to take his break, and he took out just one cigarette and put it between his lips.

And then he lit a match.

1

London, six weeks later

Why are you staring at me that way?"

Laura hardly looked up from her dinner to ask this. She arched one eyebrow over one olive green eye.

"Your hair," lied Reggie, "is in your champagne."

She laughed, and Reggie hoped it was because she remembered a September picnic in Kensington Gardens, when her red hair had indeed been in the champagne, and pretty much everywhere else.

He wanted her to think of that, because tonight, with moonlight streaming into his Butler's Wharf penthouse, he was beginning to fear that she did not intend to let it down at all.

Nor had she the week before. And so Reggie had begun to stare.

But now there was a noise from the kitchen, and Mrs. Hampstead—who should have been getting ready to bring out Blackwell tarts—brought the phone instead.

"It's your brother," she said.

"I'll return it in the morning."

"Your brother!" Mrs. Hampstead said emphatically, thrusting the phone again between Reggie and Laura. "He says it is urgent."

"Tell him I'll call him back," repeated Reggie. "In the morning."

"Suit yourself. Just as though he's not the only brother you've got."

Mrs. Hampstead had an uncanny knack for spouting phrases that Reggie used to hear from his mother.

"Quite right, Mrs. Hampstead," said Laura. "Reggie, there's no use in being stubborn."

Reggie looked across and tried to read Laura's expression, but she did not meet his gaze.

He accepted the phone and spoke brusquely.

"What is it, Nigel?"

"I can't explain it over the phone," said Nigel. "You'll have to see it for yourself."

The concern in his younger brother's voice was evident, but to Reggie that was not proof of a crisis. At thirty-three, Nigel was just two years younger than Reggie—but the brothers did not always rate the crises of life on the same scale.

"I'm sure it can wait—," began Reggie.

Laura looked up from her plate. "It's all right," she said, and she glanced at her watch as she said it. "I should be going anyway."

Reggie tried quickly to see her eyes, but she looked away again.

"I'll be along shortly," he said, annoyed, into the phone.

Laura gathered a cream-colored wrap around bare, freckled shoulders, and they took the exterior lift down from the penthouse.

They walked from the shining metal-and-glass lift onto the wharf and then got in Reggie's XJS.

For a long moment, as they drove along the Embankment, with the damp air and river scents being stirred up by a light rain, neither of them spoke.

Then Laura said, "You shouldn't be so sharp with your brother."

"Was I sharp?"

"Yes. And he only got out a month ago."

"I'm aware of that," said Reggie, and he was, though he was tired of having to think about it. "My mind was on something else," he said.

"I'm tired tonight anyway," Laura replied, and then added, "I'm sure it will be late when you're through."

Reggie thought she said this as though she were relying on it. This was worrisome. He said, "I was just beginning to think I'd found him a position he couldn't bollix up. And this was only because his predecessor came back from holiday in America and stepped in front of a double-decker. You can't count on breaks like that for all your positions." Reggie realized he was speaking sharply again, and he fell silent.

"The poor man," said Laura, and Reggie, to his astonishment, realized that he was becoming jealous now even of her sympathy. Sympathy for a stranger, for that matter. For a dead stranger, in fact.

"Must have forgotten which way the traffic moves," added Laura.

"Mashed like a potato," Reggie said tightly.

He turned right onto a narrow Chelsea street and then into the drive for Laura's ivy-covered brick mews.

They walked on damp flagstones through the front courtyard. Then Laura stood in the doorway, kissed Reggie once lightly, and said good night. He wondered just what alternative plans she might have for the remainder of the evening—but he managed not to ask.

He got in his car and drove around the eastern perimeter of Hyde Park toward Marylebone. He continued almost to Regents Park and then turned south onto Baker Street.

He drove half a block and then parked. He was now at Dorset House—a structure that headquartered the Dorset National Building Society and that made up the entire Two Hundred block of Baker Street.

It was late as Reggie entered the building, and the lobby was deserted except for a security guard, who nodded as Reggie passed by.

Reggie crossed to the lifts, his footsteps echoing on the marble floor.

He had just recently leased the next floor above for his new law chambers. The location was uncommonly far from the Inns of Court—few barristers in London had chambers beyond easy walking distance of the Inns and their clubbiness—but Reggie was willing to break that convention. And the lease from Dorset National was at a very decent bargain. Such a good deal, in fact, that at first he had been suspicious—but he was beginning to accept it now as just good fortune.

He took the lift up one floor and stepped out—almost knocking down Ms. Brinks, who was trying to step in.

"Oh," she said. "So sorry, I wasn't expecting—"

"I wasn't either," said Reggie. "Just on your way out?"

"Yes," she said. "But since you're here . . ."

"Yes?"

Reggie waited as his very efficient secretary—she had many years on the job and was often happy to say so—sorted quickly through the stack of papers in her arms.

"Perhaps you'd like to sign these?" she said. "Your broker at

Lloyd's sent them over. I wanted to have them ready for you Monday morning, but here you are now. He's uneasy about your presence in the construction trades, and thought you might prefer to underwrite something at lower risk."

"Such as?"

"A media conglomerate, I believe he said. Entertainment and such."

Reggie took the papers and began to look them over. Ms. Brinks—fiftyish, thin as a rail, and hyperactive by nature—waited impatiently.

"He says it's a low rate of return, but lower risk," she continued. "After all, who ever filed a claim over a flick?"

"Yes," said Reggie, signing the forms and giving them back. "Thank you, Ms. Brinks. My brother still in?"

"Yes, I think so."

"Good night, then."

"Good night."

Ms. Brinks took the lift, and Reggie continued on his way down the corridor, between shoulder-high gray cubicle partitions. The cubicles were dark and mostly empty—they were left over from Dorset National's previous operations there, and Reggie's chambers wasn't large enough to make use of them. Not yet.

At this hour, the main lamps were off. But there was residual light coming through the windows on the Baker Street side, intermittent glimmers from the senior clerk's PC at the opposite side, and, at the end of the corridor, the light escaping through the blinds and doorway of Nigel's office.

The air-conditioning was off as well. The temperature was tolerable, but the air was nevertheless stifling, the lack of circulation allowing scents of printer toner and old paper to accumulate.

He hoped this wouldn't take long.

The door to Nigel's office was half-open. Reggie stopped in the doorway and took a moment to note whether Nigel's working habits had improved.

They had not.

Crumpled balls of paper and confection wrappers littered the floor around the wastebasket in the near corner, where Nigel had attempted bank shots and missed. On his desk, a package of sweet biscuits spilled crumbs onto a stained blotter. And the incoming-letter basket fairly overflowed with correspondence that Nigel had yet to act upon.

Next to the incoming basket, beneath a scattered handful of chocolate Smarties, was an opened letter addressed to Nigel from the Law Society.

That had to be the reason he had called.

Nigel was doing something with the drawers of a tall wooden filing cabinet, his back toward the door. Reggie rapped his knuckles on the door frame. Nigel swiveled his desk chair to face Reggie, in the process mangling half a dozen blank forms that had slipped to the floor.

"Oh," Nigel said almost immediately. "You were with Laura."

"And you realize that just now because . . . ?"

"That perplexed look you've had of late."

Reggie didn't want to talk about it. "Is it the disciplinary tribunal?" he asked, pointing at the Law Society letter.

"That? Oh, yes."

"Well?"

"Well what?"

"What does it say? Have they scheduled your reinstatement hearing?"

"Yes. The tribunal convenes Monday morning."

"Excellent. It's about time you wound that up. You can drop all this clerical stuff and get back to what suits you."

"Of course," said Nigel, with no particular emphasis.

"Did they say anything about the substance of the charge?"

"Apparently they feel I've done my penance; they're no longer threatening to revoke my solicitor's license permanently."

"As expected. They've been sensitive to this 'inappropriate conduct' stuff ever since that lawyer in Staffordshire made page one of the *Daily Mail* by shagging a client's wife. He probably shouldn't have, given the client was in the House of Lords. But your hearing should be just a formality. You'll make nice, and I'll sit at the table to show support. No doubt at all you'll be reinstated."

Nigel listened to all that without objection—though he had begun to drum his fingers, and one knee jittered slightly. "I'm sure it will all be fine," he said now. "But, as to the reason I called—"

"It wasn't this?"

"Of course not," said Nigel, and he attacked the mess on his desk, shoving aside the tube of Smarties and the sweet biscuit crumbs. He opened the folder he had just taken from the file cabinet, and he began to push letters from it onto the blotter. Then he stopped.

"Perhaps I shouldn't have phoned. You won't understand this."

"You mean I won't agree," Reggie said suspiciously.

"No, you would agree if you understood. But you won't understand."

"Nigel, Laura is waiting. Will you tell me what is wrong?"

Nigel separated the letters and displayed them on the desk in front of Reggie.

"Part of my job is to reply to correspondence that should have been delivered elsewhere—or rather, not at all."

"What's the problem? If it's misdelivered, send it back."

"I can't. It's in the lease."

"What is?"

"That the tenant receive these letters, and not complain to the postmaster to get them stopped, but instead respond to them—with these bloody forms I have around here someplace."

"I still don't know what you're talking about."

"The in-basket is full of them. Just take one off the top."

Reggie did so. He began to read one letter—and then he stopped abruptly. He stared at the name of the addressee for a moment, and he gave his brother an incredulous look.

"Nigel, is this a joke?"

"It's not a joke."

Reggie read aloud the address on the envelope: "Mr. Sherlock Holmes, 221b Baker Street, London."

He tossed the letter dismissively back onto the desk in front of Nigel.

Nigel was unfazed. "Look at the others," he said.

Reggie picked up another letter and read the address: "Sherlock Holmes, Consulting Detective, 221b Baker Street."

And another: "Mr. Sherlock Holmes, Bee Keeper, c/o 221b Baker Street."

Nigel nodded and folded his arms as though he'd made his point.

"Are you telling me everything in this basket is addressed to him?" demanded Reggie.

"Yes—they're pretty much all like that, although most aren't so much interested in the beekeeping aspect."

Reggie stared at the letters in his hand and then back at Nigel again.

"You mean simply because our address is—"

"Yes," said Nigel. "Simply because you've located your new chambers in a building that takes up the entire Two Hundred block of Baker Street."

"But surely no one could actually believe—"

"Apparently some would do."

Reggie looked again at the letters that had piled up in the basket. There were dozens of them, in all kinds of formats—scrawled in longhand and typed on ancient Remingtons; laser-printed and hand-lettered on lined yellow pads.

In fact, the letters to Sherlock Holmes outnumbered all the legitimate correspondence. This was annoying.

"Doesn't it occur to these people that if he were real, he'd be long dead and rotten?"

Nigel shrugged. "What can I tell you? Dorset House has been getting and responding to the letters for years. The Baker Street Tourist Board loves them for it."

"Then let them handle the responses. Why should we worry about—"

"Because the letters have always been delivered to this floor of this building—and now you've taken a leasehold on it. And as you know, the lease specifically says that the occupant of these premises takes responsibility for the letters."

Reggie said nothing for a moment, and now it was Nigel's turn to give his older brother an incredulous stare.

"You did know this, of course," said Nigel. "I mean, you did read the full lease agreement before signing?"

"Of course," said Reggie.

"Article 3d, paragraph 2a, of addendum G?"

Reggie was silent. He knew what had happened, though he was loath to admit it—especially to Nigel. The lease terms had been too favorable—and he had been too eager.

He sighed and sat down. "It just seemed so damn inconsequential at the time," he said.

"It's true that most of the letters are trivial," said Nigel. "A surprising number of cat owners seem to believe he must be not only real and alive but also eager to come out of retirement to track down a stray tabby that is just out having the time of its life anyway. But—"

"My mistake," Reggie interrupted. "I'll get it stricken from the lease in the next go-round. And in the meantime, I'll speak to Ocher—handling these bloody things can be assigned to someone else. You should have more responsible tasks." He stood and picked up his overcoat.

"But that's not the problem," said Nigel.

"What, then?" Reggie stopped in the doorway.

"It's these," said Nigel, holding up three letters. "All of them, ostensibly, from the same person. This one came this morning. It references another that was in the file from a month back. But both of them refer to yet another, which I finally tracked down, filed out of order in the archive drawer. And that one— the original letter from the archives—was received here nearly twenty years ago."

"And that creates a problem because . . . ?"

"See for yourself."

Reggie picked up the archived letter and read it quickly. It was handwritten and a bit faded—but quite legible, with a return address in Los Angeles.

"She's looking for her father. He disappeared shortly before Christmas. She wants help in finding him. She encloses something she calls 'Daddy's maps' to assist in that search." Reggie stopped reading. "To find the father who abandoned her, she's writing to a character of fiction."

"Yes."

"It's touching. Or pathetic. But—"

"Pathetic, perhaps," said Nigel, "if she wrote that letter as an adult. I would guess she was no more than eight years of age at the time, from the obvious pride and care she took in her cursives."

"That and the fact that she appears to have signed in wax crayon."

"Yes. Now look at the other two."

Reggie glanced at the next two letters. There was no crayon now; both were laser-printed and signed in ink. "She asks if we still have the enclosures sent in her original letter, and that we kindly return them if we have them. Then she asks the same question again, a bit more insistently." He put the letters on the desk.

"Do you see the problem?" asked Nigel.

"I suppose," said Reggie. "But it's no great crisis. Return the enclosures if you can dredge them up; if not, send the standard form with apologies."

"You're missing the point," said Nigel. "She didn't write the recent letters. She wrote only the first one, as a child. These last two are written in her name, but they are clearly forgeries."

Reggie sighed. "I blame myself," he began. "I should have found you a position that was a little less—"

"If you'll only look!" said Nigel, standing and leaning precariously across the desk to display the letters just inches from Reggie's face. "The signatures are all wrong. They're careful and deliberate and perfect, exactly like the others except for the crayon. But no adult continues to sign exactly as they did as a child. It cannot be her signature, and Mara did not write these!"

"Mara?" said Reggie.

Nigel turned red and inched back into his chair. "That is her name," he said.

Reggie could only stare and try to discern if Nigel's mental state was real cause for concern—or if he was just on another annoying but nonlethal tear, which would occupy his interest for a few days but do no harm other than distracting him from more ordinary or more responsible activities.

"Nigel," Reggie said carefully, "surely you have not contacted this young woman?"

"No," Nigel said flatly. "I couldn't reach her. I left a message on her machine."

"Are you out of your bloody mind?" said Reggie. "Your legal career is on the line, and you're mucking about with people who write to a character of fiction as if he—we—our address—were some sort of general help center!"

"No one is doing any mucking here. I only—"

"Nigel, this is a law chambers."

"In this one very specific instance, I think—"

"Never mind my chambers' reputation, just think for a moment of the lawsuits you could inspire by encouraging some mental eight-year-old to think that Sherlock Holmes actually exists."

"She's not a mental eight-year-old; she's an actual one. I mean she was. She's not now, of course."

"The Law Society will see a pattern here—you meddling again where you don't belong. Under the circumstances, that should be the last thing you want."

"I said you would not understand," Nigel said in an exasperated tone. "But at least look at the enclosures." He held out an aged clasp envelope, raggedly torn across the top corners. "There's something here that—"

"No—I bloody well don't want to know," said Reggie. "If you must, forward the matter to the police in the area. Send them the letters, send them your theories if you wish, and then let the matter drop."

Reggie found himself pacing angrily toward the window. He stopped and looked back.

Nigel was pretending to contemplate the stains on his desk blotter.

"I want your word on it," said Reggie, "that you will let the matter drop."

"I will," said Nigel, without looking up.

Reggie turned toward the door, then stopped. He spoke too harshly with his brother, Laura had said. He took a long moment unfolding and straightening his overcoat.

"Nigel," he said, "do you remember how you broke your leg?"

"Yes," said Nigel. "You knocked me over in a rugby scrum."

"Not that time," said Reggie. "Earlier. When you were five. You'd been watching an American serial of *Superman.* Too many times. You got Mum's red tablecloth, tucked it into the back of your collar, climbed onto the roof, and tried to fly. Do you remember?"

"Vaguely."

"Bad idea, roof jumping," said Reggie. "Squash on Tuesday?"

"I expect so," said Nigel. And then, after a short pause: "I'll just tidy things up here a bit."

Reggie nodded and exited Nigel's office.

He walked back through the rows of cubicles to the lift. As he pressed the button for the ground floor, he heard someone call out.

He was sorry to see Robert Ocher hurrying up from a side aisle.

Ocher was senior clerk. He was an irritating man but skilled at negotiating Reggie's fees—and that was a powerfully redeeming quality.

"Busy office tonight," remarked Reggie as Ocher joined him to wait for the lift. "Working late, are we, Mr. Ocher?"

"No, no. I mean, no more than usual, just trying to get a jump on things, you know. I take it you only popped in to see your brother?" said Ocher, fidgety in his typical way. "I trust everything is going well, since they let him out of—" Ocher stopped; he knew he'd made an error.

"It was hardly Broadmoor, Mr. Ocher. My brother's hospitalization was completely voluntary."

"Yes, of course. I only meant that—"

"I know what you meant," said Reggie.

The lift arrived, and they both stepped in.

"When I said my brother would be helping out with administrative tasks," said Reggie, "I didn't intend that he would be answering letters addressed to Sherlock Holmes."

Ocher gave Reggie a surprised look. "I assumed that you knew. I mean, the lease itself says—"

"Yes," said Reggie. "I know. I'm surprised at the number of them."

"Oh, well, there has never been a shortage of crackpots in the world," said Ocher. "Meaning the letter writers, of course, not your brother." He forced a little laugh. "When Parsons was here, he easily dispatched the letters in a few moments each day and kept things in quite good order. They piled up a bit with him gone, and I did speak to your brother about that earlier— but of course it's all quite manageable. I instructed your brother to send just the form reply, leaving ample time for more essential tasks. I trust that is satisfactory?"

"Yes," said Reggie. "Temporarily."

"Oh, of course," said Ocher. "I realize that. Assuming the disciplinary tribunal finds no misconduct regarding that thing in Kent—"

Reggie gave Ocher an irritated look, and Ocher made a quick adjustment.

"Not that anyone could blame your brother, of course."

"You say that as though someone has."

"No, of course not," said Ocher, backpedaling as quickly as he could. "One cannot be faulted for doing one's job too well."

"Exactly," said Reggie. "Nigel will be reinstated. In the mean-time, I'll want you to find someone else to handle those bloody letters."

The lift had reached the ground floor, and the doors opened.

"Of course," said Ocher

"Thank you," said Reggie. He stepped quickly out into the lobby, and Ocher, wisely, stayed in and allowed the doors to close.

2

Reggie was annoyed as he got in the Jag. He was annoyed over Nigel's interruption of the evening with Laura, annoyed that Nigel was treating a letter written to Sherlock Holmes more seriously than his own career, and annoyed, generally, over Nigel being Nigel.

But as he drove out onto Baker Street, Reggie realized what annoyed him most was hearing anyone else blame Nigel for what had happened in Kent. It was bad enough that his brother blamed himself.

Reggie reminded himself that he couldn't suss out all his brother's issues in one night. There was just no use dwelling on it.

And he had other concerns.

He drove to Chelsea, parked, and got to Laura's doorstep. It had been only an hour or two; she might still be awake.

She was. She came to the door quickly, and Reggie saw that

she had not changed out of her evening dress; if anything, she was more radiant than when they had parted earlier.

"I'm glad you stayed up," said Reggie. "How did you know I'd return so soon?"

"I . . . didn't." She bit her upper lip, said, "Come have some brandy, then," and moved quickly off toward the drawing room.

"What did Nigel want?" she asked as she handed Reggie his glass.

Reggie thought about that for a moment. "A distraction," he said.

Laura was for some reason still standing; Reggie crossed in front of the fireplace and sat in his usual position on the sofa.

"What sort of distraction?"

"A distraction from the prospect of resuming his legal career, I think. His final hearing before the disciplinary tribunal is pending, and I've no doubt he'll be reinstated."

"I meant, how did he want to be distracted? Just go down to the Cork and Thistle and get pissed?"

"Nothing so rational," said Reggie. He told Laura about the letters from Los Angeles and Nigel's insistence that the woman there was in trouble.

"Is she pretty? This letter writer from Los Angeles?"

"I don't know. I don't think Nigel would know either, he hasn't seen her."

"Oh. Well, if it's not about that, then perhaps it's the Walter Mitty effect."

"Which is?"

"A study at Harvard or somewhere in America. They surveyed people in different occupations about their work, and then they asked about their daydreams. The more mundane the occupation, and the lower the person's self-esteem, the more dra-

matic and heroic and outlandish the daydream. I mean, after
discounting all your basic sex fantasies, of course. They called it
the Walter Mitty effect."

"So you're saying Nigel has low self-esteem," said Reggie.

"Not necessarily. It's just an alternative, given that you've
discounted the possibility that she's pretty."

"A week or so back," said Reggie, "I had a conversation with
Nigel that seemed, well . . . oddly phrased."

"Odd in what way?"

"He said, 'You have given Ms. Brinks a raise, I perceive.'
And then he took pains to explain that by observing what she
was wearing, and some change in her complexion, and an automobile repair receipt on her desk, he was able to deduce that I
had very recently given Ms. Brinks a raise."

"And had you?"

"No, as a matter of fact. But that's not the issue. The
issue—"

"You should, you know. Give her a raise."

"Nigel said so as well. But—"

"Ahh," said Laura. "Then I think your oddly phrased conversation was simply Nigel being too clever in making a point.
But if you're interested, I think I can explain the change in
Ms. Brinks. I think she's having an affair. I'm sure I saw her and
some tall man in a baseball cap tucked away in the deepest,
darkest corner of Mancini's last week."

"Really? I didn't think she was the type."

Laura laughed. "You mean you didn't think she was the age,
Reggie. But it just doesn't cap out that early. Only men are under thirty forever, and only in their own minds."

Reggie wasn't sure what that last remark meant. He decided
not to ask.

"If Nigel is finding his current job mundane," he said instead, "and he bloody well should—all he has to do about it is take his legal career back."

"Oh yes. No such thing as a mundane lawyer."

Reggie let that go. "He doesn't have to spend his days filing things. He can get his solicitor's license back immediately if he doesn't botch it up."

"That would be nice. Then he can boss your Mr. Ocher instead of the other way around."

"What do you mean?"

"I mean I hear him sometimes in Nigel's office, while I wait for you to finish with a client. He treats Nigel like a subordinate. I think the man has some sort of misplaced power complex."

"Most chambers clerks do; it's in the job description."

"Someone should revise it for him. Nigel is worth ten Ochers. Working with that man would screw up anyone's self-esteem, unless you were allowed to kick him in the backside every now and then. Say, hourly."

"I agree. But I gave Nigel the most responsible position he was willing to accept. And if he chafes under the direction of the Ochers of the world, all he has to do is stand up and take his career back. It's not as though he hasn't got the mental faculties to— Aren't you going to sit down?"

She hesitated. "I didn't expect you back this evening," she said. She looked at her watch as she said it.

"You could look out for him a bit, you know," she continued, reinforcing Reggie's recurring suspicion that before his mother died, Laura must have rung her up and requested a list of the things she could say to get under his skin. "Your brother is not like you. Things don't always come easily for him."

"Do you think everything has always come easily for me?"

"I don't know. Has there ever been anything you truly wanted, Reggie, which you could not attain?"

Reggie was sure there was, but before he could think of it, they heard the front door chimes. Laura did not seem at all surprised, and she went to answer it.

She returned with a guest. Reggie recognized Lord Buxton even before Laura introduced him—tall, bulky, arrogant—his photo had been appearing regularly of late in the *Times*. Always in connection with the takeover of one unfortunate media corporation or another. A company could not be a small fish in Buxton's pond for long.

Now Laura got a brandy for Buxton. At the last instant she freshened Reggie's as well, but it seemed almost an afterthought.

There was an awkward pause. Laura said something about the weather; Reggie and Buxton both stood with their brandies and murmured something in general agreement with her.

Then Reggie mentioned Buxton's recent American acquisitions, which included a theater in New York and a production company in Los Angeles, and Buxton thanked him for the remark, though Reggie had not intended it to be congratulatory.

Buxton's first production in America would be *The Taming of the Shrew*.

"Laura has the fire for Kate," said Buxton, "and I intend to contemporize it. Might start right in on the motion picture version, too. Add car chases, perhaps have Kate burn down Petruchio's house. It's for an American audience, you see. American audiences are different from you and me."

"Yes," Reggie said, "they have more money—"

"Laura, I do like his business sense."

Reggie didn't much like the manner in which Buxton addressed her or the suggestion that Buxton would know anything of her fire. "And less taste," he added, whereupon Laura cleared her throat. Buxton gave her a knowing look and laughed from his belly. Laura seemed to be looking at something on the floor.

She was standing now by the mantel on one side of the hearth and Reggie on the other, and Buxton crossed between them and set his glass on the mantel next to hers.

"Well, I must be off," Buxton said. And then, to Laura, "Can I drop you anywhere on the way?"

She's standing in her own home, thought Reggie. Where in bloody hell do you think you would get to drop her?

"Thank you, no," said Laura. She picked up her own glass and smiled. "Good night, Robert."

"I'll see you in New York, then," Buxton said as he picked up his coat. "Let me know if you have difficulty arranging a room—or anything."

"Good night," she said again in her firm voice. He paused for a moment, as if expecting something more; then he nodded quickly and slightly in Reggie's direction and exited.

Laura immediately gathered up the two empty glasses and rushed by Reggie without a glance or a word. He pursued her into the kitchen.

"I'm going." She whirled to face Reggie, the greens in her dress shimmering like a tropical leaf in the rain. "It is an excellent role, and I've already accepted."

"Going to America to do Shakespeare somehow strikes me as casting pearls—"

"That is precisely why they need to see it done right," she said sharply.

Then she seemed to reconsider, and she stepped in closer to Reggie. "Or better, anyway," she said. "It's only for a short time, after all. And there could be a film role in it."

"You can't go to New York," he said. "It's a slime pit. They plunk each other like grouse on the motorways."

She pulled back. "That's Los Angeles. And I've been to football at Manchester. A few rowdy Yanks won't scare me."

Reggie was silent. Then, "I've never taken you to a Manchester match."

"There are places you have not taken me, Reggie," she said, "where I have nevertheless been."

Laura crossed to the front door now, and Reggie had no choice but to follow.

"When do you leave?"

"Monday. I'm afraid I'll be mostly packing until then. And getting ready to 'contemporize' Shakespeare."

"When is your flight? I may be able to drive you," he said, immediately wishing he'd phrased it in a more committal way.

"One-ish, but you don't have to do that."

"It's no trouble."

"Thank you, Reggie," she said quite firmly. "But good night."

She shut the door, and Reggie found himself standing alone, outside, on the chilly step.

And as he drove back to Butler's Wharf, an image came to mind, pretty much unbidden, of himself, alone in his flat for the next half century, playing snooker in the billiards room with no one, putting a clever spin on the cue ball so that Reggie could not get a shot on the seven. Hair going thin and gray. Stubble on the chin. Stale cigar smoke and the odor of old clothes everywhere.

Had he already waited too long?

A prickly sensation on the back of his neck told him he might have made a mistake. It was a sensation he did not experience often, and he did not like it.

He slept only fitfully that night, and his usual four-mile run along the Thames the next morning did not make the sensation go away.

So he did the run again on Sunday, and by the end of it he had his plan.

He would be careful not to ring her. In these things, as in all things, there was strategy to be considered. It was important not to seem too desperate.

Anyway, she would be packing, and it wouldn't do to get stuck having to explain himself over the phone.

Better to catch her at the airport tomorrow.

It would be a surprise.

All the ambivalence she had shown of late would vanish; she would call off the trip, and then she would ring Buxton— no, too personal, she would fax him—and Buxton would have to find someone else for his damn play—and for whatever other purposes the pretentious bastard had in mind.

Reggie still had Nigel's hearing to attend, but it should be a quick formality. He would be out by half-past nine and easily make Heathrow before Laura.

The next day, Reggie drove to the City in plenty of time. He parked in a space reserved for him at Lincoln's Inn by a young female barrister who had once been his pupil—and something more. As he did so, it occurred to him that he would have to arrange for a new spot. He had not seen the young woman since meeting Laura. And he knew he would not see her again—given what he was going to say to Laura that morning—except in court.

Reggie walked to the Law Society building and went inside to the tribunal's meeting room. The Society had recently re-modeled its digs, and the room smelled distinctly of thick, new forest green carpeting.

Nigel had not yet arrived, but that was not cause for concern. Nigel was usually prompt, but never early.

Reggie took his seat, down left, facing the tribunal that would decide whether Nigel kept his solicitor's license.

The three members of the tribunal were seated behind a new speaker's dais, and not in the traditional deep burgundy leather, but in new, ergonomically sophisticated, plush velvet chairs with adjustable armrests that to all appearances were designed to collapse under the least bit of pressure.

On the right was Samuelson. Reggie had handled briefs for him in the past. This would be an advantage. Samuelson would want Reggie's services again in the future.

On the left was Woolrich, the oldest of the three, who looked ready to nod off. Reggie guessed he would follow the path of least resistance, whatever direction it took.

The two tribunal members on either side seemed to be having some difficulty with the movable armrests. In the center was Breckenridge, who had apparently given up trying to adjust his chair—the height of which made him appear at least a head shorter than the other two—and he sat, with a look of some annoyance, staring at the new built-in dais microphone in front of him.

Breckenridge was the main challenge. Early in Reggie's career, Breckenridge had shopped a brief at the chambers where Reggie was a junior; the clerk had tried to pass the brief to Reggie, but Breckenridge insisted on someone with more experience. By chance, Reggie was later retained by the opposing party in the same matter—and things worked out badly for Breckenridge

It was two minutes till, and there was still no sign of Nigel.

Now it was time to worry.

Reggie got out his mobile phone and rang Nigel's home number. No answer.

He tried the office number. No answer there, either. But finally the call switched over to the secretary's line, and Ms. Brinks picked up.

"I'm at the hearing," said Reggie. "But Nigel isn't. Have you seen him?"

"No," said Ms. Brinks. "His office is still dark."

"Ring his flat. Call me the moment you locate him."

"I will," said Ms. Brinks.

"We'll proceed, Mr. Heath, if it's not too great an inconvenience for you," said Breckenridge.

"Certainly," said Reggie, closing his phone.

"I suppose you find it necessary to carry as much of the office business as possible with you, now that your chambers are no longer in the City proper?" said Breckenridge, sounding more smug now than annoyed.

"Not typically," said Reggie, standing to address the panel. "May I take this opportunity to congratulate you on the remodeling? It's all really quite . . . remarkable."

"Congratulations noted," said Breckenridge. "Can we get on with it?"

"If I might briefly recount the facts for the tribunal?"

"If you feel you must."

"I do so feel," said Reggie. He cleared his throat and began, fully aware that there are occasions to be concise and to the point, and there are occasions for oratory, and with Nigel still running late, this was the latter.

"A Mr. Throckmorton," Reggie began, "a carpenter by trade, was hired by the Corning family to replace rotted wood in the back wall of the pantry. The pantry was adjacent to the kitchen, and on a table in the kitchen, Mrs. Corning had placed a frozen chicken to thaw. The plastic tray on which she so carefully placed the chicken was cracked, and as the bird thawed, it leaked, all the way down to the linoleum floor.

"Very shortly thereafter, the workman—our Mr. Throckmorton—entered the kitchen, slipped on the watery-chickeny fluid, and fell on his backside. All of which was, of course, inevitable."

"Wait a moment, Mr. Heath."

"Yes?"

"Inevitable?"

"Yes."

"Why so?"

"Members of the tribunal, you and I and all in this room know, in our hearts, that fate and chance were forever altered when the first tort law was created, such that the slightest opportunity for creating an injury will always give rise to one, if there is a lawyer available."

Breckenridge rubbed his forehead. "Please continue, Mr. Heath," he said, "but without speculation as to what this panel knows in its heart. Or hearts. Or it's collective heart."

"Of course," said Reggie, and he continued.

"The only question was the extent of damages. And so Nigel called witnesses who testified that Mr. Throckmorton had debilitating pain and paralysis caused by this fall; and the Cornings' lawyer called witnesses who said there was nothing of the kind, and in my humble opinion it was, at this point, a dead heat. What tipped the scales was Nigel's summation. Nigel believed his client, and the jury believed in Nigel—and so it came back for the full amount."

"But what does this have to do with what your brother—"

"I'm almost there."

"Get on with it, then."

"Rightly proud of this success and flush with his first commission, and happy in the knowledge that the law, God's justice, and the solicitor's pocketbook were all perfectly in sync, Nigel booked a weekend for himself at the most expensive golf resort in Scotland. I forget the name of it, I'm sure some of you know it.

"It was June, and the weather was brilliant. And Nigel was

playing so well that he had caught up with the party ahead of him.

"He stopped at a polite distance and watched as the duffer ahead of him took a perfect stance over the ball, swung the driver easily back, and with a fully extended and explosive swing, sent a high arching shot a good hundred and eighty yards onto the fairway.

"And then the man turned, and Nigel saw that this man with the excellent drive was his very own paralyzed client—Mr. Throckmorton.

"Nigel immediately returned to London and told the ethics board what had transpired."

"We know this, Mr. Heath," said Breckenridge. "And you will recall that the inquiry found no proof of bad faith on the part of the plaintiff and that therefore there was nothing to be done. The law is not perfect, especially on questions of evidence, and these things do happen. In fact, all that was necessary at that point was for your brother to let it go. But he did not. Unannounced, and with no apparent business necessity, he approached the daughter of defendant Corning at university."

"There was no other way to go about it," responded Reggie. "Nigel wanted to put things right. But Mr. Corning was in hospital, having suffered a heart attack shortly after the judgment, and Mrs. Corning threw a plate of tomatoes and bangers at Nigel when he tried at their home."

"Mr. Heath, your brother intruded into the daughter's single-gender residence hall after the curfew hour," said Breckenridge.

"The hours were not clearly posted. And it was the young Corning woman, not Nigel, who was in the corridor wearing nothing but skimpy knickers."

The tribunal members exchanged glances.

"Be fair," said Reggie. "They should ring a bell or something before they do that, shouldn't they?"

"Can be very embarrassing," Woolrich mumbled, waking up a bit. "Had that same experience myself."

Samuelson nodded. "Fair warning would be the decent thing."

"Exactly. And those extraordinary circumstances caused the daughter to misconstrue Nigel's intent. He was merely trying to return his fee," said Reggie. "He felt it was his obligation to do so."

"Was it his obligation to have his hand in his pants?" asked Breckenridge.

"He was just getting the bloody check out of his pocket," said Reggie. "Everyone at the scene acknowledged that to be so when things calmed down, including the young woman herself, the residence hall guard who came running when she screamed, and all the other young women who came pouring out into the corridor. Nigel had it—the check—right there in his hand."

The tribunal members huddled together for a brief moment.

"Are we to accept, then," said Breckenridge, "that all this fuss was because your brother felt the outcome of the case was unjust to the opposing litigant?"

"Spot on, sir. I could not phrase it better myself, though I tried mightily."

"If so, it's not a characteristic that seems to run in the family, Mr. Heath. I've not heard of you having such compunctions."

"No argument there. You can see what good such concerns have done Nigel."

"If your brother takes one approach to the law," Breckenridge said in a sly voice, "and you take the opposite, doesn't it stand to reason that one of you is pursuing the wrong profession?"

"Not at all," said Reggie. "We average out. And in law, as in life, balance is everything."

"Very well," said Breckenridge. "You've had your say, and we would like very much to dispose of the matter. But we must hear from Nigel Heath himself. It is now a quarter after the hour. Where is he?"

"One moment, if I may," said Reggie. He took out his phone and rang Ms. Brinks again.

She told him that Nigel still had not shown and that there was no answer at his flat.

Reggie didn't take her word for it. He called Nigel's flat himself.

Still no answer.

Reggie put away the phone and addressed the tribunal.

"It is impossible for my brother to appear this morning. He begs your indulgence and conveys his deepest apologies and regrets."

"Perhaps you will now tell us the reason for his absence?"

"Intestinal flu."

Everyone paused. Breckenridge drilled in.

"Is your brother in hospital?"

"Ahh . . . no."

"Then you're saying he avoided a hearing that can determine his future licensing merely because he has a temporary and non-life-threatening illness?"

"Because at this moment he is completely incapable of controlling bodily fluids from either of the most likely sources," said Reggie, leaning back very slightly, enough so that he could casually caress, in full view of the tribunal, the plush and expensive green velvet of one of the newly upholstered chairs.

Breckenridge cleared his throat and shifted uncomfortably. Mr. Samuelson looked at Reggie, recognized the opportunity, and motioned for a huddle with the other two members. For a moment all three heads bowed and leaned in together, revealing one honestly balding spot, one bad comb-over of white hair over quite pink skin, and one insecurely seated toupee.

Then all three looked up, the two on either side sat back in their chairs—one of them voluntarily—and Mr. Breckenridge spoke.

"Very well, then. We will reconvene in three days. If your brother wishes to have his reinstatement considered, the courtesy to notify us would be advisable. Am I making this clear?"

"Crystal, as always."

"Then we're adjourned."

Under the circumstances, postponement was as clear a win as Reggie could expect. He exited the hearing chambers satisfied with the outcome for the moment—but annoyed with Nigel.

The hearing had taken longer than he'd intended, and it was almost ten when he reached the street outside the Law Society building.

The parade of black suits moving up Chancery Lane from the Strand—the male barristers in wigs and dark suits and the occasional chalk stripe, the women in black skirts, with long braided hair under their white wigs—had reached its morning peak.

Reggie stepped back into the shelter of the entryway to ring Laura and was relieved to find her still at home.

"I can't talk long," she said. "I'm not nearly packed."

"Has Nigel rung you?"

"That would have been nice," said Laura, "but no. Why? You sound . . . perturbed."

"The final disposition of his review before the disciplinary tribunal was this morning," said Reggie, "and he's nowhere to be found."

"Well, that's odd."

"The hearing's chaired by Breckenridge," he added, "and Breckenridge has a memory as long as his nose. If Nigel doesn't respond soon, Breckenridge will take it as a snub, and he doesn't take snubs lightly."

"You must find Nigel and tell him."

"I don't know that it will do any good. He's a grown man; if he wants to toss his career away, I don't know that I can stop him."

There was a long pause at the other end of the line, which Reggie interpreted as Laura waiting for him to say something more sensible. When he failed to do so, she spoke again.

"Well, you are his only brother," said Laura, "so I'm sure you know best."

Reggie surrendered. "I'll check his office personally," he said. "When he wants to convey something without having to hear my response, he'll sometimes leave a note." Now he paused.

"Was there something else?" said Laura.

"I would like to see you before you leave."

"That's sweet," Laura said brightly. "But you need to find Nigel, and I can't miss my flight."

"Stop at chambers on your way. We'll get a bite, and you'll still make your plane."

There was a pause, then Laura said, "Fair enough. You know how I hate airline food."

Reggie arrived at Baker Street at midmorning. Clerical workers from the mortgage company that shared the building were still arriving at work, walking through the glass entrance and past the broad marble columns, carrying white paper sacks that smelled of cappuccinos and croissants.

Reggie was already annoyed at Nigel; and hunger, as Laura

would have reminded him, made him more so. He tried to keep that bit of self-knowledge in mind as he got out of the lift and headed toward Nigel's office.

He was halfway there when a commotion became apparent. A cluster of office workers from Dorset National had come upstairs to take a look at something, and Reggie soon realized that the object of their attention had to be in Nigel's office.

As Reggie approached, the group stopped trying to peer in past the closed blinds and dispersed.

Reggie tried the door. Locked.

He looked in through the corner edge of the window, as the crowd of gossips had been trying to do moments before.

Now he could see why they had gathered.

Only a portion of the room was visible from this angle, and even that was illuminated only by the residual corridor light around the edge of the blinds—but it was enough.

Reggie saw that the drawers on the tall file cabinet had been yanked with such force that they lay open on bent hinges. And all the books on the shelf had been swept off onto the floor. Papers were scattered everywhere.

Nigel had gone off again.

His favorite print of the American West dangled from its wall frame like a flag at half-mast—damage that Nigel in his right mind would never have done. And just barely visible in the dark corner above the top edge of the file cabinet was an empty shelf where Nigel's prized Remington bronze had been on display.

"Odd, isn't it, Mr. Heath? I didn't know quite what to make of it."

Reggie turned with a start. He hadn't seen Ms. Brinks come up next to him.

"Don't let anyone near," he said to her.

Reggie took a key from her, opened the door, stepped inside alone, and shut it quickly behind him.

He stood just inside the doorway and looked left to right to take it all in. Everything was chaos—folders, forms, and legal papers of all sorts tossed about; all the books dumped to the floor, spines broken and flattened. Everything that could be had been torn, gutted, dumped, or bent.

Everything but Nigel's hearing notice from the Law Society— that document was folded over and taped securely to the near corner of Nigel's desk, with Reggie's name written on the back of it in blue felt pen.

Reggie detached the document and unfolded it.

There was a short note written on the inside. It was unquestionably in Nigel's hand, and it said this:

> *Can't make hearing. Sorry. Just let it go.*
> *N*

As he read this, Reggie heard the door latch turning behind him.

"I said no one," he called out.

The door opened anyway. It was Laura.

"You shouldn't invite me to brunch and then tell me to sod off," she said. She stepped inside. "Do you know you have people gathered about as if— Oh my."

"I pushed him too far, didn't I," said Reggie.

"What do you mean?" she said.

He handed her the note Nigel had written. "You said it yourself—he only got out a month ago. I leaned on him just a bit—and now this. It's just the same as last time. He's trashed his office, and by now I'll bet he's checked himself into the asylum again."

"Recuperation center," said Laura, reading the note.

"Whatever."

She gave the note back to Reggie. "Well," she said, "if he doesn't want to be a lawyer, I guess you can't make him be."

"Agreed."

"But I think you're wrong about what's happened here. I think it's a burglary."

"What is there to burgle?"

"I don't know, but—" Laura stopped suddenly. Her nose wrinkled.

"What?" said Reggie.

"That smell," she said.

She walked toward the other side of the desk, the side that had not been visible through the window.

She stood near the shelf where the Remington bronze should have been. Then she looked downward, behind the desk.

She gasped and put her hand to her mouth.

Reggie crossed to the other end of the desk, following Laura's stare. Then he froze.

On the floor behind the desk was the bronze of American Indians hunting buffalo—a replica, but even so not inexpensive by Nigel's standards—and something that would never be found on the floor of his office. But that was merely odd.

What stopped Reggie and Laura in their tracks was what lay next to the bronze and the damp, thick scent that accompanied it.

It was Ocher. Or at least had been. He was lying silent and still on the floor, and with pupils fixed as stone.

The bronze Remington sculpture was coated on one long side and a corner with something dark, reddish, and crusted around the edges.

"It is . . . it is Ocher, isn't it?" said Laura.

"Yes. You aren't going to faint, are you?"

"Why on earth should I faint?"

"You're rather leaning against the file cabinet. I thought perhaps it was for steadying."

"I'm trying to look casual. For your secretary's benefit. I'm afraid she'll hurt her nose, mushing it up against the window like she is, and— Oh, too late, here she comes."

Ms. Brinks was in the doorway. Before Reggie could stop her, she stepped up to the desk and tried to lean over to see what Reggie and Laura were looking at.

"Oh!" said Ms. Brinks. "Oh my." She jerked backward at first, then just stared. "Is he . . ."

"Yes," said Reggie. "Please go out and ring the police, will you? And make sure no one else comes in here."

Ms. Brinks exited, and Laura knelt along with Reggie over the body.

"Should we try . . . I mean . . . that resuscitation thing?"

"I'm afraid that ship has sailed," said Reggie.

"You're not saying that simply because you never liked him, are you? I mean, I can do it if you don't want to. Although I think I heard him say once that he eats kippers for breakfast."

"He has no breath and no pulse, his pupils are completely fixed, and his skin is like a Yorkshire pudding that's been in the fridge. Whatever good points he once had, they're all completely gone, along with his more predominant qualities."

Laura leaned in for a closer look. "Yes, I see now. You're quite right. Oh, do you suppose this is—"

"Don't—," began Reggie as she reached for the bronze, but it was too late.

"I'm only touching the edges," she said, holding the bronze

quite gingerly in three slender fingers. She turned it base upward. One of the sharp corners at the heavy bottom edge was
thick with recently congealed blood.

"Rather nasty," said Laura.

"Yes," said Reggie. "But let's leave it as we found it, shall we?"

"Of course," said Laura.

She put the object back on the floor where she had found it.
She regarded it for a moment, then said, "No, I think it was
more like this."

She adjusted it ever so slightly, then she stood and looked
from Ocher's body to the mantel where the sculpture had been
displayed.

"You don't suppose it could have simply—fallen on him, do
you?" she asked.

"Not with that much force," said Reggie.

Laura considered that. "I suppose then suicide is out of the
question as well," she said without much enthusiasm. Then, for
a short moment, neither of them said anything.

"Well," ventured Laura, "this might have been a burglar,
and Ocher catching him."

"Yes."

"But if it was not a burglary, then the next likely scenario
would be . . . well, Ocher is—was—a very unlikable man, any
number of people might have wanted to bash him with something sharp and heavy."

"In Nigel's office."

"You'd bash him where you find him, I would think," said
Laura.

"Well, you're right about the unlikable part. But the geogra-
phy is unfortunate."

She gave that due consideration, then said, "Nigel could not
have done it."

"Of course not," said Reggie.

"He would never abuse his Remington that way."

"You're right," said Reggie, "but I hope he's got a better alibi than that."

"What's making that annoying hum?" said Laura.

Reggie listened. He knew the sound, but he was so accustomed to hearing it in Nigel's office that he hadn't noticed.

It was Nigel's computer. Reggie had assumed it was off, but he looked now and saw that, yes, the computer was still on. Only the monitor had been turned off.

Reggie pushed the monitor's button, and it began to flicker. Then the display came up, and right in the center was the text of an opened message. It was from Transcontinental Airlines. It read:

> *Thank you for confirming your reservation on:*
> *Flight 2364 to Los Angeles*
> *Departing at: 8:45 A.M.*
> *Do you wish to perform another transaction?*
> *YesNo*

"Bloody hell," said Reggie.

"Why on earth Los Angeles?" said Laura.

"The bloody letter," said Reggie. "He's gone to Los Angeles over the bloody letter to Sherlock Holmes."

Laura pondered that for a moment, then said, "And do we think that was before . . . Ocher was killed? Or after?"

Reggie looked at Laura, and they both grasped the implications of what she was asking.

"Of course it had to be before," she said quickly.

"Yes, it must have been," said Reggie. "Ocher heard something after Nigel was gone. He came in, around the desk, and then someone concealed here, behind the file cabinet, struck him with the first object at hand."

"Yes," said Laura. "Because otherwise, if Ocher were here first, and Nigel came in after, that would mean it was Nigel who—"

She didn't try to finish that sentence, and now there was a knock at the door.

Ms. Brinks stuck her head in. "The police are here," she said.

Reggie nodded to Laura in the direction of the corridor where the police were approaching.

"I'll just say hello to them," she volunteered, and stepped out of the office, closing the door and taking Ms. Brinks with her.

Reggie knew he would be alone in the office only for a moment.

Nigel had gone to Los Angeles—but where?

Reggie turned to Nigel's filing cabinet. It had been gutted, all its hanging folders yanked out and their contents dumped on the floor.

He began to look about for the envelope in which Nigel had been keeping the letters. He didn't see it.

And then he did.

It was under Ocher. Under Ocher's left forearm, to be exact, as if for some reason he had been clutching it when struck.

That was disturbing.

Reggie reached down and tugged on the envelope—gently at first and then with a bit more force—to pull it out from under Ocher, just enough to look inside.

It was empty. The enclosures it had contained—which Reggie had refused to look at the other night—and the letters, including the letter writer's name and return address, which was almost certainly Nigel's destination—were gone.

Reggie could hear Laura trying to chat up the police outside in the corridor, but it apparently wasn't slowing them much; they were right outside the office now.

There was no time for anything more. Reggie gave the computer's plug at the wall outlet a quick nudge with his foot. The monitor's display crashed out in a hazy blitz of blue and black, and Reggie managed to step away and into the doorway just as the two officers—one of them a woman, which perhaps explained why Laura had not been able to delay them longer—pushed open the door.

"Thank you for coming so quickly. I assume you have an inspector on the way?" Reggie said to the male sergeant.

"Detective Inspector Wembley will be here, sir."

"You didn't touch anything?" said the female officer, crossing around behind the desk to view the body.

"Just as we found it," said Reggie.

"I picked that thing up for just a bit, though," Laura said innocently, pointing at the statue.

"Inspector Wembley won't like that," the male officer said in an annoyed tone directed at Reggie rather than Laura. "Not quite untouched, then, is it?"

"Reggie didn't say it was untouched," offered Laura. "He only said it is as we found it, and it is—I put it back quite exactly. Although I admit you do have to watch Reggie and his words; he's a QC, of course, and likes to prove it more often than really necessary."

"Yes, we know Mr. Heath is a queen's counsel," said the female officer to Laura, rather dryly. "We got that from the name-plate."

"Did you say Wembley?" Reggie asked the sergeant.

"Yes, sir. Do you know him?"

"We may have met. Ms. Brinks will be available to him here

when he arrives. I'll be in my chambers office, at the opposite corner."

"Very good."

Reggie walked with Laura back to his own office and shut the door behind them. They were alone, for the moment.

"You might have left out the dissertation on the sculpture," he said.

"I was being diverting."

"You're always diverting."

"I mean diversionary. I was creating a diversion," said Laura. "You couldn't tell?"

"Diversion from what?"

"From them seeing you were impeding their investigation. The computer was on when I left, and off when I came back. I'm sure you did what was necessary, but I didn't want them to notice. They might have touched it and found it still warm, you know."

"You're being quite tactical, given that we know Nigel didn't do it."

"So are you. The police can make mistakes, we both know that, and we're trying to help them not make one here. But at least I'm not doing anything that could be considered obstructing. You did, and I wish you wouldn't. It's difficult enough just trying to protect one of you."

Reggie sat down. After a moment, he said, "Then you think it's possible Nigel needs protecting?"

"I didn't mean it that way."

Reggie nodded. "It doesn't help that Wembley is investigating."

"Why?"

"I destroyed him in a cross a few years back, when I was doing criminal."

"So you're worried about a karma thing, or do you think he holds a grudge?"

"Shouldn't matter, I guess. No doubt he's forgotten all about it."

There was a short pause. Then Laura said, "You know my plane leaves in little more than an hour."

"I know," said Reggie.

"I could hardly leave if I didn't know Nigel would be all right."

"I will see to Nigel," said Reggie. "You must go to New York, exactly as you had planned. If you delay it, Wembley will think you are hanging about out of concern for Nigel, and that will just increase his suspicion."

"What will you do?"

"I'm going to Los Angeles. Wembley won't like it, but he's got nothing with which to stop me at the moment. I think it's a safe bet that Nigel went there to see the girl. That's where I'll start. With luck I'll find him and figure out what's going on before Wembley does."

"Wouldn't it be better to stay and wait for your brother to contact you?"

"Have you ever known Nigel to ask for help when he should?"

Laura had no answer for that.

"No," said Reggie, "I haven't either, and I've known him thirty years longer than you. And you know he's been like that even more so since . . . well, since you and I . . ."

"No," said Laura. "I don't think I do know that. But I know you think it."

Laura said that as if there were more to discuss on the issue, but Reggie avoided it. "Point remains," he said, "whatever Nigel's dug himself into, he'll only dig it deeper if I don't reach him. Wembley will already think he's found means and opportunity. I won't be able to stop him from grilling the staff, and if he asks the right questions and gets the wrong answers, he might think he's found motive as well. As you said, they make mistakes."

Now Ms. Brinks was at the door.

"Inspector Wembley is here," she began, but that was as far as she could get.

"I'll only need a minute, Heath," said a voice from behind her, and now the door opened fully and the detective stepped in without invitation.

Yes, that was the Wembley, Reggie remembered.

"How are you, Wembley?"

"Better than your clerk," said Wembley. Then he turned toward Laura. "You're Laura Rankin, aren't you?"

"Yes," said Laura.

"I saw you in *Chicago*. The play, I mean. It was a bit over the top for my taste, but not you—you were captivating."

"Thank you," she said. "It's always comforting not to be lumped in the over-the-top category."

"It was you found the body?"

"No," replied Laura. "Reggie found the—Mr. Ocher. I came in after."

"Oh." Wembley nodded.

"He was a horrid little man, you know. Mr. Ocher," continued Laura.

"Really?" said Wembley.

Reggie knew Laura was being diversionary again, and he tried to give her a cautioning look behind Wembley's back—but she ignored it.

"He had more annoying little qualities than I can even begin to recount," she said to Wembley.

"Knew him well, did you?"

"Only from my visits to Reggie's chambers. I mean the legal chambers, of course. Not Reggie's other chambers."

"So you didn't get on with him, then?"

"Not a bit. I rather despised him, and I'm sure he felt the same about me."

"Laura—"

"Well, I don't know that he didn't."

"You'll understand that I have to ask you this," began Wembley. "Just as a matter of form—"

"Yes?"

"Where were you last night, and early this morning, say, between the hours of—"

"Home in bed," said Laura. "Rather, alone. No one saw me there at all."

Wembley had a look on his face that said "More's the pity." Reggie decided it was time to interrupt.

"Miss Rankin is due in New York," he said. "She has rehearsals starting immediately. There's no need to delay her, is there?"

"Not on my account," said Wembley. "Professionally speaking. But it's the City's loss whenever you are away, Miss Rankin."

"Thank you again, Inspector Wembley," said Laura. She kissed Reggie lightly on the cheek and turned toward the door.

"The hotel you're at?" Wembley said suddenly as she turned the latch.

"Something over Central Park," she said. "Reggie always knows how to find me if I'm needed." She stepped out and closed the door behind her.

There was a pause for just a moment after, before Wembley said, "You've done well for yourself, Heath."

He seemed to be looking about at the room as he said it,

but it wasn't clear that the chambers was what he was referring to.

"Sit if you like," said Reggie.

Wembley declined and then said, "We'll hear what forensics has to say, of course. One doesn't want to be hasty—how do the Americans say it, to . . ."

"Rush to judgment."

"Yes. But it's rather hard to see it as accidental."

"I'm sure you must be right, but it's not my field. I don't know much about criminal matters."

"Quite. I recall how little you knew," said Wembley. Then, "Did Ocher have conflicts with anyone I should know about?"

"I don't know much about his personal life."

"I meant in the workplace."

"Ocher annoyed pretty much everyone he worked with, none more so than I. He thought it his duty as senior clerk, and quite right about it, too."

"Hmm." Wembley, standing in the middle of the room, put his hands in his pockets, hooked by the thumbs, rocked back on his heels slightly, and took a moment to look about at the appointments for Reggie's chambers.

Then he began again.

"So Mr. Ocher was in your brother's office when he was killed?"

"I don't know. That's where we found his body."

"Does your brother generally lock his office?"

"I'm not sure."

"There was no sign of forced entry, you see."

"I don't know that Nigel does lock his office, but in any case, Ocher has his own key."

Wembley nodded slightly. "Anything taken that you know

of? I mean, it does look like a possible burglary, I'll grant you. But was anything actually taken?"

"I don't know."

"Hmm," Wembley said again. "Quite right. Yes, I expect I'll need a word with your brother, won't I? Is he about?"

"I'm afraid not."

"Expect him soon?"

"I'm afraid he's . . . on holiday."

"That is unfortunate. When did he leave?"

"I think last night," Reggie lied. "But I don't know exactly when."

"Returning?"

"A few days, I expect."

"Where is he taking this holiday?"

"He didn't say."

"Not close, then, you two?"

Reggie shrugged.

"Have him ring me when you hear from him, will you?"

"Certainly," said Reggie.

"Computer was warm," said Wembley, turning suddenly. "Know anything about that?"

"No."

Reggie stood and opened the office door; Wembley exited, and Reggie watched until he had seen him enter the lift, the doors close, and the indicator lights show that the lift was actually on its way down.

Then Reggie went to his own files and opened his list of contacts from the inception of the Dorset House lease. It was a very thorough list, with contacts for people with all sorts of connections with the Dorset National Building Society. Now there was one that he needed.

He found it.

It was an address in Theydon Bois. Out of the city, but not all that far.

Reggie took the back stairs out of the building, looked quickly about for Wembley, and then got in the XJS.

With any luck, he'd get what he needed and still make an evening flight from Heathrow.

3

Reggie got out of the city and drove to Theydon Bois in good time. Just past the Shepherd's Arms pub, he navigated a little circus where three roads converged and then drove halfway up a small hill to the address referenced in the Dorset House lease.

It was a smallish two-story structure, in various shades of tan and red brick—nicely maintained, with a flagstone courtyard in front, surrounded by an unintimidating three-foot iron fence.

Two small children ran from the courtyard into the house as Reggie approached; moments later, a woman in her late thirties came to the door. She had a naturally pale and unfreckled face, with thick, attractive auburn hair, cut short in the way many women would do when they've begun a family—but still with a flip above the shoulder.

"Yes?" she said.

"I'm Reggie Heath," said Reggie, offering the woman his business card. "Are you Mrs. Spencer? Formerly with Dorset National?"

"Yes," she said, looking at the card. "You found me. I hope you're not here because you think I have need of your services," she said with just a little bit of a laugh.

"Not at all," said Reggie. "I came to ask you about the letters."

"The letters?"

"The Holmes letters."

She looked at Reggie's card again. "Well, I guess I might tell you," she said. "After all, you've taken a leasehold on them, haven't you? Would you like some tea?"

"Thank you," said Reggie as he followed her inside. "I won't keep you long."

She seated him in front of the French windows overlooking the courtyard and her two playing children.

"I did leave very explicit instructions on how to handle the letters, you know," she said as she joined him there with the tea. "I was careful about it, especially because the lease was changing hands."

"I hope that wasn't a problem for you—," began Reggie.

"Oh, don't worry," she said. "You didn't cause me to lose my job. I left just before, to be a full-time mum. There was a temp brought in to replace me."

"Yes," said Reggie. "Mr. Parsons. Other than him—was it just you answering the letters—the whole time you were there?"

"Yes."

"Did you keep records?"

"Certainly. And Mr. Parsons was to do a complete historical inventory and archival of them when you took over the lease. It should all be in the tall filing cabinet."

"I saw that," said Reggie. "But I'm afraid a bit of it has been lost. Did you have any other sort of backup? Copies of the letters, anything like that?"

Her eyes widened slightly, and she put down her tea. "Why would I have such a thing?"

"I didn't mean you personally, necessarily," said Reggie, sur-prised at what seemed a defensive posture. "I just meant—is there any other record at all? A log of the addresses? Backup copies of the letters?"

"No," she said, glancing out the window. "Dorset National did not ask me to keep a log." She took a moment now to unlatch the French windows and tell one of the children in the court-yard to leave the cat alone.

In a courtroom, Reggie would have regarded this move as an evasion.

"Sorry," she said with a slight smile, brushing the curtains back in place. "They tend to pull its tail a bit."

It seemed a long shot, but Reggie had to try. "Mrs. Spencer," he said, "is there any chance you made copies of the letters for yourself?"

Her cheeks turned red, and she looked as though she had got caught cutting to the front of the queue at the bakery.

"Is it truly important?" she said.

Now it was Reggie who hesitated. It wouldn't do to tell her what had transpired in chambers. "Really just bookkeeping," he said. "Not important at all."

"Oh," she said with a slight laugh, and then there was a brief pause as they both pretended the important thing was to adequately stir the sugar in their tea. Then Reggie looked up.

"But did you?" he said.

She sat back, looked at Reggie, and sighed. "One moment," she said.

She got up, went to a bookcase, and took a laptop out of a satchel there. She started to set it up—and then she stopped.

"You won't tell Dorset National about this, will you? I mean, not yet, at least. I'll tell them myself, if the time comes. But before I left the company, I scanned all my favorites, from the very beginning of the letters, into a file. I was thinking that someday I might compile them all—into a book, or some such thing."

"A book about crazy people who write letters to a character of fiction."

"No, not at all. A book about people who for one reason or another are a bit naïve in some particular area. We all have our blind spots, don't we?"

"No doubt," said Reggie.

"What information is it you need?"

"What's missing is a file from twenty years ago," said Reggie. "Although I'm sure that was before your time."

"Just slightly." She laughed. "I started when I was nineteen. But I scanned some that were already in the files from before I arrived. So you might be lucky. Here—does this have what you need?"

She put the laptop in front of Reggie, and he began scrolling rapidly through the file.

"These are just the letters themselves, of course," she said. "People often sent various kinds of collateral material with them—evidence of things that they thought Sherlock Holmes would want to consider—but I didn't attempt to scan any of that."

"This should give me what I need," said Reggie. "For the bookkeeping, I mean."

He scrolled down two more clicks—and there it was. The twenty-year-old letter from the eight-year-old girl in Los Angeles: Mara Ramirez on Mateo Street. He knew it immediately from the careful crayon script and the plea for Sherlock Holmes to find her father.

Reggie jotted down the letter writer's name and address. "You've been a great help," he said, standing to leave. "Thank you."

She gave him a quizzical look as she escorted him to the door.

"You're quite welcome," she said. "But was that all that you needed—just the one address?"

"Well . . . yes," said Reggie, wishing he had covered his intent better—but he couldn't see how it would matter to her. "It's the one missing, and if one's missing, they're all missing, I like to say."

"You don't look like someone who would say that," she said, and laughed. "But I'll take your word for it that you do, given you came all this way for just the one letter."

Reggie paused now. He had what he needed, but he couldn't help asking.

"In all the time you were handling the letters—did you ever feel tempted to answer one of them yourself, rather than just send the official form?"

She looked at Reggie suspiciously now, and she took a moment before answering.

"If I would have done—you can be sure that Dorset National would have taken a very dim view to learn of it. There's a firm rule about always just sending the standard form letter. I was very specific about that in the instructions I left."

"Yes," said Reggie.

"I used to refer to it as the 'prime directive' myself," she said with a smile that seemed to reference a joke that Reggie did not get. "Dorset National lawyers had concerns about potential liabilities, as I guess you might imagine."

"Understandably," said Reggie.

"Which is why, of course, they also included that clause in your lease that terminates the leasehold, and brings all the rent for the entire term immediately due and payable, if that rule should ever be violated."

"What?"

"I believe they call it a liquidated damages clause, in which—"

"I'm familiar with the term. Are you telling me that there's such a clause in the lease pertaining to these letters?"

"Why, yes," she said, and now she looked at Reggie with her pale brow furrowed. "I hope there's no reason to say this," said the woman, "and I would certainly not be the one to snitch to Dorset National—but I trust you are truly just . . . tidying up—and not attempting to contact one of these people directly. That would be—"

"Bloody foolish," said Reggie.

He thanked the woman again.

And then he drove to Heathrow, with the address for the Los Angeles letter writer in his pocket.

4

At Heathrow, the only available evening flight required a layover and was not scheduled to arrive at Los Angeles until the following morning. Reggie knew this would put him nearly a full day behind Nigel, but it was the best that could be done, and he took it.

His seat was behind an American woman and her two young boys, probably ages four and six. In what seemed to Reggie a major tactical error, she had positioned herself on the aisle and the two boys next to each other on the inside seats.

Now an elbow was launched from one inside seat at the occupant of the other, and with that effort the little culprit threw himself back in his seat, causing it to crash into Reggie's knee. Reggie shifted his position. A retaliatory elbow came from the other side, with a similar effect, and Reggie adjusted his position once more.

"I told you to stop it," said the mother. "Someday you'll both be grown up, and if you don't learn to stop fighting, you won't be friends. Then where will you be?"

Do all mothers say this? thought Reggie. Do they read it in a book somewhere?

"Gin and tonic," he called out, perhaps more loudly than he had intended. The flight attendant was finished helping someone several seats away, and she came over.

"Would you like ice, sir?" She was standing near him now, quite attractive, leaning in, making him warmly aware of an intoxicating scent, and when Reggie smiled, her smile in response seemed genuine.

Reggie said that ice was unnecessary.

She smiled again. This one was not required professionally, and to Reggie it indicated possibilities. It had been his longstanding rule to always act on possibilities. Even if the odds were against—and rarely had he thought they were—one still had to presume a positive outcome and make one's move.

He had not in fact been with any other woman since Laura and had no intent to follow through on such a move—but of course that was not a reason to get out of practice.

But the flight attendant gave him his gin and tonic now, and he failed to think of anything clever to say before she moved off.

That was odd. Why was that?

But now there was another annoyance.

The two boys had been settled for a moment. But now the one next to his mother threw his right elbow again. War recommenced.

"Do I have to separate you two?" said the mother.

"No," said one brother and then the other, and they seemed to settle back again, but Reggie guessed this would be temporary, and he tried to cross his legs in advance to get out of the

way of the next skirmish. He inadvertently kicked the back of
the woman's seat in the process.

She looked around at Reggie.

"Forgive me," said Reggie.

She glanced to the side at her two boys, then smiled at Reggie.

"I hope they're not bothering you," she said.

"Not a bit," said Reggie in a bit of a lie, and then, feeling
churlish for his own initial impatience, he observed aloud that
they both had their mother's blond hair.

"Yes, they do," she said, "but I'm their grandmother."

She laughed, complimented by Reggie's mistake. Reggie
was unsettled; this woman could not have been more than ten
years older than he.

"Do you have any of your own?" she asked. "Children, I
mean?"

He said that he hadn't. She looked at him closely for a moment.

"Well," she said, "you are getting to that age."

There was no opportunity to ask what age she was referring
to, for she was suddenly distracted by the activities of the child
nearest her.

"Stop that, Richard," she said, but it was too late. Richard
had snuck down around her feet and loosed his battery-powered
Robotron upon the aisle. It must have been set on Mach cruise,
for it had already marched in a wobbly fashion past Reggie's
seat and on down the aisle.

Reggie turned, but it was beyond his reach.

It whirred and clanked on a diagonal path, two rows, then
three, finally, five rows back—then it butted up against the
metal base of an empty aisle seat, and it stuck there, making a
high-pitched whine, though its arms continued to move with
precision and regularity.

In the seat adjacent to the irritating toy sat a tall man reading a Hollywood trade magazine. Reggie expected the man to reach down and turn the device around. But the man didn't and instead kept his bald head averted to the side, too intent, apparently, on his day-old edition of *Variety*.

Reggie watched as Richard, with instructions from his grandmother to apologize to the nice man, ran down the aisle to ask for his toy back. In a whisper that carried into the next cabin, the grandmother repeated the instruction to apologize.

Richard stood in the aisle and mumbled something. "Nicely," instructed his grandmother.

"I'm sorry," Richard said loudly. "May I have my toy back?"

Now the man had no choice but to acknowledge his presence. He nodded slightly in the boy's direction.

"Here," he said. "Take your action figure."

Without dropping his paper, he pushed the toy toward Richard.

Richard grabbed it, returned at top speed to his grandmother, and surrendered the Robotron.

"They're a handful, but they're good boys," said the grandmother, and Reggie, on some instinct looking curiously back down the aisle but unable to clearly see the face of the man attacked by the toy, understood that this was the proper thing for her to say.

5

Reggie exited the terminal at LAX under a hazy sky but fierce heat.

He quickly discovered that his mobile phone didn't work—apparently the Americans had a completely different system. He hunted up a public phone to ring Laura's hotel room in New York—and also Nigel's flat in London, on the chance that his brother would at some point check his answering machine. He left messages for both, and for Ms. Brinks at chambers, that he would be at the Bonaventure.

Then he found a cab in front of the terminal. He showed the letter writer's address to the driver, and in a few moments they were moving east on the Santa Monica Freeway, toward the center of a ring of dirty haze.

It was late morning, not rush hour, but they had traveled only about five miles before traffic slowed to a crawl. The driver did not seem surprised.

"Wanna know the worst jam I ever seen?"

Reggie guessed that he really had no choice and said nothing.

"It was that big fire in the new subway dig on Lankershim. Somebody left a blowtorch on or something. Closed down the Ventura Freeway, the Hollywood, killed a guy—it was a mess. It was all over the news, even CNN. I'll bet they showed it even where you're from."

"Missed it somehow," said Reggie. "I didn't know you even had an underground in Los Angeles."

"A what?"

"A subway."

"Didn't used to. Got one now from downtown all the way to the Valley, and pretty soon they'll head east."

"Clever idea," said Reggie, eyeing the lanes of stalled traffic. "We built ours a century ago."

"Whoops," said the driver. Three major motorways were converging, and the lane they were traveling in ended abruptly The driver swerved radically into a right-hand lane that was still moving.

"Almost there," he said.

Less than a mile but ten minutes later, the driver exited the motorway. Within a few blocks, they entered a modest residential neighborhood, with narrow streets, skinny palm trees, and small front lawns drying in the sun.

The driver slowed and came to a stop in front of a faded yellow wood-frame house.

"You looking to buy?" said the driver.

Reggie checked the address. It was correct—but the house was vacant, with a lockbox on the door and a FOR SALE sign staked in the lawn, bearing the name of a local real estate agent.

"What a bleeding idiot I am," said Reggie. "The address is from twenty years ago. Of course she isn't here now."

But at least he had her name. He called directory assistance, and the operator told him the only Mara Ramirez in Los Angeles was on Cawley Street. Reggie gave the new address to the driver.

They got back on the motorway, the driver took the Alameda off-ramp, and now they were on surface streets in downtown Los Angeles. They passed the county jail, the train, and a bus depot.

Then the driver made two more turns, and they were on an empty frontage road running parallel to the Los Angeles River—a dry-looking flood control channel cut through the heart of the city, its concrete sides covered in graffiti that glinted red and gold in the sun.

They were driving not on asphalt now, but over metal sheets and heavy plywood that covered a trench cut down the center of the street. The plywood rattled and stirred up powdery dust on the edges as they drove.

"All this construction is for the new extension from downtown," announced the driver.

The taxi drove another block, then began to slow.

On the right-hand side of the road was a row of sooted brick buildings—warehouses, obviously abandoned now, with faded block letters identifying what had been toy and clothing wholesalers.

On the left was the fenced end of the subway construction that they had just passed; adjacent to that were rail lines, bracketed by pillars supporting a bridge across the river channel and by ramps of intersecting downtown motorways.

"This is it," said the driver. He turned the corner onto a cross street that ended at the frontage road, and brought the cab to a stop.

Reggie was skeptical. The cross street had been thoroughly

torn up for the subway trench. There was no traffic and only a few parked cars.

He looked at the street sign and asked the driver if there was another Cawley Street in the city. The driver shook his head.

"Not with those numbers," he said.

"Wait for me," said Reggie.

"Pay me," said the driver.

Reggie paid him, then got out and stood on the corner to get his bearings.

Behind him was a brick building that housed a soup kitchen, apparently closed at this hour. Black-stenciled letters identified the structure as the EAST CITY RESCUE MISSION.

To Reggie's left was the frontage road.

To his right on Cawley Street were several small, brave businesses that had struggled to stay open for any customer who could negotiate the construction obstacles and find their entrances.

But there were no apparent customers—just an elderly woman who slowly pushed a rusty shopping cart filled with ragged possessions that were probably everything she owned. A bent and dangling orange-and-white sign on the front of the cart, identifying a grocery market, rocked back and forth as she struggled to push the cart up over a curb.

McKenzie's Shoe Repair was boarded up but displayed a banner for its new location.

Angel's Used Books apparently could not relocate. It displayed a sign that said it was closed after twenty-five years and, in bold letters, **"Thank the Silver Line!"**

A dry cleaner was simply shuttered and displayed no sign at all.

Joe's Deli was the only business that seemed still to be hanging on. In the window was a roughly lettered sign proclaiming that the deli was still open during construction and boasting the best Philly sandwich in the West.

Not content just with the sign, Joe's Deli had tacked a box of flyers, with menus and directions to the deli, against plywood construction fencing on the frontage road. But—predictably— wind and other random forces of the city had scattered the flyers from their box, trampled them under foot, and now they skittered across the frontage road and along the dusty walkway on Cawley Street, until the wind plastered them against the walls of the rescue mission, and against Reggie's pants leg.

Now Reggie looked across the street from Joe's Deli, and he saw the address—it was a small block of flats, and the numbers on the building matched what Reggie had for the letter writer.

The structure looked to be at least fifty years old, and at first Reggie had assumed it to be abandoned. But as he approached he saw that it was indeed residential and occupied—with curtains, potted geraniums, and drying clothing in the windows. There was an open, arched entryway.

He stopped some yards off and hesitated.

He knew that contact with this letter writer would put his chambers lease at risk, if Dorset National should learn of it. But presumably Nigel had come here, and that was the only lead Reggie had.

Besides, how would Dorset National likely learn of it?

Now Reggie was distracted by motion on the boarded walkway adjacent to the building—he saw brown legs against a white cotton sundress and long dark hair falling over a young woman's bare shoulders as she approached the entrance to the building.

She stopped at the post box just outside the entryway. Reggie watched her pick up her letters and then go up an inside stairwell.

Reggie detached the Joe's Deli flyer from his leg. He crossed
the street, went up the same stairs, and found the apartment
address he was looking for.

He went inside and knocked on the apartment door.

After a short moment, the tiny latch window in the center
of the door opened, and Reggie saw, just for an instant, a pair
of soft and worried brown eyes. Then the window closed.

"I have a dog," the young woman announced loudly from
the other side of the door. "He's really big." Then she added, as
if it were an afterthought, "You can't hear him barking because
he's asleep right now, but if I woke him, he'd rip your arm off."

"Then kindly let him sleep," replied Reggie, though the dog
sounded like a ruse. "My name is Reggie Heath. I believe you
have met my brother." Reggie had a sense he had said these
words before, though he couldn't immediately recall where.

The woman behind the door was hesitating. Then the shutter opened, and there were those brown eyes again.

"His incisors," she said tentatively, "are at least an inch and
a half."

"I believe my brother, Nigel, was here," said Reggie. "But
I know he left a phone message. About a letter to Sherlock
Holmes."

"No," she said. "I've had no message like that."

"But you did write a letter to Sherlock Holmes? A letter
about your missing father?"

The shutter closed abruptly.

"Mookie! Wake up!" shouted the young woman.

There was a vibration in the floor and then a sharp and
heavy scuttling across a hard surface. Then the door opened
wide, and Reggie had just enough instinct to step back as 150
pounds of what was apparently Mookie charged through. It was
the largest Saint Bernard he had ever seen.

Mookie displayed a remarkably narrow turning radius, and although Reggie initially made an adept dodge, he was obliged to retreat down the stairs as rapidly as possible. He took the first two steps backward, and then, turning to continue the rout face first, saw that he was not the only person on the stairs.

A man in a two-tone suede leather jacket was standing only a few steps below Reggie. The man had flattened himself as much as possible against the wall, but what Reggie saw in his face was more a look of hostility than any fear of the slobbering presence close behind Reggie.

In the next instant, a heavy weight struck Reggie in the back, pitching him forward into the stairwell.

He had time to get one forearm beneath him, but it was not enough.

He came to at the bottom of the stairs. His forehead was throbbing, and when he touched it, his hand came away wet with blood.

As his senses began to clear and he got to his feet, he heard their voices.

"Is he all right?"

That was the young woman's voice. Reggie saw her standing halfway up the stairwell. The Saint Bernard was pressing its considerable bulk against her legs, slobbering and grinning.

Between the young woman and Reggie was the man with the two-tone jacket, and he answered her.

"He'll live, Mara. Did he bother you?"

Mara shook her head, then she turned, and without waiting for more of a response from either Reggie or the man in the jacket, she started back up the stairs.

Reggie stumbled out to the street, looking for his cab. Thank God, it was still there. And there was the driver, already looking in Reggie's direction and getting out to help, and— No, now seeing Reggie's condition, he was tossing Reggie's carry-on out of the boot and driving away.

Bloody hell.

Reggie pressed a handkerchief against his forehead, staggered over to the one bag he'd brought from London, and took out his mobile to call another taxi.

No signal. He'd forgotten the damn thing wouldn't work here.

He looked about. There was not a public phone in sight, and given the location and condition of the street, he knew he could wait forever and not see another cab.

But three blocks up the street was a red neon sign for the Roosevelt Arms—a hotel with peeling pink stucco and rusty window air conditioners.

It was the only option. He picked up his carry-on bag and trudged toward it.

Several head-throbbing minutes later, he entered the dimly lit lobby.

He surveyed the floral-print carpeting, the five-dollar prints of waves crashing at sunset, and the purple simulated-leather chairs and concluded that if the cost of the place was like its decor, it had to be the cheapest lodging around.

Reggie considered that fact for a moment.

If Nigel was in the area, this would be his affordable choice.

Reggie approached the bored desk clerk and asked for Nigel Heath.

"Yeah. He was here. Checked out."

"When?"

The clerk shrugged. "Not long, I guess. Do you want a room or what?"

"Thank you, no," said Reggie. "Did he say where he was going next?"

"No. Promised to write, though."

"Has the room been cleaned?"

"You want a room, I got one available on the third floor. Clean as a baby's bottom."

"No doubt. But what about the room where my brother stayed?"

"I don't know if my staff has gotten to it yet," said the clerk.

This was sarcasm. Reggie recognized the tone from weekend holidays in Paris.

"May I see it?"

"You can rent it."

"Of course," said Reggie. He paid the full day's rent with his American dollars and climbed the stairs carrying his bag with him.

In Reggie's experience, American hotel rooms typically smelled too much of bleached linen and antiseptic cleaners. Unfortunately, the rooms of this hotel did not have that fault; the corridor smelled instead of mildew and substances best left unidentified.

Reggie found Nigel's room. For reasons he did not understand, he knocked first. There was no response. Of course there wasn't. He opened the door.

He realized now he had half expected that Nigel would still be there, despite the clerk's assurances that the occupant had checked out.

But there was no one.

The bed, small by American standards, apparently had not been slept in. There was nothing lying about on the faded carpeting to prove Nigel had been there, though Reggie supposed the absence of empty beer cans and whiskey bottles might in itself indicate that the most recent tenant had not been of the usual clientele.

The closet was empty; there were no toiletries left behind

in the bathroom. Some loose stationery in the desk drawer bore the logo of a local car rental agency. But nothing was jotted down. No pressure markings on anything. And still no positive trace of Nigel.

Reggie looked at the wastebasket at the side of the desk. It had not been emptied, and he removed the contents: one empty tube of chocolate Smarties.

Nigel had been here.

Reggie returned to the front desk and spoke again with the helpful clerk.

"Do you have a record of outgoing calls?"

"Sure. It's in the billing."

"I'd like to see the billing for my brother's stay."

"I'm probably not supposed to do that," said the clerk, looking at Reggie expectantly.

Reggie put a twenty-pound note on the counter.

"What's this?" said the clerk.

"Twenty pounds. At current exchange rates, that's well over thirty dollars."

The clerk studied the note. "You're telling me a pound is better than a dollar?"

"Usually."

"You don't have dollars?"

"No," said Reggie.

"Well, I need forty. I don't know from exchange rates; forty, pounds or dollars."

Reggie put out another twenty-pound note. The clerk put both in his pocket, turned away for a moment, then turned back with a printout of Nigel's stay.

It showed that Nigel had called six numbers—the first five, one right after the other, with no more than two-minute gaps between the placement of each call—and then a twenty-minute gap before the sixth and final number.

Reggie went back to Nigel's hotel room. He made the assumption that the very last in the list must have given Nigel something he was looking for—and he tried it first.

He reached Pizza Premieres, which claimed to deliver pepperoni to the stars.

Nigel might well have been looking for pizza. But that wasn't much help.

Reggie began calling the other five numbers. On the first, he reached something called Selman Productions. The receptionist pleasantly told Reggie that he couldn't speak to Mr. Selman without an appointment, and if Reggie was someone who had to ask, he couldn't have an appointment.

No help there. Reggie tried the next number.

Another production company, and with similar restrictions—no help there, either.

He tried the third and then two more after that. All production companies, all with the same result.

So Nigel had rung up five film production companies in rapid succession—and then, several minutes later, apparently having worked up an appetite with that effort, he'd ordered take-away pizza.

Reggie picked up his luggage again, dragged it back downstairs, and asked the desk clerk if Nigel had left by taxi.

This was apparently a tough one, and the clerk had to think about it.

"No," he said after a moment. "When he checked out, he was on foot. When he wanted a taxi—that was yesterday."

"You called the taxi for him?"

"Yeah, probably."

"You have a preferred provider arrangement with one of the smaller locals, I'd expect."

"Huh?"

"Do you usually call the same taxi company?"

"Usually get the same cabbie, too."

"Brilliant. Call him for me, would you? I'll pay the charges."

"Now that I think about it, might be tough to get the same guy again."

Reggie laid out another twenty pounds, and the clerk made the call.

Ten minutes later, the taxi pulled up.

"I'm looking for a fare you picked up from here yesterday," Reggie said.

"I pick up lots of fares. You got a picture?"

"No. Someone who sounded like me."

"Oh, right. I remember. The other Australian guy."

"The other British guy. I want to go where you took him."

"I don't know if I'm supposed to do that," said the driver.

Reggie sighed and pulled out yet another twenty-pound note.

6

They drove for forty minutes, moving at a reasonable speed north through the Cahuenga Pass and then slowing to a crawl when they merged onto the Ventura Freeway.

The driver had offered to take an alternate route, over surface streets—but Reggie was not often fooled by such offers from taxi drivers, was not impressed by the boast that they could drive past the studio for *The Tonight Show*, and insisted on the motorway.

A mistake, apparently.

Now, finally, the driver exited the motorway. He made two more turns, covering perhaps a mile, and then came to a stop.

"Why are we stopping?"

"This is it," he said.

"There's nothing here," said Reggie.

"Can't help that," said the driver. "This is where the guy wanted out."

Reggie got out of the cab.

The air, hot, thick, and lung-tightening, hung in a visible gray haze over the nearby San Gabriel Mountains.

The street was barricaded at all intersection points but one and was thoroughly torn up. The center of it was consumed by a cut-and-cover trench several feet across, like the one Reggie had seen downtown, blocked and covered by wooden barricades and thick plywood platforms.

"Did my brother say where he was going when he got out of your cab?" Reggie asked the driver.

"Why would he tell me? He's not my brother."

"Which way did he walk?"

"He just stood there, like you're doing. That's where I left him. And I work on the clock."

Reggie looked to the north, up the street, where an entire city block had vanished into a massive excavation. The site was surrounded by a board fence crowned with razor wire; from the center towered an eighty-foot mustard yellow excavation crane.

The gated entrance was a few dozen yards down the street. But Reggie could see no reason for that to be Nigel's destination.

Reggie looked south. For two blocks in that direction there was nothing but razed, fenced ground, where the original buildings had been leveled in preparation for new construction. But some distance farther was a corporate tower with walls of reflective glass, rising up thirty-odd stories from the floor of the Valley, dominating the skyline like a citadel. It shone dark like obsidian on the shaded side, but bright like steel on the sunlit side, reflecting images of the sage-covered hills and the solidifying layer of smog to the east.

The name of the building glinted in silver block letters on the top floor.

But if that had been Nigel's destination, why would he get out here, a quarter mile away?

"What's in the Paradigm building?" Reggie asked the driver.

"I don't know. Movies, maybe?"

"Take me there," said Reggie.

He got in the cab and rode the quarter mile to the Paradigm tower. It would have been a bit of a walk from Nigel's drop-off point, but perhaps he had gotten out at the wrong spot by mistake.

They drove south past the two blocks that had been flattened for new construction. In the next block—immediately adjacent to the reflecting tower—construction was already complete, and the new businesses here were apparently flourishing. There was a huge car park and a café that had customers queued up clear onto the pavement.

Reggie paid the driver to wait and got out of the cab at the tower entrance. He entered the lobby, and on a hunch, he pulled out the phone list from Nigel's hotel and carefully perused the building's roster for the production company names Nigel had called.

Nothing. There was no match. It was a bust.

Reggie had the driver take him back to the point where he had dropped Nigel. He got out and looked across at the massive excavation site.

"What are they digging?" he asked the driver.

"Subway terminal," the driver said. "Seen enough?"

"No," said Reggie. "Wait for me."

Reggie crossed the street, his footsteps reverberating on the wooden planking, to the entrance for the construction site.

The excavation pit was more than fifty yards across and at least a hundred in length, with sheer vertical sides. The perimeter was fenced, but through the gate Reggie could see a construction bungalow. He walked through the gate, heading toward the bungalow.

A pleasant young woman in an orange hard hat and security guard's vest stopped him and asked if she could be of assistance.

Reggie said he wanted to see the foreman. The young woman didn't ask why; she just gave Reggie a quick visual once-over, then turned and went right back into the bungalow.

In an instant she appeared again in the doorway, pointed in Reggie's direction, and then stepped aside as a tall man, face deeply tanned and lined from the sun, came charging down the steps.

He was as much as sixty years old, Reggie judged from the white hair showing under the hard hat, but he could have been much younger from the energy in his stride.

"I'm Sanger," he said, sticking out his hand, "and you are . . . ?"

Reggie gave his name. Sanger had a grip like stone.

"What station are you with?"

"Excuse me?"

"I put out a statement this morning. You want more, here's your quote, and get it right: 'Shit happens.' End quote. You want this on tape, you wait till I break for lunch. That's in about six hours. Unless I get busy. Right now I'm due in the pit. Excuse me."

Sanger began to walk away toward the excavation, and Reggie followed quickly.

"I'm not a reporter," he said as they strode toward the edge of the pit.

"You're not from Channel Seven?"

"Do I look like a television reporter?"

Sanger stopped and appraised Reggie quickly. "Yes," he said. "Except for that thing on your forehead."

"I'm not."

"Sound like one, too. CNN?"

"I'm not from a news agency of any kind."

"This is not about Sunset Boulevard?"

"I'm just looking for someone," said Reggie.

Sanger paused. "You'll have to excuse me," he said with a sort of sheepish grin. "I've had reporters up the wazoo, and I guess I'm beginning to see 'em behind every rock."

"That would be annoying."

"It is. Every damn little thing gets reported. Last week someone broke in here and figured it would be fun to pour five pounds of damn sugar into the mole's gas tank. Standard high school prank, but it made the five o'clock news. Then two nights ago an underground water main ruptures next to the new tunnel between the downtown and Hollywood sites, creating a sinkhole clear across Sunset, and some poor hooker tripped and mussed herself falling in. That made the five o'clock, the six, the ten, and the eleven o'clock news."

"Of course," said Reggie. "Nothing gets media attention like water-damaged hookers."

"Yeah, and I just hope she doesn't sue me for missing a night's work."

Sanger looked down into the construction pit now, whistled to workers below, and a motor connected to the platform whirred into gear. "So who did you say you're looking for?"

"My brother, Nigel Heath."

"Don't know the name."

"I think he might have come here yesterday."

"For what?"

Reggie had no good answer. "He was looking for work, I suspect."

"All we're hiring is subsoil engineers. That what he's looking for?"

"Possibly."

Sanger leaned casually against the precariously low guardrail. He looked Reggie up and down. "Your brother's a sandhog?"

"We don't call them sandhogs at home."

"What do you call them?"

"Subsoil engineers."

Sanger put two fingers to his lips and let out a loud and commanding whistle.

The young woman in the orange vest hurried over.

"You see somebody looks like this guy yesterday?" said Sanger.

"Hmm."

"Or sounds like him?"

"Well, I don't know until I hear—"

"He means a British accent," said Reggie, "like mine."

"Oh, yeah. There was this guy I caught running around between the cars."

"Uh-huh," said Sanger. "And was that just his way of asking for a job?"

"I don't think so. He said he was tracking a hit-and-run. Or something like that; he was kind of evasive about it. I threw him out."

"Yeah, thought so." Sanger gave Reggie a hard look, and then he said to the guard, "Do the same for this one."

"Thank you for your time," said Reggie, and the security guard escorted him to the gate.

Sweating from the afternoon heat, Reggie got in his taxi and told the driver to take him back to downtown L.A.

7

Reggie returned to downtown Los Angeles and booked into the Bonaventure.

It was less than a mile from the Roosevelt Arms, where Nigel had stayed, but it was a world of difference.

A desk clerk in the spacious lobby looked askance at Reggie's bruised forehead and mentioned, with more suspicion than concern, that the hotel had a licensed nurse on staff.

"I'm fine," said Reggie, "if you have aspirins and ice."

They did have these things, the clerk said. And with a little effort, they could set him up on an American cell phone as well.

Reggie took the glass lift up more than twenty floors.

Then he sat in a deep chair with a bag of ice and a glass of dark port.

With the uncomfortably long flight and layover, he had not slept in any meaningful way in more than thirty-six hours. Jet lag and the wine were stronger than the pain in his head, and though he did not intend to, he faded.

Then he woke with a start. The hotel phone was ringing.

He picked up.

It was Wembley.

"What time is it?" said Reggie.

"Just past eight in the morning here," Heath said cheerily. "Not sure what it is in your zone. Hope I didn't wake you."

"No," said Reggie. He knew Wembley bloody well knew it was after midnight.

"On holiday, are you, Heath?"

"Yes," Reggie said tightly.

"Might have let me know. If I hadn't managed to pry your number out of Ms. Brinks, I wouldn't be able to inform you now that we're going for a warrant on your brother."

"On what evidence?" said Reggie.

"Seems there was a dispute between the two of them—Ocher and your brother—in your brother's office, the Friday before the murder."

"What about?"

"I was rather hoping you'd fill that in for me, Heath."

Reggie presumed this was the conversation Ocher had related in the lift. It was hardly a motive for murder, and for a moment he considered trying to explain that tiff away for Wembley: Ocher trying to get Nigel to concentrate on his primary work, but Nigel being obsessed with these bloody letters that a girl had written to Sherlock Holmes.

That was all there was to it.

Well, perhaps "obsessed" would not be the best word to use.

"Still there, Heath?" said Wembley.

"Can't help you there," said Reggie. "And if that's all you've got, I'd say a warrant is premature."

"We know voices were raised; they were overheard. We've got

the dispute, whatever the specifics turn out to be, and we've got his fingerprints on the murder weapon."

"Nigel's fingerprints on a sculpture in Nigel's office? You've got nothing."

"I've got enough," said Wembley, and the cheerfulness was gone. "You'd be doing your brother a favor if you put us in touch with him."

"I've no idea where he is," said Reggie.

"I'm sure you'll hear from him. Do let us know."

"I'll keep it in mind," said Reggie.

"Enjoy your holiday," said Wembley. "I'll be in touch." And he hung up.

Reggie remained seated in his chair, and now he took the remaining gulp of the port.

He had no choice but to try a look at it from Wembley's point of view—or the point of view Wembley would likely take once he knew all that Reggie already knew—and the picture was this: Nigel continuing to play around with those bloody letters. Ocher coming in Monday morning and once again berating Nigel over a requisition form or some other such nonsense (sounding, in Reggie's imagination, uncomfortably like Reggie himself); Nigel finally deciding in a violent impulse that he would take no more of it and rising, bronze Remington of Indians hunting buffalo in hand, to bash Ocher's head in.

Utter nonsense. Nigel was not capable of it. He was not impulsive.

Well, perhaps occasionally impulsive. But he'd never done a violent act in his life. Reggie could not recall Nigel ever being in so much as a schoolyard fight.

Of course, there would not have been the time or the energy, it occurred to him now. Growing up, he and his brother had always been too busy fighting each other.

But that didn't count. Between brothers, fighting was a means of conversation. There was a familiarity that erased barriers and made some low level of violence possible between siblings that did not apply to outsiders.

Massaging a bump still present on the top of his head from the time his eight-year-old brother had knocked him with a cricket bat, Reggie insisted on his original hypothesis: Nigel was not capable of it.

Remaining certain of that would make things simpler. Instead of worrying about the possibility of Nigel being guilty, he would worry only about proving that he was not.

Now the hotel phone rang again.

Reggie picked up. It was the desk clerk. There was a fax for Reggie in the lobby.

"A fax?"

"Yes, sir. Marked 'Urgent.'"

"Who—"

"You did say that if someone named Nigel Heath tried to contact you—"

"Send it up."

The desk clerk did so. Five minutes later, Reggie stood in his room staring at the message from his brother.

"Meet me at foot of 2nd Street. 2:00 AM. Nigel."

Bloody damn. A street meeting in the middle of the night.

Why couldn't Nigel learn to carry a mobile?

Reggie got his coat, went downstairs, and was lucky enough to find a taxi in front of the hotel.

It was little more than a mile, and just five minutes of the hour, when the cab approached the foot of 2nd Street.

The street ended on the same frontage road Reggie had been on when he first arrived. Farther south was the fence that bordered the concrete riverbed, and to the east was the block of flats where Reggie had tumbled down the stairs.

The taxi stopped beneath the last weak yellow streetlamp. The cabbie apparently did not care for the area and drove away immediately.

Reggie stood for several moments at the corner. There was no other traffic on the street: no cars, no pedestrians, and no lights of any establishment.

In London, this would have been the place to go to purchase something illegal.

And as if to confirm that opinion, Reggie saw the black-and-white panels of a Los Angles police car cruise through the intersection at the next block down.

Reggie waited a moment, but the squad car did not turn again and come back in his direction.

He looked at his watch. Now it was five minutes after. And there was no sign of Nigel.

Somewhere on the next street over, a dog was barking.

He looked at the street signs over his head. Yes, this was the foot of 2nd Street.

Reggie looked southwest, toward the fence. Well, he wasn't quite standing at the foot of 2nd Street. The actual foot of 2nd Street was at the fence, another fifty yards or so, under the dark of the bridge overpass. Surely this was putting too fine a point on it, but Reggie began to walk in that direction.

As he approached, he could make out details that hadn't been visible from a distance—shards of broken bottles, newspaper that stirred in the slight wind, a couple of flattened, refrigerator-size cardboard boxes, a discarded automobile bench seat propped against one of the concrete supports.

At the end of the street, a sizable hole was visible at the bottom of the wire fence. The wind carried a stale, dank odor of old food and urine.

Odd choice of a meeting place, even for Nigel.

Reggie began to turn back toward the corner, but then he stopped—at the edge of the concrete support, next to the car seat, something appeared to move.

It was the wind, probably, but he stepped toward it.

He saw now that it was just the torn corner of a green garbage bag, covering the rubbishy contents of a banged-up shopping cart. One edge of the garbage bag had been hooked over a bent orange-and-white sign for the grocery from which it had been taken. There was a slight breeze, and the corner edge of the bag flapped slightly.

Something was odd—the sound of the flapping vinyl, perhaps.

Reggie reached down to the edge of the garbage bag—but then his fingertips touched a texture that caused him to pull back immediately.

In the dark beneath the slick black-green bag was a pale human face.

This time it was not like finding Ocher in the brightly lit office. This time it was different.

Reggie steadied himself with one arm against the concrete wall. He managed to draw a breath, and he looked again.

No, it was not Nigel. It was not.

This realization had barely taken hold when, from just yards away, brakes screeched, and the moan of an American police siren reverberated off the concrete walls.

Reggie looked up directly into the squad car's spotlight. For a blinking moment he could see nothing but that light, and his first instinct was to put up an arm to shield it.

"Freeze!"

Reggie did so. He heard car doors slam; one of the officers approached.

Reggie expected there was going to be a further reaction when the officer got a few steps closer, and there was.

"Freeze, freeze, freeze!" shouted the officer, who must have now seen the body. "Don't move! Put your hands on the wall!"

Reggie did not move at all. He could hear the adrenaline in the officer's voice, and through the glare of the spotlight he could see that the very young officer had his revolver drawn.

Reggie thought it wise to ask, as loudly as he could, which of the two contrary instructions they preferred he should obey first. "Put your hands on the wall," said the voice again. He carefully raised his right hand in full view of the squad car and placed it on the wall next to his left.

As he did so, something on the ground caught his eye. He had, in fact, almost stepped on them, and there was no question what they were.

Someone had spilled Smarties. Green-, blue-, yellow-, and red-shelled chocolate disks—and half a dozen or so were scattered exactly where Reggie was standing and within just a few feet of the body in the cart.

In the spotlight reflecting off the walls, they actually glistened.

Reggie shuffled his feet, trying to push them out of sight.

"Freeze!" shouted the officer again, and his voice had now climbed at least half an octave. Reggie hoped they would get on with it before the officer with the drawn gun could make a mistake.

Finally, someone came and pulled Reggie's arms down and cuffed them.

As the police hustled him toward the squad car, Reggie managed to turn his head and look back.

They had pulled the trash bag back from the body, and now Reggie caught a glimpse of what the man was wearing.

Now he knew. He hadn't recognized the facial features, but there was no mistaking the two-tone jacket: It was the man from Mara's stairs.

"I was just about to ring you," said Reggie as an officer pushed on his head to guide him into the back of the car.

8

At the Los Angeles Central Police Station, Reggie stared stonily at the camera for the face-front shot and then squared his shoulders and turned right for the profile.

When he had seen photos of wanted felons before on news reports, it had always seemed curious that they could manage to look so sullenly guilty. Now he knew that guilty or not, looking sullen was unavoidable.

The clerkish, uniformed man giving the photography instructions was as matter-of-fact as if Reggie had simply come in for his driving license. That was irritating. Reggie's own adrenaline was flowing now, more so than when weapons had been drawn at the overpass.

Now he was ushered into a narrow room with darkened glass in one wall and told to stand with his toes to a yellow line. Along with four other individuals in the room, Reggie stood and faced the glass, and then on instruction he did the profile maneuver again.

If the young woman with the dog was on the other side of the glass, she would surely have no difficulty picking him out. Of the four other men standing in the lineup, none resembled him in the slightest; one was wearing a policeman's shoes, and only one stood within two inches of Reggie's height. And the bruise inflicted by the bloody dog was still visible on Reggie's forehead.

After a moment, an instruction came from the other side of the glass:

"Number one, say something."

None of the men said anything. The voice came again:

"Number one, say, 'Do you have any Earl Grey tea?'"

This did not sound promising. Reggie had not uttered any such words since arriving in Los Angeles—or at any time that he could immediately recall—but Nigel might well have.

He looked to the man at the far left, who looked back and shrugged. Reggie looked at the man wearing the policeman's shoes, at the far right, who displayed a look of intense frustration but stared straight ahead and said nothing.

The voice again:

"Number one, would you please say—"

"No one bloody knows which of us you have designated as number one," said Reggie.

This apparently caused some commotion. The intercom crackled, and he was told to step forward and did so. He stared straight ahead at the glass for several seconds and then stepped back again.

It would have been comforting to see the same procedure repeated with the other individuals, but it didn't happen. Instead, the side door opened, and everyone but Reggie was invited to leave.

Reggie was escorted to a plain room and then introduced to

Detective Mendoza—a sixtyish man with white-gray hair—and Detective Reynolds—a dozen or so years younger than Mendoza and some fifty pounds heavier.

Reggie was invited to sit at the table, and Mendoza sat across from him, perusing Reggie's passport.

"What's your address, Reggie?" said Mendoza.

"Nine Shad Thames. But I didn't catch your first name."

"You here on business or pleasure . . . Mr. Heath?"

Reggie replied that his visit was recreational. Offhand, he couldn't think of a business reason that would survive scrutiny.

"You should have checked with the tourist bureau," said Mendoza. "There's no forms of recreation I know of to be had that close to the river channel. Unless, of course, you were interested in purchasing some form of illegal substance, which is something we tend to frown on locally. Is that what you were doing, Mr. Heath—trying to purchase a little chemical recreation?"

"No."

Reggie considered whether to say anything about Nigel. On the one hand, he was concerned that Nigel had not shown at the rendezvous. On the other, there were the bloody Smarties—and the nagging fear that Nigel could be in some way connected to the clammy corpse under the overpass. Best to say nothing—and hope that Wembley had not yet contacted the Los Angeles police about either of the Heath brothers.

"You seem uncomfortable, Mr. Heath. Is there any reason why you feel you might need the presence of an attorney?"

"It's a moot point. I am one."

Mendoza raised an eyebrow very slightly and sat back in his chair; the other detective just smirked.

Altogether they did not seem as intimidated as one might have hoped.

"That's fine," said Mendoza. "Saves you a quarter, if you want to ignore that thing about having a fool for a client. But no one has charged you with anything here. So why don't you just tell us what happened?"

"I went for a walk and was handcuffed at gunpoint. But I believe you know that."

"You were found in the presence of what would appear to be a homicide victim," Mendoza said dryly.

"Charge me with finding a corpse, if you have a law against that. But I know nothing about it."

"A witness has already identified you by voice."

"In regard to what?"

Mendoza did not say anything in response; he just leaned back with a show of confidence, folded his hands at the back of his head, and looked appraisingly at Reggie.

Reggie gave the same look in return and after a moment concluded the detectives were bluffing. The lineup must have failed visually, even though the detectives claimed to have a match on the voice.

Of course, even at home, strangers had occasionally confused Reggie's voice with Nigel's.

Better to avoid that subject entirely.

"I've done nothing," said Reggie. "You've already had me on display, and your supposed witness could not claim to have seen me before in any sort of incriminating circumstance. Otherwise, you'd have placed me under arrest. So I take it I'm free to go."

He stood and reached across the table for his passport.

Mendoza pulled it back. "If it's all the same to you, we'll just hold this here until you're ready to leave."

"No, I'll take it with me."

"I guess you're not very familiar with the police procedures in the States, Mr. Heath."

"I know that you can't keep that without an order from a magistrate," said Reggie, hoping it was true here.

"No problem," said Mendoza, smiling and handing back the passport. "But when you think you're ready to leave the city, you be sure to give me a call."

9

Sleep-deprived and unshaven, Reggie left the police station.

There were now two murders to account for. The police on both affected continents apparently were not in communication yet—but Mendoza might at this moment be checking with Scotland Yard.

Whether the authorities would eventually try to distribute the culpability evenly—like Mum distributing biscuits, one for Nigel and one for Reggie—or just gang up both murders on one or the other was still to be determined, but neither prospect was appealing.

Reggie could see one thing in common between the two events, though, and that was the young woman who both wrote the letters and—apparently—knew the second victim.

He took a taxi back to Mara's flat. If he was to get any information from her at all, he would have to reach her before the police did.

He went up the stairs and knocked on the same door he had the day before.

No response.

He knocked again, and still no response.

That had to mean she was out walking that dog. He would have heard it rushing the door otherwise. She would be back. After all, how many places could she go with a 150-pound Saint Bernard?

Reggie came back downstairs and crossed the street, to wait at the desperately open Joe's Deli.

He walked across the plywood excavation covering and stepped over bags of tunnel grouting. When he entered the café, he brought with him a little swirl of gray dust.

Inside were mustard-colored vinyl booths, a tan-flecked linoleum floor, and fans circulating overhead slowly and unsuccessfully against the heat.

The near wall was covered with signed photographs of would-be actors, directors, producers, and other celebrities of types that Reggie could only imagine. Judging from the ties they wore, some of them had been hanging there for many years. One or two of the photographs actually looked just vaguely familiar, though Reggie could not place from where. He guessed that even the locals would not recognize most of them.

The waitress, a plump woman of about fifty in a dress of tiny red and white checks, hurried over from behind the counter.

"You can sit anywhere you like," she said, trying to convey, despite evidence to the contrary, that this was a rare privilege.

"Should I know them?" said Reggie.

"What? Who? Oh, on the wall?" She shook her head with a sort of knowing smile. "I have no idea at all who any of those people are. Most of them have been hanging there since the day we opened."

"Actors?"

"All of them movie biz of one kind or another, I guess." She shrugged. "They could be anything by now. Sit wherever you like," she said again.

The establishment had been built to handle fifty or so at rush hour, and from the apparent age of the place, it had survived for some years at that capacity. But at the moment, though it was prime time on a weekday, it was empty.

This was a bad sign for breakfast, but good for Reggie's other purposes, and he took a booth by the window, with a clear view of the entrance to Mara's building.

The woman came over with a glass pot of some sort of thick black fluid and began to pour a cup of it for Reggie.

Reggie preferred coffee, even American coffee, to badly made tea, but this stuff looked dangerous.

"I don't suppose," he began, "you would have any Earl Grey—" And then he stopped. The woman was suddenly staring, and now she took a step back, and he immediately knew why.

"It's you!"

"No, it isn't," said Reggie. "I've never been here before in my life."

"From the police station!"

"Yes, but—"

"I'll call them right now if you make another move."

"I'm not moving," said Reggie, "and just think about it. Yes, I was in the lineup, but you did not pick me. And that's why they let me go. And that makes us friends. Doesn't it?"

"But I told them you sound the same," she said.

"Do I look the same?"

She was calmer now, and she took a step closer to study him.

"You had the same jawline, but you weren't quite so tall, and—"

That would be Nigel, but Reggie said nothing.

"—your hair wasn't so thin."

Reggie wanted to object to that, but he decided to let it go.

"When did you see me—I mean, this shorter but thicker-haired version of me?"

She said that he had sat at that same table the day before in the afternoon, and the day before that as well, and she remembered him clearly, because he had tipped very generously, even though they had no Earl Grey tea.

And then Reggie abruptly asked for the check—through the café window he could see the Saint Bernard coming around the corner, dragging its attractive young owner at the other end of the leash.

Reggie overpaid his bill and quickly crossed the street.

Mara was just starting up the stairs as he reached the curb. The Saint Bernard turned around to face him, straining the leash and causing Mara to turn as well.

"Please," said Reggie, "I mean no harm. If you don't trust me, come across to the café and talk with me where others are present. Well, some, anyway. Bring Cujo with you if you want."

She looked at Reggie, and then in both directions of the empty street, and then at Reggie again. There was doubt in those burnt sienna eyes, but she was considering it.

"What do you want?" she said.

"I must find my brother. He came here believing you were in some sort of trouble. And now . . ."

"And now—what?"

"Now he is."

She hesitated, pulling back on the dog's leash. "What kind of trouble?"

"Well, I'm not sure the exact details are all that important," said Reggie.

"Give me a ballpark," she said. "Are we talking life and death, parking tickets, or what?"

"He's gone missing," said Reggie. And that part was true enough; it wouldn't do to tell her all of it.

Mara studied him closely. The dog stood solidly with its weight against her legs and studied him, too.

"They have lousy coffee," she said after a moment. "You can come upstairs."

She turned abruptly and started up the steps, pulled along rapidly by the dog, leaving Reggie flat-footed at the base. He took the stairs several steps at a time to catch up.

She opened the door to the flat, and Reggie immediately identified scents of turpentine, paint, and canvas. She had set easels along the largest window. Her paintings depicted a bright yellow wood-frame house; a child alone on a swing at dusk; and a huge backyard pepper tree with fallen clusters of tiny red berries and small green leaves.

"I work at an art gallery," said the young woman as Reggie noticed the paintings. "But the owner doesn't show my work, she says I need to get out of my domestic period. That one's the house I lived in when I was a kid. But this is the last of the domestic series, so you better buy it now before I get famous and expensive."

"The house or the painting?" said Reggie.

"I meant the painting, of course—my mom and I had to sell the house years ago. But if you're actually interested, I drove by it last week. It's vacant and up for sale again. I almost wanted to go in and take a look."

"Revisit happy childhood memories?" said Reggie.

"Yes," she said, "mostly. You can sit if you like."

There was a multicolored braided rug on a hardwood floor, a small table with cane-backed chairs, and a comfortable-looking couch. But the Saint Bernard jumped onto the couch, and Reggie was obliged to accept one of the less comfortable-looking chairs.

Reggie looked about the room for some hint of bereavement. He hadn't seen it in her face. So either she didn't know yet or the dead man meant nothing to her.

"He was a complete stranger," she said.

"Who?" said Reggie.

She gave Reggie a puzzled look. "The man you said is your brother. He was a complete stranger, and I had no idea what he was talking about, so I sent him away. That was about it. Do you want some water?"

Reggie said yes, and though he knew she expected him to remain seated, he followed her into the kitchen. Mookie followed also, keeping his substantial girth between Reggie and the young woman and effectively sandwiching Reggie against the kitchen counter as Mara opened the refrigerator door.

The kitchen was narrow, but it was immaculate.

There was a wooden sash window at the opposite end of the room. It was closed, but Mara opened it now, revealing the rusted iron railing of the fire escape. Beyond the iron railing was a narrow alley and, across that, what looked to be an abandoned warehouse.

Mookie stopped staring at Reggie for the moment and began to nose his supper dish about on the floor.

"Just what was it my brother said to you?" said Reggie.

She studied Reggie's face uncertainly for a moment. "He asked about some letters," she said finally as she handed him a bottled water. "Seemed like a decent guy, actually. But he asked if I wrote a letter to Sherlock Holmes last month." She stopped with that and glared defensively. "I'm not stupid. I don't wait up for Santa Claus, and I don't write letters to characters of fiction."

"Perhaps you waited up for Santa Claus when you were a child?"

She looked at Reggie for a moment, then nodded.

"Yes," she said. "When I was only eight and didn't know any better. I mean, I read a lot, but—you know, it's not like I knew about the world. And I was desperate. So I wrote a letter to Sherlock Holmes."

"Just the one letter when you were eight? You didn't write again recently?"

"Of course not. Why would I?"

"No reason," said Reggie. "What else did my brother say to you?"

"I really didn't give him the chance to say much of anything," she said.

"You're sure there was nothing else? You've told me nothing that can help me find him."

"Well, you guys weren't much help finding my father!" she blurted, and then she quickly recovered. "I mean—whoever got my letter wasn't. And the police didn't do jack."

"It must have seemed that way when you were eight," said Reggie. "I'm sure the locals did the best they—"

"I'm sure you don't know what you're talking about," Mara said heatedly. "First they said they had to wait awhile, then they said he must be on a bender and sleeping it off, then they said he must have run away because he lost at Santa Anita."

"Sorry," said Reggie, "I didn't mean to—"

"Well, all right, he drank a little. And he went to the track once in a while. I drink wine with my lunch—well, sometimes—and I bought a lotto ticket once. Does that mean if I disappear, nobody should come find me?"

"Someone would certainly come find *you*," said Reggie, and then he immediately wished he hadn't—or at least not with the inflection he had given it.

Her eyes narrowed, and her chin tilted up.

"But the point now is," Reggie said quickly, "Nigel came here in response to your letter. If I knew exactly what you sent—it might help me find him."

"Why do you need me for that? Don't you have the letter?"

"It's gone, actually. And whatever you sent with it. There was an enclosure, wasn't there?"

"There was something I sent with it, yes," Mara said after a moment.

"I think if I had that—I'd be able to figure out where my brother is—or at least what he's trying to do."

Reggie moved closer and made eye contact to say that. Mara looked directly back at him.

"Can you be trusted?" she said.

"Yes," said Reggie.

She was still studying him closely.

"I can sort of see the family resemblance," she said, "though you don't have your brother's eyes, exactly."

She got up and crossed to the mantel above a gas fireplace. She moved aside framed photographs and several old books that hid a tin box. Then she came back and sat on the couch with one leg tucked underneath her, the Saint Bernard lying comfortably with its head at her knees.

She put the box between herself and Reggie and opened it.

Reggie leaned forward and caught a glimpse of the contents as she sorted through them. There was a vehicle ownership certificate, some ticket stubs, a small gold butterfly pin, and—

Suddenly she stopped. Then she started from the top again. She thumbed carefully through, past greeting cards and ticket stubs, handwritten notes that might have been poems—until she had reached the bottom.

She looked at Reggie with what he took to be genuine surprise.

"It's gone," she said.

"Are you sure?"

"Of course I'm sure," she said, annoyed. She withdrew the box protectively to her lap; she stared at the contents with a puzzled expression, then at Reggie with an accusatory one.

"I just got here," said Reggie. "Just what is it that's missing?"

"The thing you're asking about," she said.

She got up and walked to the window near her paintings. "My father was in his study," she said. "I came in, and he had these sheets of really thin paper that he was looking at. They were on the desk, on the floor, all over the place. I wanted him to play. I sat down and started drawing on one with a crayon. He got really angry, he said the papers were very, very important, and he picked them up and put them in the bottom drawer of his desk."

"You seem to remember it very clearly."

"I should; I thought it was the reason he went away."

She paused when she said that, then continued. "After he went missing, I made copies of all of it. I walked all the way to the stationery store and made them. It took a ton of dimes. And then I came back, and—you have to understand, I was barely eight, and I read a lot, but mostly just novels, and—"

"I understand," said Reggie.

"I sent one copy in my letter to Sherlock Holmes. And I kept the other copy in this box; you couldn't miss it if it was here."

"Does anyone else have access to your apartment? A boyfriend, or—"

"None of your business," she said. Then she added, "No. No one else has access."

"Have you had a break-in?"

"No. I mean, I don't think so."

Reggie considered it for a moment. He wanted to be careful

about this, but there seemed only one possible connection to make.

"This neighbor of yours—the one I saw on the steps the other day—"

"What about him?"

"Has he had access?"

Mara looked at Reggie, then out the window as if to express her amazement to the world, and then back at Reggie again, and Reggie realized he might have phrased it better.

"You've got to be kidding," she said with precise emphasis.

"I don't mean access to—you—that is, I only meant, could he have had the opportunity to—"

"Look, it's like this," she said. "The guy moved into the building a month or so ago—and right away he's hanging around the mailbox when I come home, every single day. And playing that 'I really want to get to know the real you' shtick to the hilt."

"Always at the mailbox?"

"Well, yes. But he pretty much never has any mail. I can tell he's just waiting there for me."

"To chat you up."

"Exactly. And he had a shtick."

"Good shtick?"

"Not that good. But I did make the mistake once—just once—of letting him come up for coffee. And he laid it on real thick about getting to know the real me. Asking about my family—and we're talking about how I grew up, and how tough it was when my dad left, and did I ever hear from him again, did I get to have a quinceañera, what kind of stuff did I keep from when I was a kid, and—"

She stopped abruptly when she said that and stared down with realization at her box of keepsakes.

"Did you show any of this to him?" said Reggie.

She nodded. "I showed him my maternal grandmother's recipe for Irish burritos—and next thing I know, he's got his hand on my knee. And then—"

Now there was a sharp, authoritative knock at the door.

"And then I threw him out," said Mara, and she might have continued—but now the knock at the door was even more commanding. She got up quickly and started toward the door, Mookie trotting alongside.

She left the box behind, and Reggie looked in closely. In a bottom corner, a scrap of thin photostat paper was wedged into the crease of the box. As if someone had pulled something out hastily, and this piece, caught in the crease, had torn off and been left behind.

The dog stuck its head between Mara and the door and emitted that now familiar rumble from its throat. From his vantage point, Reggie could not see who it was, but he could hear the voice. It was Lieutenant Mendoza, introducing himself to Mara.

Reggie extracted the bit of paper from the joint of the box and stuffed it in his jacket pocket. Then he got up and went quickly into the kitchen, out of the line of sight should Mendoza step in.

Mercifully, Mendoza did not step in. Not yet. But he was still within earshot.

Reggie heard Mendoza ask if Mara knew her neighbor well—a man named Howard Fallon.

Mara replied that she didn't know any Howard. Her neighbor's name was Lance—Lance Slaughter.

That was the name on the man's Screen Actors Guild card, Reggie heard the detective say. But the name on his driver's license was Howard Fallon.

So Mara's neighbor had been using a stage name.

And a bad one at that.

Mendoza then said something in a softer voice that Reggie did not quite catch. For a moment, as near as he could tell, neither Mara nor Mendoza said a word. But the dog started a low growl.

"I . . . really didn't know him very well," Reggie heard Mara say.

Reggie held his breath. He supposed Mendoza would ask now if Mara had noticed anyone of British extraction hanging about.

But Mookie was getting louder, and Mara told him to hush. Reggie strained to hear. Mendoza was giving her his card. He was going away.

Reggie waited until he heard the receding footsteps; then he stepped out from behind the kitchen door.

Mara, still standing at the open doorway, stared at Reggie. Mookie was pressed protectively against her legs.

"You knew this?" she said; then she demanded, "Did you know about this?"

"About what . . . exactly?" Reggie said in his closest approximation of an innocent voice.

"Get out," she said. "Now." The dog was not growling; it was looking at Reggie as though it had sighted a rabbit.

Reggie found as much space as he could and edged out the doorway.

Then the door slammed shut, and the young woman turned the locks behind him.

10

Reggie hurried down the stairs and then checked for the detective's car before stepping out of the stairwell.

He didn't know why Mara had not revealed his presence to Mendoza; for all he knew, she had changed her mind and was calling the police right now. It was probably not a good time to be seen about.

And he was beginning to wish he'd rented a car.

He walked four blocks and caught the first taxi he found.

"Where to?"

"One moment."

Reggie called the local SAG office on his new mobile, provided the stage name used by Mara's neighbor, and got the name and address of the talent agent who handled Lance Slaughter.

As they drove, Reggie reached into his coat pocket and found the slip of paper he had taken from Mara's box of keepsakes.

It was just a scrap, one corner and a few square inches, but it was enough to make a very general guess at its purpose.

The copy was not great quality, but he could see that the original had been printed with thin vertical lines—one column listing depths and the other displaying a series of faded hand-written marks—chemical symbols, percentages, and other no-tations.

And in the corner heading was a date and something that was probably an identifier—or at least might be to someone who knew the acronyms.

Reggie called Ms. Brinks in London, catching her just as she was about to leave for the day.

"I need your help," he said.

"Of course."

"I'm going to send you a fax," he said. "Some sort of geo-logical analysis, I think. Find someone who can tell you exactly. Ring me back as soon as you can."

The cabbie found a place for Reggie to send the fax. Then they drove north on La Brea and turned right on Sunset, head-ing for the agent's office.

It was Reggie's first time in Hollywood. He was not im-pressed. The architecture was less than ordinary, and the streets were dirty.

They drove two blocks, then stopped at a three-story pink stucco building dating probably to the thirties. At the entrance were placards for a dance studio and an actor's studio on the ground floor. The Silberman Agency—and several similar establishments—was listed for the first floor up.

The dance studio was just now letting out. Young women in form-fitting spandex were escaping rapidly in all directions. Into compact Hondas on the adjacent residential street, into other studio classes in the same building, and one or two striding boldly and quickly down the boulevard, looking neither right nor left but drawing hostile glares from two ladies of the afternoon posing at the corner.

A slender young woman, wearing faded jeans over dance leotards, her high cheekbones pink and glowing from her workout, and with hair that fell in perfect dampness behind her ears, opened the door and stepped out as Reggie was going in.

Of course, what had he been thinking? The city's reputation for glamour had never been for its architecture.

Reggie smiled as she passed by, and she avoided eye contact with the air of a woman who knows she's been smiled at by someone beneath her.

This was a tough sort of glamour. Reggie couldn't recall being hit with that degree of indifference since his first year at Cambridge.

The building had no lift; Reggie took the stairs to the office marked for the Silberman Agency. From the size of it, the agency was not likely to be mistaken for William Morris.

The woman seated behind a desk in the outer office—or maybe it was the entire office—swiveled in her chair and asked Reggie how she could help him. He asked to speak to Leslie Silberman.

The woman first studied Reggie's face for a moment, then leaned back in her chair and conspicuously appraised the rest of him.

"We've got about a dozen of your type already," she said. "But Spielberg isn't on the line right now, so I'll forgive you. Can you do anything special? Martial arts? Impersonations? You can drop the British accent shtick."

"I'm not an actor. I'm looking for one."

She pushed out a chair for him. "Just tell me what you need."

"An actor by the name of Lance Slaughter?"

She frowned. "Lance Slaughter. Aka Howard Fallon. Classic reality show reject. Yeah, I represent him. Pretty much."

"I'm hoping that you can—"

"I don't think he's available," she interrupted, "but I got a dozen better of the same type. No one broke any mold when they made Howie, whether they should've or not, know what I'm saying?"

"I'm not interested in anyone else."

She shrugged agreeably and turned to a file cabinet to locate the actor's folder. "Just so it's clear from the start that all payments to Howie are going through me as his legal agent and representative. The standard deal. Clear enough?"

"Of course."

"Yeah, well, I got burned by this guy once already," she said as she gave Reggie the folder. "I got him an assignment early in the summer, tremendous break for the kid. A full year of busting my tail for him, one day this guy from something called New Vista Productions calls. Heard of them?"

"No," said Reggie.

"Me neither, and that shouldn't be. But what they ask for fits Howie's profile perfectly. So I set up a meeting; he goes and reads for the part, and that afternoon they call back and say he wasn't right after all.

"I figure the kid feels real bad that he didn't get the part, and I make a special effort to find something else for him, which isn't easy, reason being he has the talent God gives a clam. I find something, a walk-on, that maybe he can do if he remembers not to open his mouth.

"I call his numbers. Disconnected. No message machine, nothing. I figure the kid's given up and gone back to Omaha, or wherever. Two days later, I'm having lunch at Hanrahan's, I walk outside, and there the creep is. He's driving a brand-new

Porsche. He's stopped at the light. I go up to him, ask him what the deal is, and he says he doesn't need an agent, he's got his own connections. He says he's got an in that I'd kill for. I ask who, then the light changes; he gives me the finger, honks that obnoxious Porsche horn, and drives off.

"I know what this means. This means Howie and New Vista decided to cut out the middleman. So I go back upstairs and I call the only number I had for New Vista, and guess what?"

"Disconnected?"

"Damn right. I thought maybe they were on the Paradigm lot, because I saw a Paradigm parking sticker on his car—but nobody at Paradigm had heard of them, and at a certain point it's just not worth the trouble."

"Paradigm. I think I've been there," said Reggie. It was the general area where he had tracked Nigel's cab. "That's the tall glass thing in Burbank?"

"Well, that's the corporate headquarters. The lot is just south of it. Same parking for both. But like I said, they'd never heard of New Vista—somebody's tax dodge, I bet."

Reggie opened the folder and turned quickly past the glossy head shots to the résumé.

"He hasn't much professional experience, has he?" said Reggie.

"You kidding? The highlight of this kid's résumé is the ability to carry four dinner plates simultaneously. In fact, zero screen credits was something they were looking for."

Now she reached across and took back the folder. "Which makes me wonder," she said, "why you or anyone else would be wanting to hire him. So what's this really about? And don't give me any nonsense about looking for a fresh face. You're no casting director. And if you really were looking to hire this guy, you would have just phoned."

"You're right," said Reggie. "I'm making inquiries for a friend. I think your Mr. Fallon has been doing some moonlighting."

"What sort of moonlighting?" said the agent.

"I don't know yet. Maybe something you wouldn't want to accept a commission for. Thank you for your help."

"You know, you've got a nice voice; you might consider voice-overs."

"I'm hoping it doesn't come to that."

"But like I said, you should tone down the accent. I've heard better."

"I don't suppose you've heard one exactly like it recently?"

"No. And I'd remember."

Reggie exited the office and took a cab back into the Valley, traveling the same route he had taken earlier.

The Paradigm studio lot comprised several acres of square stucco buildings, wood-slat bungalows, and exterior sets. It was just on the other side of the parking garage for the corporate tower that Reggie had already visited.

There was a guard booth, but the guard was preoccupied with a delivery van.

Reggie strolled in casually as if he belonged. He walked past several aluminum-faced production stages until he found a row of off-pink wood-slat bungalows—surprisingly casual and un-substantial structures, given the money amounts he knew such ventures involved.

But then this was the production lot. The real money and power had to be in the tower.

Reggie found the bungalow for Selman Productions—the first company Nigel had phoned from the Roosevelt.

At a receptionist's desk, in front of stacks of scripts with ti-tles written on their spines in black felt pen, sat a tanned young woman, perhaps twenty-five, with suspiciously perfect white teeth and a professionally flirting charm done so well that Reggie couldn't tell at all whether it might be directed at him personally.

"Mr. Selman isn't in," she said almost musically. "The whole office is out protesting the Great San Fernando Shaft."

"The what?"

"This monster hole they want to dig in the Hollywood Hills. For one of the subway lines; I forget which. All the canyon people aren't real thrilled about it. You hadn't heard?"

"No."

"That must be because you're from out of town. But trust me—if you want to get invited to parties, you're against it."

"I'll keep that in mind. What about the little ditch at the end of the street? Am I against that as well?"

"Oh, no. Not that one. We're all for it. I've got a memo from our corporate owners to prove it."

"I see. I'm for the ditch. I'm against the Great San Fernando Shaft."

"Right. Also known simply as the Shaft, as in . . . well, you know."

"Yes, I get it," said Reggie. "I'm sure everyone gets it."

She looked at Reggie to verify that his pun was intentional, then smiled.

"So. Do you have an appointment?"

"No, but perhaps I won't need to speak to Mr. Selman at all," said Reggie. "I'm just looking for someone who might have been here yesterday. His name is Nigel Heath."

The young woman shifted just the slightest bit of her charming resources to saying no, she could not give out that kind of information about Mr. Selman's appointments.

"I doubt that my brother had an appointment," said Reggie.

"Your brother. Hmm . . ." She studied Reggie a bit more closely, and something seemed to be clicking. "So—someone who sounds like you, looks sort of like you, only a little bit—" She hesitated for just an instant.

"Shorter," Reggie interrupted.

"Younger," she continued.

"Slightly."

"Uh-huh. Well, I think we're talking about the pizza guy. Although, come to think of it, not the regular pizza guy."

"A substitute pizza guy?"

"Apparently."

"What did he want?"

"What all pizza guys want, I hope—to deliver. Although it was looking doubtful at first."

"How so?"

"I saw him through the window, driving real slow, up one end of the parking lot and down the other, like he's looking for a parking space or something. Finally he stops right in front of the entrance, like every other pizza guy in the world, comes running in, drops the pizza on my desk, and then takes off again without even waiting for a tip. But at least he got the order right. One pepperoni with onion, and one veggie."

"What did he do then?"

"Beats me. Finished his route, I guess. Bunches of people eat pizza on this lot."

"I expect so. Would you mind taking a look at this?"

Reggie showed her his list of the names of all the production companies Nigel had called.

"If I wanted to deliver pizza to every production company on this lot," he said, "would this be an accurate list?"

"Not much of a pizza list if you don't write down what they ordered," she said. "But if you're asking whether that's a list of all the production companies on this lot, the answer is yes. No secret there; you can get the same from a phone book."

Reggie thanked the young woman and left Selman's office.

He returned to his cab. He considered, and then immediately rejected, the idea of visiting each of the companies in turn. The result for each would almost certainly be the same—Nigel drives the truck slowly, Nigel runs in with the pizza, Nigel leaves. There was nothing useful in that.

And in any case, now his mobile was ringing.

It was Ms. Brinks.

"I showed your fax to a friend at King's College," she said.

"That was quick," said Reggie.

"Of course," said Ms. Brinks. "You know I don't dally. It's from some sort of a geological survey report."

"And?"

"That was pretty much all he could say, not being at all familiar with the area. But I checked about, and I have the name of someone local to you. Professor Rogers at the Pasadena Geological Institute. He can see you today. He said he has an opening at one."

"It's past eleven now," said Reggie.

"Well, he's gone for the rest of the day after that. Said to be quite the expert—had a top-notch firm before he became an academic, according to his curriculum vitae. And the institute looks to be only about fifteen miles from where you are."

"Fair enough," said Reggie.

Reggie's cab negotiated its way through the motorway exchanges to get out of downtown Los Angeles, and then they drove toward the foot of sagebrush-covered mountains, dirty green and brown.

Reggie got out of the cab into air that was visible but dry and that stung the eyes.

The institute was housed in a dispersed arrangement of Spanish-style structures with red tile roofs and white plaster archways, and a plaza that reflected too brightly as Reggie walked across it to the geological sciences building.

He located the main office for the department and learned that Rogers was the department chairman. Reggie was admitted almost immediately.

Rogers, a smallish, white-haired man of about sixty, cordially offered a chair in front of the desk and asked how he could be of help.

"I've only got a scrap of it," said Reggie. "You may not be able to tell me much."

Rogers smiled condescendingly. "Better let me be the judge of that, shall we? After all, you came all this way."

Reggie gave Rogers the piece of paper he had stolen from Mara's keepsakes.

Rogers looked it over with a bemused expression. "It's part of a geological analysis," he said. "Is that what you wanted to know?"

"I had taken a wild guess for that much," said Reggie. "But what you're looking at is twenty years old. What I need to know is, what significance would it have to anyone today?"

"Did someone tell you it is significant?"

"Not in so many words," said Reggie.

Rogers shrugged. "There's not much remarkable here," he said, perusing it. "You've got clay, and some sand, more sand, a layer of flinty shale, some groundwater, some gaseous concentrations—all pretty much typical for the general area."

"What area is that?"

"Excuse me?"

"The general area?"

"Could be almost anywhere in the Valley—or any number

of valleys in Southern California, as far as that goes. I'd have expected a little igneous stratification—granite—if it were the mountains."

Rogers gave the sheet back to Reggie now, and he began to gather together some papers of his own.

"What would have been the purpose for this particular analysis?" asked Reggie.

"Anything that breaks ground," said Rogers. "Just from this scrap, there's not much I can tell you. I'd have to know where this data is from, and need a lot more of it, for any kind of real analysis. Right now I have a seminar, but if you'd like to come back tomorrow with the complete document, I'm sure I could be of more help."

"I wouldn't want to take any more of your time."

Rogers shrugged. "No big deal. Just drop it by."

Reggie said that perhaps he would do that.

But truth was, he was not inclined to wait that long if he could help it.

He walked down the corridor toward the exit. In the open lab to his right, a graduate student was shutting down the devices she'd been working with and was about to leave. Reggie paused at the entrance of the lab. No one is more eager to tell all they know than a dedicated graduate student.

Reggie knew she had to be a graduate student because the age was right, because she was working alone in an open lab, and most important, because of the tired shadows under her eyes.

She had short brown hair, a pleasant face, and a complexion that said that while everyone else was at the beach getting tanned and toned, she was working long indoor hours and living on caffeine and junk food.

He liked her immediately.

"I'll be done here in a minute," she said without turning away from a spectrograph, as if Reggie were another student waiting to use the equipment. But then she glanced over at him and revised her appraisal. "You looking for someone?" she asked.

"Anyone who can tell me what this is," said Reggie, holding up the page fragment.

"Torn," she said.

"Thank you. If it were complete and I had the remaining pages, what would I have?"

"You're serious? It's a geological analysis." She took the paper for a closer look. "Pretty old one."

"Is there a usual purpose to this sort of map?"

"Sure. Somebody wondered what it would be like to dig through the stuff."

"For what purpose? A construction foundation? Office building, housing, or—"

"No, no, deeper. Tunneling. Please tell me you're not a student in our program."

Reggie admitted that he wasn't and asked what else she could tell him.

She settled back on her lab chair.

"Well, it's from 1976—these numbers in the corner are the date and county." She smiled. "Okay, you probably knew that. And it's somewhere in the Valley—this note here about 'Fernando formation' is referring to the typical kind of clay composites you find around here. The site number—which you're missing, it would be on the opposite corner of the sheet—would tell you exactly where. But even without that, I suppose the data could be cross-matched."

"Where might I do that?"

"You might not do it at all, if you're not a student here. We have a database that goes a long way back, but you need an account. Or are you an alumnus?"

"No, not that, either."

"You might ask Professor Rogers about this; he used to do a lot of work in the area. I bet he could place this right off the top of his head."

"He didn't quite have the time to do that," said Reggie.

"Oh. Well, he's like that sometimes. Be grateful he's not sitting on your thesis committee."

She'd packed her kit and was ready to leave, but she paused.

"So," she said after studying Reggie for a moment, "just what is it exactly you want to know about this?"

"For a start, what the missing part of the page says."

"I think I can manage that. I have to go teach Intro—tell a bunch of undergrads what a rock is—but I'll be in the library later tonight."

"And the remainder of the entire report would be helpful."

She laughed. "Don't push your luck," she said. "If you want major printing, you'll have to buy your own card. Where can I reach you?"

"Here," said Reggie. He gave her his card and wrote down the number at his hotel. "I'm Reggie."

"Anne," she said.

"Thank you. Your help is invaluable."

"Right," she said with a quick little laugh, "I'm the expert." Anne brushed her hair back and went away down the corridor, her satchel swinging from her shoulder, with an attitude that made Reggie nostalgic for university.

11

Reggie's taxi took him back to the Bonaventure.

He entered the lobby, intending to order room service and call Laura, but he didn't make it to his room—the American detectives were at the lobby desk, and Reggie spotted them too late.

"Just the man we wanted to see," said Mendoza, stepping up alongside Reggie before he could get to the lift.

"Lucky me," said Reggie. "Will this be quick, or should I call my embassy now?"

"You're not under arrest," said Mendoza. "We just want to talk."

"We did that."

"We have information you might want to hear."

This seemed doubtful, but it seemed better to be forewarned.

"Join me for coffee if you like," said Reggie.

He pointed the detectives into the hotel's formal dining room.

The waiter came over to declare the area off-limits until dinnertime but went instead to get the coffee urn when Mendoza produced his badge.

Reynolds looked about as they took their seats. "Five-star kind of place, isn't it? I'd blow my whole vacation budget—if I had a vacation budget—if I stayed here a day."

"You said you had something to tell me."

The waiter brought the coffee. Reggie resisted the temptation to reach for it immediately; they would think his mouth was dry.

"At first, it was you I liked for our friend under the overpass," said Mendoza, "but it seems you're off the hook."

He paused, waiting apparently for Reggie's reaction.

"Pass the sugar, would you?" said Reggie.

"Want to know why?" asked Mendoza.

"If you want to tell me. Robbery is my guess, if we're going to make a game of it."

"Bad guess," said Mendoza. "Still had his wallet, and his money. No, what gets you off the hook is, we have a witness that places a guy in a nearby café, just hours before the murder, who sounded just like you," said Mendoza, "but it wasn't you. It was your brother."

Reggie said nothing. The witness had to be the waitress at the café—but he couldn't see how they'd made the connection to Nigel.

"I expect you can understand our confusion at first," said Mendoza. "We were working from a sketch based on our witness's description. The guy in the sketch looked an awful lot like you, once you get past your having a little less hair, and of course that could've just been a rug."

"I don't require a rug."

"And no one gives a rat's ass. Point is, things have cleared up considerably." Mendoza paused, for effect, apparently. "You should have told us you have a brother."

"I don't see how my family structure concerns you."

"And that he was here in Los Angeles."

Reggie didn't respond to that.

"And that he was at that café, just sort of hanging around for two days before the murder."

"My brother's a grown man; I don't have a bell on him. He was in London when I saw him last."

Mendoza said nothing; he poured himself some coffee and sat back for a moment. Then:

"He's sort of the black sheep, isn't he?"

"I don't know what you mean."

"Oh, you don't have that expression? It means—"

"I get the bloody expression; I don't get how it applies."

The detective shrugged. "Not even by way of comparison? I mean, you yourself are a pretty successful guy. By most standards."

"Hell," said Mendoza's partner, handling the fabric of Reggie's coat lapel, "I know I couldn't afford this stuff."

"Remove your hand," said Reggie. And Reynolds did let go of the lapel, but Mendoza didn't stop talking.

"You took highest honors at Cambridge. A barrister at age twenty-four. A QC—that's sort of like senior partner here, right?—at thirty. Really big companies call you when their mergers and acquisitions fall through and they just get pissed at each other and finally have to duke it out in court. Lots of money in that." He paused, then, "A little out of your element right now, maybe."

"Not entirely," said Reggie, though he hadn't touched criminal law in years.

"Hey, you're only one guy, you can't do everything," said

Mendoza. "But you don't rest on your legal laurels when it comes to making bucks—you also made a bundle in foreign securities. And you're an actual Name in Lloyd's of London. Very impressive. I'll bet you were a rugby captain or something like that when you were at Eton, right?"

"Something like."

"Now your brother—he's a different story."

The detective paused and picked up another folder, in a manner that Reggie guessed was a practiced effect. "Takes him six years to finish the program at King's College. You have contacts, and you get him a job as a junior solicitor. He sticks with that for a couple years, more or less. But then something happens. He breaks down in the middle of Piccadilly Circus—as if anyone could tell, from what I hear of the place—and it's off to the funny farm."

"The what?"

"We having a language problem again?"

"It was a health and recreation center in Bath."

"Of course, a health and recreation center is what you call it. I stand corrected."

"Will you be getting to a point soon?"

"I'm getting to motive. Means and opportunity, those I already had—a witness that places your brother in the vicinity; a murder weapon that we'll tie to him when we find him, and—"

"My brother doesn't own a weapon, he wouldn't know what to do with a bloody gun. They aren't household items where we—"

"Did I say it was a gun?"

Everyone paused. The two detectives looked expectantly at Reggie; he looked expectantly back at them.

"Fine, I'll bite," Reggie said finally. "How was the man killed, then?"

"You saying you don't know?"

"Of course I don't know."

"His larynx was crushed," said Mendoza. "A hard blow from something with a long, rounded edge, right across here." Mendoza touched one finger across that area on his own throat.

"I'm sure in time you'll develop something a little more precise," said Reggie.

"Like the long end of an umbrella," said Reynolds.

"An umbrella," seconded Mendoza, nodding. "He also had some cuts where he hit his head on something—but it was the forceful contact with a long, rounded edge, like on an umbrella shaft, that killed him."

"I take it you attach some special significance to umbrellas, but the nature of it escapes me," said Reggie.

"Nobody in L.A. carries an umbrella," Reynolds said in a self-satisfied tone. "So our killer is from out of town. From someplace where it's green and damp and rains all the time, where everyone always carries an umbrella."

"I've heard that's Seattle," said Reggie.

"There's more," said Mendoza. "We found these."

He took a plastic bag out of his pocket and spilled several small, disk-shaped objects onto the table. Most of them had been more or less flattened, but one or two were intact.

"We found these at the crime scene. Know what they are?" asked Mendoza.

"I'm sure you'll tell me."

"I'm sure I don't need to. They're Smarties. Not M&M's, not Pokies, and not Hersheyettes—my own personal favorite, God rest them, which you can practically only get at Christmas. But Smarties. A fine chocolate candy, I'm told, which you cannot buy in the United States, because the shells on the nice little blue ones—or maybe the red ones, I forget—contain a dye not approved by the FDA. Which means our killer arrived recently from someplace—you can probably guess where—where you can buy Smarties in any Seven-Eleven."

"What's a Seven-Eleven?"

"So that put him—or at least some Brit, and he'll do for the moment—not just in the area, but at the actual scene of the crime. All we needed now was motive."

The detective paused, arms folded, and leaned back smugly.

"I know you're going to tell me," said Reggie.

"Your brother had a thing for the girl. This guy was in the way. So he killed him."

"That's absurd."

"Why?"

"Nigel's much too good a sport for that," said Reggie.

"Uh-huh. Well, I ran it by our profiler. She sees a classic stalker personality here," said Mendoza. "She said, 'Look for a triggering event. An emotional trauma of some kind that pushes him over the edge.' So I did. And I found it."

Mendoza paused and looked at Reggie for a reaction.

"Enlighten me," said Reggie.

"Every now and then even a loser gets lucky. Really lucky. For your brother it was an actress, London stage mainly, I guess, although I'm pretty sure I've seen her on TV, in some shampoo commercial or something. Dark red hair; pale skin; kind of reminds you of a really nice Washington apple after you've taken the first bite. She took him to Cannes, which is the thing to do, I guess, and they had a hot little affair during the film festival there. But then when they came back—"

"Who told you this?" Reggie interrupted.

"Excuse me?"

Reggie hesitated. "I can't see what possible source you could have for any of this," he said.

"*Daily Sun*," said Mendoza. "And the *Globe*, too."

"The *Sun*?"

"You don't follow the London tabloids?"

"No," said Reggie.

"You should. You really should. Keep you abreast of things, I expect. I mean, for every five stories about a space alien conspiracy that killed Di, there's always at least one celebrity story with a grain of truth. Your brother never warranted coverage, of course, but apparently the lady did. Just a few lines in a couple of those 'who's doing whom and where' columns, but it was enough."

Reggie had nothing to say to that.

"Anyway," said Mendoza, "that's not the interesting part. What's interesting is when it ends. They come back to London after, and she dumps him within a week. Don't know why yet. But that's our traumatic event. He quits his job, bums around for a while, then tries to come back to work. But when he does, he ends up frightening this poor girl in Kent so much that a complaint is filed with the Law Society. Then comes Picadilly Circus, and next thing you know, he's on extended holiday on that funny farm—or health and recreation center—call it whatever you like."

"Bloody rubbish," said Reggie, more vehemently than he intended.

"Meaning none of it's true?" said Mendoza.

"Meaning your facts are wrong, and even if they're not wrong, they don't mean what you think they mean."

"It isn't true, but if it is true, it doesn't count? Uh-huh. I guess lawyer logic is the same on both sides of the Atlantic."

"The thing in Kent was just my brother trying to give back his fee."

"Say again?"

"He won his case, but felt justice wasn't done. He wasn't pursuing the girl at all; he was trying to give her family the fee he had made, to set things right."

Mendoza and Reynolds looked at each other, then at Reggie.

"I take it back," Mendoza said with an amused laugh. "Lawyers are not the same on both sides of the Atlantic. But I still say he killed our Mr. Fallon because he's obsessed with the young woman who lives in the building."

"You've got that wrong as well."

"Okay," said Mendoza. "I'm a sucker for a good laugh. If he's not stalking her, just exactly what is he doing here?"

Tactical error, Reggie realized. He should have said nothing, but Mendoza's recounting of Nigel's downfall had rattled him. Now he was stuck in it. The only question was whether it would sound more credible to let Mendoza drag it out in pieces or to spill it all at once.

"He came here in response to a letter. When she was a child she wrote a letter to Sherlock Holmes. I lease that address, and I receive those letters. Nigel answers them. He read her letter and came here in response to it."

Mendoza and Reynolds looked at each other again.

"Oh, this is way too rich," said Reynolds.

Mendoza looked at Reggie again, and now he was well past amused. His expression was almost merry. "You're saying your brother thinks he's Sherlock Holmes?"

"Absolutely not," said Reggie. "I'm saying he read her letter, concluded she is in trouble, and came here to help."

"You mean he deduced it," said Reynolds, with a joking wink at Mendoza. "When Sherlock Holmes does something, it's always a deduction, right?"

Mendoza smiled slightly and stood.

"You can make up whatever kind of story you want to cover

his ass," he said to Reggie. "But my guess is, if you don't already know where your brother is, you soon will. And when he contacts you, you'd do well to let us know."

"You're the detectives," said Reggie, "you find him."

"We'll do that," Mendoza said.

"And you can deduce this," said Mendoza's partner. "Turns out you've been holding out on us—we get to charge you with accessory." Then he put a single dollar bill on the table.

"Hope that covers the coffee," he said. "It does where I eat."

The two men started to leave, then Mendoza paused and turned. "I almost forgot," he said to Reggie. "Inspector Wembley sends his regards."

Mendoza and his partner walked out.

Reggie just sat there. He was angry, but the detectives were gone and there was no one to vent it on.

Now he got up and, avoiding the lift, took the stairs at a furious pace up to his hotel room. Nine flights three steps at a time took some of the edge off, but not all of it.

Reggie paced to the window, back and forth, and then on impulse checked and saw that yes, as rapidly as he had left London, he had nevertheless brought an umbrella. Nigel would have also, and probably the big golf one from his office. It was routine.

He stopped pacing and sat down, tensely, in the deep leather chair facing the window. He stared out at long shadows being cast over Figueroa Street by billboards in front of a low sun. The shadows gradually merged and disappeared, flood lamps came on to illuminate the shapely young woman on the Jordache billboard, and Reggie still sat staring, gripping the arms of the chair, trying to make one thought go out of his head:

That Mendoza might be right.

Certainly he had part of it; he had the Law Society and the girl in Kent. The surface of it, at least.

But it was the part about the affair with the actress setting everything off that bothered Reggie.

Because the actress, of course, was Laura.

And Reggie knew who was the cause of that relationship ending. He had just never before tried seriously to think of the event from Nigel's point of view.

He did so now.

It was Nigel who had met her first, now that Reggie took time to remember it.

Nigel had returned with Laura from Cannes, just as Mendoza described, and then, in a moment of reckless enthusiasm, he had rung Reggie up.

"She will be onstage tonight at the Adelphi," Nigel had said. "You must come see her."

A few moments later, thinking better of it, Nigel rang Reggie again, only an hour before the performance, to retract the invitation.

And Reggie would have honored the request, if he had received it. But it came too late; he had already departed for the theater.

And there, on Nigel's initial invitation, Reggie sat in the front row with Nigel and saw Laura for the first time.

After the performance, Nigel was to go backstage. He did not ask Reggie to accompany him, so Reggie walked instead through the lobby, thinking of this remarkable woman he had seen.

And then, on the street in front of the theater, amid tuxedos, bouquets, and flashbulbs, there was Laura. Nigel had gone through the back to find her, but a publicity agent had pulled her out through the front. She lost her balance turning from a camera, and Reggie caught her arm, the momentum of her near fall carrying her body, just for a moment, up against his.

She had blushed at first, laughing lightly, thanking him for breaking her fall. And then she asked Reggie if she knew him from somewhere.

"I believe you have met my brother," Reggie replied.

Much later that evening, Reggie returned home and found the retraction from Nigel. But it was too late. He had already met Laura, they had all three gone out for hours after the play, and from Reggie's perspective at the time, they had all had a wonderful evening.

But for Nigel, the damage was already done.

Reggie had put this out of his mind long ago; but he remembered it now and realized that, even at the time, Nigel had had second thoughts and recognized the danger in inviting his older brother to meet such a woman.

Had Nigel considered him that much of a threat?

If he had—he would have been right, as it turned out, wouldn't he?

They had been in competition, he and Nigel, all their lives, now that he thought of it. In one arena and then another and at progressively more significant levels, but all their lives.

And in each arena, in sports, which was the first in order, and in women, which they discovered next, and in their careers, there had come a moment when Reggie realized that he had won.

At first it had surprised him. Nigel had the better serve in their youth—Reggie should never have been able to defeat him in squash. But he did, and then he had become accustomed to it. And having defeated Nigel, who was no slouch, Reggie went out thinking he could defeat anyone else. He expected the success, and it came about. The victories in this sibling competition seemed to expand into victories in the world at large.

Had it simply become the opposite for Nigel?

Three months after the encounter at the theater, Reggie and

Laura were on holiday together, and Nigel was throwing away his legal career.

Would any of it have happened if Reggie had not gone to that theater and snatched Laura away?

But it wasn't as though Nigel could have held her for long in any case, Reggie told himself now, and then wondered if he was right even about that. Perhaps he was wrong about all of it. Perhaps he was the last person in the world who could give an accurate assessment of his brother's strengths and weaknesses.

Could Mendoza be right about everything?

Certainly this young woman in Los Angeles could be captivating. Given an undeniably attractive subject, and Nigel's tendency to infer moral issues and subtle motives where other people would see nothing out of the ordinary, was it too much of a stretch to suppose that lacking other means to attain her, he would construct an imaginary danger from which he could rescue and win her?

And no one was more likely than Nigel to be carrying around a half-eaten tube of Smarties.

Bloody good thing I'm not the prosecutor, thought Reggie. It was simply rot, all of it, and if he weren't so bloody tired, he wouldn't even be considering the matter. He was allowing distinctly separate events to blend, and that made them unsolvable.

He'd hardly slept. His thinking process was becoming a soup.

He needed to clear his head. He had to move.

Reggie left his room and went back down the stairs, out the lobby, and onto the street and began walking at a furious pace southward, pushing through the evening crowd of downtown pedestrians, disturbing the shoppers who clustered at the curbside clothing stores and vegetable stands below Broadway.

He crossed Alameda. Both the vehicular and pedestrian traffic began to thin. He was entering the area of the warehouse district near Mara's flat, a mix of decrepit buildings, avante-garde cafés and cheap American greasy spoons, and then the occasional artist's loft, but mainly the still abandoned dark brick warehouses.

He stopped. On the opposite corner, dim yellow light from a streetlamp revealed an old woman in too many layers of dusty clothing, dragging her belongings behind her on a flattened cardboard refrigerator box.

Reggie had seen this homeless person earlier, when he'd first come to downtown from the airport. But at that time she had been pushing a heavily laden shopping trolley.

Now she wasn't, and Reggie knew why. The cart she had pushed when he had first seen her—the one with the bent orange-and-white sign—was the same one that had later contained the body under the overpass.

Reggie crossed the street to the woman.

She tilted her head slightly when he approached, but she kept her eyes averted until she realized that he wasn't going to simply walk by. Then she looked up at him suspiciously.

"You've lost your shopping trolley," offered Reggie. "Your cart, I mean."

"Didn't lose it. Someone stole it. And I can't get another, because the grocery boys see me coming and take the carts away."

"Where was it when it was taken?"

She gave him a quick, hard look, then turned her back and tried to ignore him.

"Perhaps I can help," said Reggie.

She said something under her breath that sounded like "liar." But then she pointed in the direction. "By the Dumpster," she said. "Over there in the alley."

The alley she pointed at was on the side of Mara's apartment building.

Reggie took the time to walk three blocks, steal a new

shopping trolley from the grocery market's parking lot, and wheel it back to the old woman.

Then he crossed quickly toward Mara's building.

At the entrance to the alley, he slowed his pace. This alley ran along the side of Mara's building; another alley ran behind the building. A few yards before the intersection with the second alley was the Dumpster the woman had pointed at.

Its contents were overflowing, and it stank. But Reggie wasn't interested in whatever might be inside it. He stared at the ground and walked slowly around the perimeter to the other side.

On the dusty asphalt where the Dumpster abutted the wall, he found two sets of small parallel grooves, each about half an inch in width—faint but present, they were certainly marks left by the wheels of a shopping cart.

Reggie followed them for several yards, until they stopped just beneath a fire escape. Here the marks were trampled and mashed out. And there was something else—several small, dark, dried splotches that might have been a number of things but which looked a lot like blood.

He squatted, leaning forward with his elbows on his knees. Yes, it was almost certainly blood.

No need for a taste test.

So the body had been stuffed in the shopping cart to be moved, then wheeled to beneath the overpass. And either the killer was interrupted before he could hide it properly—or else he really didn't care so much if it was discovered; he simply didn't want it discovered where the killing occurred.

The murder had been committed either here on the ground or on the fire escape above.

It was Mara's fire escape.

Reggie looked across the alley. Not much going on there. Just the abandoned warehouse building, with its windows boarded up. In fact, the whole block on that side of the alley was abandoned.

So why was there a single light from a second-floor window at the far end of the abandoned building?

Reggie blinked. No question, there was a light, behind one of the few windows still intact.

He stepped out of the shadows to get a better view and stood looking directly toward the lighted window.

And immediately the light went out.

Reggie began walking rapidly toward the street at the opposite end of the alley, counting the windows as he went. There was no doorway from the alley to the warehouse building; to get inside and find the source of that light, he would have to get in through the street entrance.

He reached the street and then paused. A pair of headlights had appeared at the opposite end of the block. He waited until they had passed, and then he went quickly to the entrance of the old warehouse.

There was no longer any real door over the entrance, though clearly it had once been boarded up; but the accumulated debris would be enough to keep any but the most desperate from venturing inside. There was still a sign announcing the building was condemned and suggesting all sorts of legal remedies against anyone who should trespass, but the sign's rust, dirt, and .22-caliber bullet holes made it seem an empty threat.

Reggie stepped over the debris and into the building and immediately gagged at the stench of rotten food, stale alcohol, and urine. There was a narrow path through the rubbish and up a stairway. He leaned outside, took a deep breath of the marginally cleaner air, and then turned and began to walk up the stairs as quickly as he could in the near pitch darkness.

Reggie reached the second floor without having stepped on any obvious bodies. He wasn't quite certain that he had managed not to trod on anything of organic origin—but that seemed a bit much to ask in the circumstances.

He tried to move quietly as he reached the second floor. Whoever had been responsible for the light would still be there, unless he had taken a back way out.

The hallway was dark in both directions, and in both directions the doors had been either broken out completely or smashed.

Except for a door to Reggie's right. That door was relatively intact. And it was completely closed.

Reggie moved silently and cautiously to the side of the door, then paused. If his guess was right, the person watching from this window was likely the person who had killed Mara's neighbor.

It didn't seem wise to knock. Reggie put his hand tentatively on the doorknob.

"Go away," said a muffled and vaguely inebriated-sounding voice from inside.

There was obviously no opportunity for surprise now. Reggie tried to open the door, but the latch didn't turn.

"I said get lost," came the voice again, sounding even more sodden. Reggie stepped back and, not at all sure that it would work, kicked hard at the latch.

The door broke open.

"Bloody damn," said the voice from the back of the darkened room, clearly recognizable now.

Reggie just stood there for a moment. He wasn't all that happy with this turn of events himself.

"Nigel," he said. "Nigel. What in hell have you—"

That was as far as Reggie got. There was a sudden commotion from the stairs, and four police officers came charging down the hallway and through the doorway Reggie had just kicked open; one held Reggie in place against the wall, and two others held guns on Nigel as the fourth handcuffed him. It was all complete in a matter of seconds.

"I wish," said Nigel to Reggie, just before they were both ushered down the stairs, "you were as good at not being tracked as you are in tracking."

12

It was eight in the morning at the metropolitan jail.

Reggie had been released after another interrogation from Mendoza—who threatened charges of obstruction, although Reggie knew he didn't have enough to make it stick.

Nigel, however, was under arrest.

Reggie sat in the waiting area until the door from the inmates' quarters opened and a guard appeared.

And there was Nigel.

Except for the tangerine jailhouse jumpsuit, Nigel appeared quite normal. No, more than normal for Nigel—he looked composed. Focused.

He seated himself on the opposite side of the visitors' window from Reggie.

Reggie wasn't sure why, but he found it vaguely annoying that Nigel did not look even a bit haggard.

"What in bloody hell were you thinking?" said Reggie.

He was referring to the dead-of-night meeting at the overpass—but Nigel seemed to give the question a broader interpretation. He leaned in close to the window partition, to avoid the guard overhearing—and then he spoke almost eagerly.

"You were right," said Nigel. "After you left my office the other evening, I thought it all through—and you were right. I don't mean just about the letters. I mean about everything. About how it came to be that I was sitting in a clerical office in my brother's firm at ten on a Friday evening with nothing better to do than respond to letters written to a character of fiction and obsess about what may or may not have been happening twenty years ago in the life of someone living five thousand miles way and whom I've never met."

Nigel paused. He was making so much sense that Reggie did not even try to interrupt.

"I know I've been casting about in one direction and then another for years," Nigel continued. "I know it, and it's long past time for me to focus. After all—as you know—one can get by on charm and good looks for just so long.

"So that night I resolved to just dispose of the letters and put them out of mind, no need to even read them, really. Just open-insert-seal, open-insert-seal. Then I dumped them all in the basket for the Monday pickup. It took no more than forty minutes when I did it like that; you were right, Ocher was right, it was nothing.

"On Monday morning I came in very early, to get myself into properly humble form for the tribunal. The whole floor was still dark, which felt odd, but . . . well, truth is, I've never been the first one in before, so how would I know?"

"Go on."

"I opened my office door and flipped the light switch—but my desk lamp didn't come on. Figured I must have kicked the plug the night before. I opened the door further to get a little more of what light there was—and that's when I saw."

Nigel's demeanor as he said this was not what Reggie would have expected. "Saw what?" he asked.

"Someone had forced open the lowest drawer of the filing cabinet," responded Nigel. "The other drawers were open, too, but I knew immediately what was taken. The lowest drawer—which I had locked, and where I kept the letter—was broken open; the hanging file had been removed and was lying there on the desk, but it was empty. Both the letter and the documents that came with it were gone."

Nigel gave Reggie a look to make sure he understood the significance of that—and then he continued.

"There was no time to waste. The hearing was out of the question. I wrote you a note, and—"

"Wait a moment."

"Yes?"

"That's all you saw that was unusual?"

"Isn't that enough?" Nigel looked puzzled.

"Just . . . continue," said Reggie.

"As I said, I saw that the letter and the enclosures were gone," said Nigel. "And I knew what that meant. It meant that as right as you are about everything else, about that one thing, that letter, you were wrong. It was real, it was not something that could be ignored. And it couldn't wait. I booked the next plane out. Sorry I couldn't call, but you wouldn't have understood, there was no helping the disciplinary hearing, I knew that, and if I'd told you, you would have just felt obligated to talk me out of it, or to do something about the hearing itself if you had to, and there was no point to it. I had to go, and that was all. So I went."

"And you just left your office at that point?"

"Of course I left my office."

"Did you ever get the light on? Walk around the desk, assess the damage, and perhaps—try to pick things up at all?"

"No, as a matter of fact," said Nigel, getting a bit annoyed. "I know I'm not neat, but there are priorities. Why?"

Reggie nodded. "Just go on."

Nigel looked at Reggie suspiciously, but he continued.

"When I arrived in Los Angeles, I did not get reckless. I remembered what you said about possible liabilities—and aside from that, there's this lease provision about not personally contacting—"

"Yes," said Reggie. "I know."

"So I didn't even try to go to her directly," said Nigel. "I just went to the café across from her building. I ordered their sandwich-and-coffee special and waited. Then I saw what they call coffee, and I asked for tea instead. The tea was . . . well, you can imagine. But I stuck it out. After a bit I see this bloke come out and start loitering around the entrance to the building, where all the flats have their post boxes. Then a young woman comes walking down the street. I pay attention; she's the right age for our letter writer. And the neighbor is paying attention, too. When he sees her, he ducks up into the stairwell and then comes right back out again—as though he had just then decided to step out and check his correspondence. He tries to chat her up—but she's clearly having none of it; in fact, she just looks annoyed, and she goes up the stairs.

"He stays below, just standing there, deciding what to do. Then he walks over to the entrance for the side alley. First he looks about to see if anyone is watching—and then he goes into the alley. You understand? He just goes into the alley, for no good reason I can think of."

"Yes."

"I don't like it; I need a better angle to see what he's doing.

So I leave the café and cross the street, using the parked cars for cover, and just when I'm thinking I'll have to take the chance and go into the alley to see what's going on—he comes out.

"I duck down behind an SUV; I see him looking around like someone who doesn't want to be seen. And then he jumps into this car—a Porsche, mind you—nearest the alley and drives off.

"But I got a good look at his car, and I saw a parking sticker—something called Paradigm Pictures.

"Then I went into the alley. And it was just like I thought— she has a fire escape there, and he was casing it. I'm sure of it."

"Why?"

"What else would he be doing?"

"Is there a rubbish bin? Could he have just been throwing something away?"

"There is, but he didn't have anything in his hands when he went in. And I saw something odd on the ground near the fire escape. Some sort of caked dirt."

"You think it's odd to find dirt in an American alley?"

"This kind. It was clay, with flecks of something—gypsum? I'm not sure, but it wasn't what you normally see on top of the ground, it was something you see dug up. But nothing's being dug up in the alley."

"So you figured he tracked it in from somewhere?"

"Someone did."

"Was it still fresh?"

"Not sure," said Nigel, looking a bit annoyed, as though Reggie had thought of something he had not. "Well, all right, then— it looked pretty dry. But it was odd for it to be there. And—"

"What did you do next?" Reggie interrupted

Nigel hesitated. Then he took a deep breath, looked Reggie directly in the eye, and said, "I went up to talk to the girl. I know I wasn't supposed to, I know it's a violation of your lease, should anyone find out—but no one should find out. And it was looking urgent."

"All right," said Reggie, and there was not much more he could say. He himself had made the same decision. "What happened?"

"She wouldn't talk to me. Said she'd put the dog on me if I didn't leave."

"Yes, I'm familiar with it. A huge hound."

"It's not a hound. It's a Saint Bernard."

"We're agreed that it's a very large dog, Nigel. Continue."

"I went back to the café and stayed there, watching, until they closed and kicked me out. At that point, since she wouldn't talk to me, I thought the next best thing was to track her neighbor to see what he was about. I got his name from the flat he came out of—Lance Slaughter, if you can believe that. And I'd seen the Paradigm parking sticker. I went to the Roosevelt Arms, checked in, and got a cab to the Paradigm lot, thinking I'd look for his car. But they wouldn't let me in."

"What about the excavation site? What were you doing there?"

"That was the clay I was telling you about. I'd already seen it in the alley behind Mara's flat. And when I left Paradigm, and the cabdriver took that last turn off of Lankershim, I saw it there, too—in the diggings from that huge excavation site. I got out and managed a look around before getting tossed by security—but the car wasn't there.

"So I went back to my hotel for the night. The next morning I rang every studio on the Paradigm lot, and asked about an actor named Lance Slaughter. Didn't learn anything; it doesn't work that way—they either wouldn't talk to me at all or just didn't keep that kind of information. So I figured out a plan to get onto the lot and search for his car."

"Pizza Premieres."

"Yes. I checked out of the Roosevelt Arms and bribed a driver to let me take his route. I spent half a day scouring the lot and delivering pizza—but I didn't see any sign of Lance or his car. So now I was at a loss; I couldn't think of anything else to do except keep watching her place. I went back to the café. But when they closed, I had to find another spot."

"And you chose the warehouse for that?"

"It was the only possibility. I needed a sight line on the alley. The place stank, and I had to pay a vagrant to use his space— but I set up there that evening, and eventually I see the bloke return. In the dead of night. He goes to the alley entrance like he did before, and looks in. Then he takes out a mobile phone, calls somebody, talks for a minute—and only then, after all that, does he go into his own flat.

"There's no phone near the warehouse; just a late-night pharmacy with a fax machine three blocks west. I know, I should get a mobile. But if I had rung you at that point, you would have just told me to turn things over to the police. And I didn't really have anything to give them yet. So I ran to the pharmacy and sent you the fax to meet me at the overpass, where we'd have a clear line of sight and I could keep an eye on Mara's fire escape.

"In the meantime, I waited and watched from the warehouse. I couldn't see the fire escape clearly from there, but I could see the entrance to the alley—and I didn't expect anything to happen before you and I had a chance to meet. But I was wrong. At half-past one in the morning, I saw him come out of the entrance to the flats and go round into that alley.

"I was caught off guard. I got out of the warehouse as quickly as I could, but it takes a while, with all the rubbish and derelicts lying about—and I couldn't see the alley while I was exiting. By the time I got a line of sight again . . . well, whatever happened had happened. I didn't know someone would kill the neighbor and wheel his body up right where I had asked you to meet me."

"The police think it was you, Nigel. They think you're an obsessed stalker and that you killed her neighbor out of jealousy."

"They'll never make that stick."

"And on our own side of the pond, Wembley's building a nice theory about how you bashed Ocher with your Remington."

Nigel seemed genuinely puzzled. "My Remington?" Then, "What do you mean, bashed Ocher?"

"I found his body in your office, Nigel."

Nigel took that in for a moment, looking as though he truly had no idea. And then he half stood out of his chair.

"You're saying someone killed Ocher?"

"Yes."

"In my office?"

"Yes. You didn't know this when you ran out? Sit down, the guard is watching."

"Reggie, Ocher passed me in the corridor as I was leaving that morning. He checked his watch in that 'amazed to see you here at this hour' sort of way."

Reggie wanted to evaluate the implications this had for the order of events, but now Nigel suddenly leaned forward.

"When can you get me out of here?" he said urgently.

"After arraignment, assuming they allow bail," said Reggie. "But that's just for the wanker under the overpass. If Wembley has begun extradition proceedings—"

"Then we can't wait," said Nigel. "If I can't go to Mara, you must."

"Nigel, if the police find either of us hanging about—"

"She is in danger now!"

Nigel stood again as he said this, leaning forward with his

hands pressed on the partition table between them, and Reggie saw that the guard was beginning to take notice.

"Keep calm," he said. "I'll do it. Just sit down."

"Good," said Nigel. He sat down, and then, after just an instant's hesitation: "Good," he said again.

13

Reggie exited the jail, called for a cab from the steps, and then rang Laura at her New York hotel.

Finally someone picked up.

It was Buxton.

"Heath! Good to hear from you!"

When Reggie asked for Laura, she was on the phone immediately—close at hand, apparently; in the same room, if not on the same piece of furniture.

"Catch you at a bad time?" said Reggie.

"Of course not," she said. "Why do you ask?"

"No reason."

Reggie told her about finding Nigel. And there being a dead body under an overpass. And Nigel being arrested for it.

Reggie heard an intake of breath and then a pause on the other end of the line. Then Laura said, "How do we get your brother out of jail?"

"Arraignment is tomorrow morning," said Reggie, "but bail is problematic."

"Why so?"

"Nigel is a foreign national accused of a capital offense."

"Isn't there someone you can ring?"

Reggie didn't answer immediately. The answer he was obliged to give was embarrassing.

"No," he said after a moment. "I don't know anyone in such places here."

"Oh," said Laura.

There was another pause, and then she said, "Shall I ask Robert? Perhaps he might have more effect. I mean, he might know someone—"

"No, don't. I'll manage it."

"Right, then."

There was an awkward pause.

"I have to go," said Reggie. "Nigel assigned me a task."

"Right, then," Laura said again, with no apparent disappointment. "But ring. Let me know."

"Of course," said Reggie.

Reggie shut off his phone, waited for the cab to arrive, and then rode to Mara's flat. He knocked on her door, waited, then knocked again.

No one answered.

But, significantly, there was no sound from Mookie, either. So she might just be out walking the dog again.

Reggie crossed the street to Joe's Deli and settled in to wait. He got a late breakfast—what passed for eggs and bangers, once he'd made himself understood.

He sat at the table and watched her flat through the café window. An hour passed. Then another. More time went by, the coffee was eating a hole in his stomach, and still no sign of Mara.

And now Reggie's mobile beeped.

It was Anne from the geological institute.

"I have news," she said. "But it's sort of complicated. Can you come out?"

"I may have to stay put for a bit. Can you give me a hint?"

"Well . . . bottom line is, something's not right. I can't explain it clearly over the phone. I'll need to show it to you in person. I've got a couple hours open until my evening seminar."

There was a tenor to her voice that made Reggie take notice.

He looked across at Mara's flat again. It was a weekday, still early in the afternoon, and she most probably was at work at the gallery she had mentioned. She might not be back for several hours more. And wherever she was, Nigel's concerns notwithstanding, she had her 150-pound dog to protect her.

"I'll see you in one hour," he said.

It took somewhat longer than that. This city needed more cab ranks. And apparently it had a morning rush hour, and a lunch rush hour, and presumably another at the end of the workday.

Or perhaps, like London, one long one from dawn till after midnight.

Finally, Reggie reached the campus. Anne was in the lab, eating while she worked in front of a computer terminal.

"Sorry to keep you waiting," said Reggie.

"Want half? Peanut butter."

"No, thank you."

"You won't believe what I found for you. Or maybe you will—but I don't."

"Did you find the page?"

"No. And that's a little spooky."

"What do you mean?"

"Your fragment has a partial identifier—right here in the corner—that says it has to be somewhere in the L.A. or San

Fernando basin. The other corner is missing, so we don't know exactly where, but when you have enough data, it's just like a fingerprint—all I have to do is enter the data you've already got and find the report in the database that has that exact same sequence of values."

"Right. So where is it?"

"Bring that chair over, I'll show you the problem."

Reggie did so, and he watched as she punched numbers into the terminal.

"I'm entering the measurements from that fragment of yours, in sequence, and I'm searching for one exact match in all the recorded surveys for the area within the last twenty-five years. Look at what I get."

Reggie looked at the display. "It says, 'No Match.'"

"Right. No match at all."

"Thanks for trying," said Reggie, getting up. "I wish I could have given you more to go on."

"What? No, you don't get it. This can't be. These things all get recorded. The set of measurements on the sheet you gave me has to have an exact match in our database. But it doesn't."

Reggie sat back down. "What sort of measurements are we talking about?" he said.

"Everything you need to know if you're thinking about drilling or digging or tunneling into a specific location. The water table. The concentrations of gases. The composition— granite, clay, sand."

"But the set of measurements I gave you doesn't match anything in your database?"

"Exactly," she said.

"Possibly just an input error when the data was recorded?"

"If it was just one error, my wild-card search would have picked it up," she said. "This is multiple discrepancies."

Reggie considered it. "This means that either someone deliberately falsified the entries in the database, or . . ."

"Or the database entries are correct, and that piece of paper you gave me is forged data," said Anne.

"Why would someone do that?"

She sat back in her chair, put on an air of suspicious authority that made Reggie want to smile, and said, "You tell me."

"It's hard to see," Reggie said respectfully, "what advantage someone would gain by trying to present an altered original after the data has already been recorded."

"I guess," she said. "But this thing you brought me is torn from a copy, not from an original. I didn't notice at first, because I've never seen this kind of copying paper. Before my time. But this is a twenty-year-old photostat."

"Fair enough," said Reggie. "But even so, I think we need to look at this the other way around. What if this is an accurate copy of the original document—and the official database is what someone altered? Would there be a reason for someone doing that?"

She thought about it for a moment. "Well, sure, lots of reasons, if you want to make that assumption. This valley is so highly developed, no matter which way you turn, there's nothing anywhere that doesn't have tons of money involved. So, yeah, I could think of some reasons why someone might want to alter one of these things—if they thought they could get away with it. You'd alter the data so that someone would dig and build where you want them to dig and build."

"What sort of change would you make—I mean, to influence the choice of one location over another?"

"If you wanted someone to dig, you'd show more clay and less water and gas. If you wanted them not to dig, you'd show just the opposite."

"Is there any way you can tell where this site is?"

"Not from just this," she said, pushing her chair back from the terminal. "Bottom line is, you need to find the rest of your survey map. And you need the original—the original showing two signatures, one being the guy who did the survey, and the other being the supervisor who signed off on his work—if you want anybody to take this seriously."

"I'm working on it," said Reggie.

"When you find it, you better let me know," she said, gathering her things. "Might be it will matter somewhere."

"I'll do that," said Reggie.

"Last chance," she said, showing Reggie the last bit of her sandwich.

Reggie shook his head.

"Going, going, gone," she said, and she popped the rest of it into her mouth.

14

The ride back from the institute hit the late-afternoon rush hour, and it was dusk when Reggie returned to Mara's street.

The detour to the geological institute had been worthwhile in his opinion; at least he had a glimmer of why the map sent twenty years ago to Sherlock Holmes might be important to someone now.

But he had not intended to be away so long. He paid the driver quickly and got out.

The rescue mission on the opposite corner had opened its soup kitchen; and a few lights were coming on in the block now. Not so Mara's window; it was still dark. But Reggie could make out white curtains stirring in the breeze. Her kitchen window was open, and he was almost sure it had been closed before.

He hurried up the stairs.

No one answered on his first knock. He knocked again. Still nothing. He called her name. Nothing again.

He tried the door. Locked.

Reggie came down the stairs and went around to the alley entrance.

It bothered him that the window was now open but she was not home. It was possible, of course—even likely—that she had come home, opened the window to let in the breeze, and then gone out again. It worried him nevertheless.

But if he could get up on the fire escape, he could look inside through that window.

He went into the alley. It was dark now; one weak lamp cast a yellowish glow on the ground at the entrance but did nothing to illuminate the upper reaches.

He identified the fire escape below Mara's kitchen window—the fire escape where, in Reggie's opinion, her neighbor had been killed earlier.

It was a railed platform, eight feet across and entirely dark except for a shred of residual light from the end nearest the entrance to the alley. The distance from the platform to the ground—some ten feet or so—was intended to be bridged by a heavy metal ladder that would drop down on release of a lever. But to release the ladder, of course, you had to already be on the fire escape.

Reggie looked up at the fire escape. He could probably manage it—struggle up onto the platform and get a look in the window—if he could get a grip on the edge of the platform, but it was a tad too high.

He took an orange crate from the nearby Dumpster, positioned it beneath the platform, and pushed off from it. It was just enough—the crate broke, but Reggie got enough of a jump to catch on to the metal base of the fire escape with both hands.

He pulled himself up chin high, turned his right elbow perpendicular to the platform base, and levered himself all the way up and onto the platform.

Now he was standing on the platform, next to Mara's open kitchen window. He parted the curtains and looked in.

Nothing appeared to be amiss. The kitchen and what he could see of the living room were as orderly as they had been before.

But he couldn't see much from this angle in the dark. He got down on his knees, put his arms on the windowsill, and began to lean in for a better look.

As he did so, it occurred to him that Mara's neighbor might have been doing this exact same thing before he died.

And then—suddenly—everything went hot, stinging, and black.

Reggie came to an instant later—it might have been just an instant—lying flat out on the iron grille of the fire escape.

A dull, heavy ache was spreading from the back of his head to his temple, and his collarbone hurt, too, from contact with the rounded edges of the windowsill over which he had been leaning. He touched the back of his head and felt a bleeding cut where his scalp had grazed the lower edge of the window.

The window itself, he saw as his vision cleared, was now shut. Someone had struck him, then pulled him back out of the kitchen window—and then closed it from the outside.

Beneath him, the platform grillwork rattled as that person clambered down the metal drop-down stairs.

Reggie saw the man jump to the ground on the last step and run up the alley. The man wore an old gray windbreaker and jeans. He ran quickly but not smoothly—middle-aged or older, thought Reggie. And as groggy as he was, he knew he could catch the man within a few hundred yards. Reggie clambered down the stairs in pursuit.

He reached the street.

He saw no one in either direction.

But across the street, half a dozen or so raggedly dressed men had gathered in front of the rescue mission. The man in the dark windbreaker did not appear to be among them, but people were going in and out of the entrance. Reggie walked quickly in that direction.

Reggie supposed as he approached the entrance that he would find himself more than a little conspicuous here, but almost no one gave him a second glance as he went in.

The mission was configured for the evening meal, with large, square, mustard yellow plastic tables and seating for perhaps a hundred.

There were easily a dozen men eating at the tables who were of the same general height and appearance as Reggie's assailant. Without having seen the man's face, he had little hope of picking him out.

Reggie walked past the tables to the serving line, where mashed potatoes, something like minced meat with gravy, and green beans were being spooned out by a man with a short salt-and-pepper beard and deeply lined face.

"Get your tray first," he said as Reggie approached in line.

"I've eaten," said Reggie. "I'm looking for a man in a dark gray jacket who entered in a hurry within the past few minutes."

"I don't keep track," said the man. "You're holding up the line. Step back if you don't want any."

Reggie grabbed a tray and got back in line. He slid the tray along until he faced the same food server again.

"See the building across the street?" asked Reggie.

"What of it?"

"A young woman lives in a flat there. Pretty, mid-to-late twenties, with long dark hair, walks a Saint Bernard every day that weighs more than she does. Have you seen her?"

"No," said the man. He picked up one of the thick white

plates and shoveled food onto it; then he looked up with a glare at Reggie. "Little old to be following twenty-somethings around, aren't you?"

"I'm not," said Reggie, meaning following her around—although the suggestion that he was too old for her was annoying and worthy of a denial itself. "So you haven't seen her, then?" he said to the food server.

"No," said the man. "Don't hold up the line."

Reggie took his tray and moved on.

He glanced back at the food server, who paid him no further attention and continued shoveling up the stuff for the next person in line.

From all he had seen of his attacker, it might have been the food server himself. Or it might have been almost anyone else in the room. But even if he could identify one suspect as more likely than the others, he couldn't call the police—not unless he wanted to try to explain to Mendoza what he himself had been doing on Mara's fire escape.

So he took his tray and located a seat in front of the window. From there he had a decent vantage point on both the entrance to Mara's building and the side alley.

As Reggie considered whether he was hungry enough to eat what he had before him, he looked through the window and saw a taxi moving slowly down the frontage road. It came to a stop two blocks away, near the overpass where Reggie had gone to meet Nigel two days before.

The passenger door opened, but the passenger stayed inside.

Reggie stood up in front of the window and watched. It was not a location where one would expect a typical sightseer to stop.

The taxi held its position for a moment longer, and then the passenger door closed. The driver turned the cab around, coming back now in Reggie's direction, and turning onto Mara's street.

When it had just passed the mission, the taxi stopped. The passenger window rolled down, and then the driver backed up and pulled to the curb directly in front of the mission.

Reggie, still standing in front of the window, stared as the passenger got out of the taxi.

On the pavement, staring back at Reggie through the window of the shelter, was Laura.

15

I'm famished," said Laura. She was seated next to Reggie inside the homeless shelter now.

"Aren't you supposed to be in New York?" said Reggie.

"With Nigel about to be carted off to jail on two continents? Give me better credit than that," she said. "I caught a flight first thing. They can spare me a day or two. I rang your hotel, but you weren't in, so I thought I'd take a look at the place where you said you tried to meet Nigel. Lovely spot, wasn't it? And I saw a mashed Smartie wedged into a crack, without even trying. Really, Reggie, if I can find these things, certainly the police—"

"They did."

"Well, there you are. And then I'm on my way back to the hotel and I see you here having a lovely dinner without me." She reached over, grabbed one of Reggie's eating utensils, and took two spoonfuls of what he was eating. "It's rather like shepherd's pie, isn't it?"

"I'll get back in the queue and get you a second helping if you like."

"No, this will tide me for a bit." She finished it off and pushed the plate out of the way. "Now," she said, "how do we get Nigel out of jail?"

"The arraignment is at eight in the morning," said Reggie. "We'll see whether bail can be set."

"But then what?"

"You mean how do we prove him innocent?"

"Of course that's what I mean," she said. Now she noticed Reggie's most recent bruises. "Oh, that looks nasty," she said, and gingerly touched the back of his head.

"Let's take it as a given," said Reggie, "that with no other murders being attributed to Nigel in the first thirty-three years of his life, two in a matter of days cannot be coincidence and must be somehow related."

"Agreed."

"And so it's not just some workplace squabble between Nigel and Ocher that got out of hand."

"Clearly," said Laura.

"So the letter is the key. The letter and the map that was missing from his office."

"The letter that you said was nonsense," Laura said with an unaccusing face but with what sounded to Reggie like an emphasis on the "you."

"Yes," said Reggie. "Which I told him to ignore, but of course he would not, thereby involving him, and me, and you, apparently, if you have your way about it, in something that I just can't see having a very good end."

"Well, you needn't get snippy about it. I didn't say you were wrong to tell him to leave it alone."

"All right, then," Reggie said after a moment.

"Don't pout. Tell me more about your dead body."

"Just bruised a bit; hardly dead. I can prove that to you later if you like."

She smiled, but only a little. "I mean the one you discovered. The one you discovered here."

"He had some interest in our letter writer. I'm chalking that up to the map as well, until we know otherwise."

"Oh? Our girl's not attractive, then? The croaked bloke wasn't just trying to get her into a bit of a romp?"

Reggie shrugged. "I don't think it was that," he said. "But yes, she's attractive. And it's a problem—because the police here think that is motive for Nigel, that he flew out here to stalk her and that he committed murder in an attempt to eliminate the competition."

"Why don't you just tell them the truth?"

"That he read a letter written by a child to Sherlock Holmes twenty years ago and was so concerned by it that he felt he had to come here himself? I did tell them. They consider it improbable, to say the least."

"If the truth is improbable," said Laura, "I suppose we have to prove that the police theory is impossible?"

"Ideally, but I'll settle for presenting a more plausible alternative," said Reggie. "I've been waiting for her to come back. Nigel thinks she is in danger, and even if she is not, I need her to tell me who the map was for and why her father created it."

"Do you want to try again to get inside her flat? I learned a trick once with a charge card."

Reggie looked across at Laura and mentally registered one more reason why she was unlike any other woman he had known. And for a moment, given her almost eager willingness to do so, he considered accepting her offer to break the law in a foreign country.

But as they looked through the window at Mara's building, they saw a marked police car roll up to the entrance, pause, and then cruise slowly to the front of the alley. The cruiser shined its spotlight into the alley for several seconds before rolling slowly on.

"No, it won't do," said Reggie. "Not now. Someone must have seen the commotion. And I can't be found camping on her doorstep."

"Well, if there's nothing to be done here," said Laura, "then there's the arraignment tomorrow to look forward to. And I still have my cab outside."

They walked outside to Laura's cab. They got in, and Reggie told the driver they were going to the Bonaventure.

"I'm at the Beverly Hilton," said Laura.

Reggie looked at her with surprise. "I'm at the Bonaventure," he said. "Didn't I tell you?"

"Yes," she said, "you did." She averted her eyes for a moment.

"Beverly Hilton, then," Reggie told the driver.

But Laura said, "Yours is before mine, isn't it? I suppose we should drop you first."

"Still the Bonaventure, then?" the driver chimed in.

"Yes," Reggie said tightly.

So they drove to the Bonaventure. Reggie got out of the cab, and Laura rode away to Beverly Hills.

Laura had known where he was staying—and had booked a room across town.

There were, of course, more urgent matters to worry about.

But piling the Laura worry on top of the Nigel worry wasn't making either of them feel lighter.

16

Back in his hotel room, Reggie opened the minibar.

With nothing more that could be done tonight, his intent was to review what he had accomplished in America since arriving—to assess the status of one problem at a time and see where it all stood.

And although he did not want to prejudice the result of that assessment, he had a sense that he would need, at minimum, the Glenfiddich. After a moment's reflection, he took both Glenfiddiches. And then, thinking again about Laura booking at a separate hotel, he took the two American bourbons as well and brought them all back with him to the leather chair by the window.

He poured the first Scotch and began his assessment.

And it broke out like this:

Regarding the simple purpose of getting Nigel to report to the disciplinary hearing and get his career restored: That was already a bust, whether or not Nigel cared—if the Law Society had not heard yet of the goings-on in Nigel's chambers, they soon would. And a criminal indictment—either in London or in America, and even if Nigel was ultimately acquitted—would certainly fry any remaining sympathy the tribunal had toward him.

But on the scale of things, that concern was becoming minor.

Because the next item was Ocher's murder. In that regard, all Reggie had only accomplished was to learn that someone for some reason twenty years ago had—apparently—put one set of data into a map that the eight-year-old Mara had sent to Sherlock Holmes and another set of data into a geological database that construction firms throughout Los Angeles used in planning their digs.

Certainly there could be a connection between those occurrences. But Reggie didn't even have the map itself. As far as the court in London was concerned, if Nigel was charged, Reggie had nothing exculpatory at all.

He finished the first Glenfiddich. The minibottles in this hotel seemed smaller than normal. He poured the second.

The next item was Mara's murdered neighbor. Well, there was a winner. Instead of clearing Nigel of Ocher's murder, Reggie, by his mere presence at the wrong time under that overpass, had made both him and Nigel suspects in another. Not Reggie's fault, true, but that was not the point. The point was that between them, Reggie and Nigel had dug the hole deeper.

Not to mention Reggie's unintentional assistance in leading the police to Nigel. No question whose fault that was.

And then there was Mara herself, who had sent the original map that was at the root of it all—and now Reggie had lost track of her as well.

It was time to get up from that chair. Reggie knew it, but he remained seated. There was one more thing to worry about.

Laura.

But he couldn't even begin to suss that out at the moment. He opened the two minibourbons and poured them both together into his glass.

Some time passed after that; Reggie was in no condition to judge precisely how long. And then suddenly he was awake— to early morning light and to the scent of something, somewhere, that was burning.

He was up in an instant—there was no smoke in the room.

He went to the window, where the pungent, syrupy odor was stronger. It smelled like burning creosote, as if they were tarring the street below.

But they weren't. There was in fact no one in the street at all, at the beginning of a workday.

Reggie went downstairs.

Other hotel guests had begun to accumulate in the lobby. It was a subway fire, someone said. The bellman said the police wanted everyone to stay inside.

But they had left no one there to enforce the order.

There were no pedestrians when Reggie stepped outside, and there were no cars. Everything was blocked off.

From the smoke and the fire trucks still blaring their way in, the source was farther south. Reggie began walking quickly in that direction. He got around the first set of barricades at Alameda with no trouble.

In a few more blocks, the burning odor became so strong that it stung, and now Reggie could see the reason why.

The street itself was on fire—or more precisely, what was beneath the street. Orange-and-blue flames licked through thin fissures in the asphalt and around the edges of the iron sewer covers.

He walked on all the way to the frontage road bordering the subway dig.

But the smoke was from the left, and he turned in that direction. He passed a cut-and-cover trench, from which a line of ungrouted holes sprouted low, even flames, like the jets of a gas stove.

Now he was at the center of it all, just yards from the new tunnel opening.

A policewoman noticed. "See the tape?" she yelled. "Get on the other side of it!"

"Channel Seven," said Reggie. It seemed worth a try, since a decent jacket and properly spoken English seemed to indicate a newscaster in Los Angeles. "My crew got here ahead of me, they should be around here somewhere."

"Right over there—" She pointed. "But try to stay out of the way."

At the other side of the street, the Channel 7 news van had in fact just arrived. Channel 7 had the prime spot, at the edge of the barricade closest to the tunnel. Reggie got there just as the reporter began.

"I'm just yards away from the second subway fire this year. Six weeks ago a blaze in the North Lankershim site, at the opposite end of the Silver Line, claimed the life of a worker there. Today, at the downtown site, in a scene reminiscent of Dante's *Inferno*, we may be looking at a tragedy just as bad. Behind me—"

Reggie pushed forward through the gathering crowd for a better look. There was a particularly advantageous position— where two barricades intersected—that provided an angle on the tunnel entrance itself.

The available space there was already occupied by an old man with a stubby white beard and a shorter, slender person in a hooded sweatshirt. But as Reggie approached, the old man shuffled off to the south, muttering, and Reggie shouldered his way in to take his place.

He immediately got an elbow in his ribs from the hooded sweatshirt.

"I'm standing here, jerk."

Reggie looked down, and the hooded face looked up for the first time.

It was Mara.

They recognized each other immediately. She did not seem pleased. Reggie saw her eyes shift to the south for an exit route and then back toward the tunnel. She hesitated but remained in place.

"I've been looking for you," Reggie said. "My brother thinks you're in danger."

She did not respond right away. Reggie watched her expression, and he saw her think about saying one thing and then settle on something else instead.

"Not your concern," was all she said.

And now she wasn't even looking at Reggie; she was focused on the tunnel entrance, where two police officers came into view, followed by medics bearing a man on a stretcher.

Mara pushed forward, past the news cameras, to get a better look.

Reggie tried to follow to keep track of her. But suddenly they were caught in a pool of blinding white light as the Channel 7 news crew came up behind them. Reggie shielded the glare from his eyes, and after a blinking moment he saw Mara turn and begin to walk quickly away from the scene.

He ran and caught up with her, walking briskly alongside.

"Please talk to me," he said.

"Stay away from me," she said, not slowing her pace.

"Do you know the man on the stretcher?"

"No."

She was heading toward the edge of the barricade; there were police cars parked there and uniformed officers standing about. And there was a pale blue 1960s Volkswagen Beetle that Reggie had seen outside her apartment and guessed was probably hers.

She had been walking quickly, but now she suddenly slowed.

Reggie followed her line of sight and saw the point of concern.

Between them and the blue Volkswagen was Detective Mendoza, standing by a barricade and talking to a Valley Transportation Authority official and a man in a hard yellow hat.

"You'd better leave me alone," she said to Reggie. "I see our friend over there."

She had a point. But something in her demeanor made him think she had not stopped short for his benefit.

"Considerate of you, but it's no problem as far as I'm concerned," Reggie said, bluffing.

"Sure it is," she said. "He probably thinks you killed my neighbor."

"You think otherwise, or you would have called Mendoza over by now. And whoever killed your neighbor had something to do with you—or with the letter you wrote to Sherlock Holmes."

"What makes you think so?"

"That's why he was always at your post box—to intercept whatever you received. And he talked his way inside to steal whatever you kept from years ago."

She ignored this and started walking again, but this time on a trajectory that would take her to the car without crossing conspicuously in front of Mendoza.

Reggie kept pace.

"I know why I'm avoiding Detective Mendoza," said Reggie as soon as they approached her car. "Why are you?"

"I'm not. And if you don't get lost now, I'll start screaming and we'll see who is more afraid of the law."

"I have just one question, then I'll leave you alone."

"Make it quick."

"Where is your father?"

"My father left twenty years ago," she said, getting very angry now. "We had that conversation already."

"I think your father is back—or at least, I think you think he's back. That's why you came here tonight. That's why you were at the tunnel trying to see who they loaded into the ambulance."

She had no immediate response to that; Reggie could see her trying to think of something.

"Maybe I'm practicing to be a lawyer," she said. "You know, chasing ambulances."

"I don't think that's it," said Reggie, and if that was all she could muster, he knew he must be hitting close.

"Even if my father were back, why would I think he'd be in the tunnel?" said Mara. "He was not a sandhog."

"Your father was a geological surveyor."

"Yes."

"Did he survey this tunnel?"

Mara looked back at the tunnel, at the smoke still pouring from the entrance.

"I was eight. I didn't read the things. I don't know what he was surveying. It could have been anything. Anywhere."

"The map your father made is the key to proving that

someone other than my brother had the motive to commit two murders. Without the map, he goes to prison."

This seemed to give her pause.

"That could really happen? Your brother could be convicted?"

"Odds are, yes. For at least one of them."

They had reached her Volkswagen now. She stopped.

"I'd help you if I could," she said. "But the map is gone, you saw that."

"What was taken from your flat was a copy. Did you send the original to Baker Street?"

"Of course not. I was a child, not stupid. I didn't send my original through the mail. I made two copies. I sent one and kept the other copy in that box."

"What about the original?"

She looked as though she hadn't thought about that in many years. Then she said, "I put it in a safe place."

"Where? What safe place? A bank?"

"I was eight. You think I had a safe deposit box?"

"Then where?" said Reggie.

She hesitated. For a moment, she looked as though she might tell him what he needed to know.

"People may have died because of this map," said Reggie, pressing his case. "Important data may have been falsified."

Now her expression changed—and Reggie knew he had blundered.

"You're saying that my father falsified a geological map?"

"No," Reggie said quickly, attempting a tactical retreat. "Not necessarily."

Too late. Her expression had hardened.

"Your brother should not have come here," she said. "And neither should you."

With that, she opened the Volkswagen door abruptly into Reggie's knee, got in, and locked the door.

"Agreed on that," said Reggie, but he knew she didn't hear him, because she was already driving away.

17

It was already twenty minutes of eight when Mara drove off, and Reggie finally had the chance to remember his brother's scheduled arraignment.

He found a cab and made it to the courthouse just two minutes before the hour.

Laura was sitting on the steps waiting for him, ignoring the second looks from the pin-striped attorneys going inside.

"You didn't sleep well, did you?" she said, assessing him.

"No," said Reggie. "I think that must be the general rule over here."

They went inside and took seats in the crowded courtroom. The detainees for the eight A.M. arraignment were just at that moment filing in.

Nigel was not among them.

The first arraignment took place. Then another. An armed robbery, a carjacking, and two felony drug possessions with intent to sell.

Nigel had still not appeared and his case had not been called.

"Is this right?" said Laura.

"No," said Reggie.

They exited the courtroom and walked down the corridor to the court clerk's office.

"When is the arraignment for Nigel Heath?" Reggie asked.

The clerk pressed a couple of keys at her terminal. "That was yesterday. Night court."

"What? It was scheduled for eight this morning."

"What can I tell you? It was moved up."

"Why was it moved up?"

"I don't know, light docket, maybe. I don't control these things."

"Was a bail amount set?"

The clerk, annoyed now, pressed more keys. "Bail was set in the amount of one million dollars, and it was posted, and he was discharged an hour after the arraignment."

This news was so astonishing that the woman was almost able to shut her window before Reggie could react.

"Who posted the bail?" he said quickly.

"I don't have that information, sir."

"It should be part of the public record."

"It hasn't been entered yet. Will that be all?"

It was all. The woman closed the window, and Reggie turned back to Laura.

"You're sure you had the time right?" said Laura.

"Of course I did," said Reggie. It was unusual for Laura to question his reliability. "It was moved up."

"Why would—"

"Might have been routine. Or someone with influence might have made it happen. But there's no way Nigel managed a one-million-dollar bail on his own."

"Well, I didn't post it."

"Nor I."

"So who would have the kind of clout to get Nigel's arraignment moved up—and post a million-dollar bail?"

"I'm wondering that, too."

They both stopped to ponder this on the courthouse steps.

"And he didn't contact you?" said Laura.

"No."

"Then—where would he have gone?"

"The girl," said Reggie, flagging down a cab. "He would go to see about the girl."

The traffic was actually light as they approached Mara's block; the fire had been all over the news, and everyone who could do so and who didn't regard fires as spectator sport was avoiding the downtown.

They stopped in front of Mara's building.

Across the street, the little café had its brave OPEN sign in the window. The cook stood in front of the doorway, smoking a cigarette on the empty walkway, then went inside.

In the distance to the south, the barricades to the tunnel sight were visible. The smoke was gone, but the burnt smell lingered.

They went up the stairs to Mara's flat.

Reggie knocked.

They waited. No response.

"They could be here, you know," said Laura. "Both of them. I mean, if Nigel got out early on bail, came here, and had a reason for not letting anyone know, he wouldn't just pop over to the door when anyone knocks."

"You have a point," said Reggie. "If you assume that she would have let Nigel in at all."

"Perhaps she likes him better than she does you," said Laura. And then, on Reggie's look: "Well, it's possible. And of course the girl might not want to talk to any of us at all, so if she's in, and saw us from the window, she'd just be sitting tight."

Reggie nodded. "So what do you suggest?"

"Better use your more annoying knock. Just in case Nigel is there."

Reggie used his more annoying knock, not all knuckles at once but in staccato succession, and loudly, three times. It was obnoxious. He knew Nigel would recognize it.

Still no response.

"Now what?" said Laura.

"Whether Nigel is here or not," said Reggie, "I still need the map. It's the only real lead we've got."

"And we think it's in here?"

"If it's anywhere. She said she kept it in a safe place."

"So . . ."

"So now one of us is going to commit a felony," said Reggie.

"Brilliant," said Laura, digging enthusiastically into her handbag for a charge card.

"Wait," said Reggie. He placed his hand on the doorknob.

"Oh, surely not," said Laura.

Reggie tried it. The handle turned.

"Unlocked?" said Laura. "Are they so trusting here?"

"No," said Reggie. "They're not."

He pushed the door open a crack. He called Mara's name. No response.

He pushed the door farther and then waited, just in case, for an onrush from the dog. But there was nothing.

They both stepped inside.

"This can't be good," Reggie said softly. "Let me check first."

He walked through the kitchen to the fire escape and looked out. No one. He checked quickly for anyone in the bedroom or bath, then returned to the front room, where Laura had already switched on the floor lamp to take it all in.

"The couch is wrong," she said.

"You need to allow for American tastes. And I think she may be on a bit of a budget."

"Her taste is perfect, and so is the arrangement. Which makes it a bit odd for the angle of the couch to be just out of kilter."

Reggie looked closely at the foot of the couch and saw the indentations in the thin carpet.

"And there's a bit of wicker broken off from the magazine basket," continued Laura. "It wouldn't just be lying there. She's too tidy for that. There's not a speck of dust in the room."

"Then the room's been searched," said Reggie.

"Very popular item, this map."

"She has a tin box on that mantel," said Reggie. "Behind the photographs, and underneath the books."

"Not any more she doesn't," said Laura, lifting up the books. "Bloody hell."

"It's moot, though," said Laura. "She told you she hid the originals when she was eight, and I think we can believe her on that. An eight-year-old girl doesn't hide things in a tin box. She doesn't have a tin box. At eight she has a little jewel case that her mother gave her, and she puts that, and anything that is too big for it, in a shoebox, and she hides the shoebox in the attic."

"So where do we look? There is no attic."

Laura didn't answer; she was busy examining the framed photos on display on the mantel.

"Is there a photo missing?" she said. "There should have been three. The two remaining are set up that way."

Reggie stepped up beside her. There were just two framed photos displayed now on Mara's shelf. One was of Mara as an adolescent, somewhere indoors, holding a puppy that had to be Mookie. The other was a much younger Mara, sitting with her mother on the front porch of a yellow wood-frame house.

"You're right," said Reggie, "there was another. A man, early thirties, perhaps. Standing somewhere outside in dry hills."

"Her boyfriend?"

Reggie thought about it. "No, the photograph was too old for that."

"Her father, then?"

"Perhaps."

"And someone took that, too," said Laura.

"Or she took it down."

"Keep it there all these years and then take it down now?" said Laura.

"Yes," said Reggie. "She could have a reason for that."

"Let's check the other rooms. I'll try the bathroom cabinet. Why don't you see how the bedroom looks?"

Reggie did so. The bed was contemporary and inexpensive; she'd put her money into the big down pillows. The window was open by a couple of inches, just enough for the thin white curtains to move gently in the wind.

"Anything of interest?"

Laura had come up behind him unnoticed.

"Nothing out of the ordinary," said Reggie.

Laura walked to the foot of the bed. "She'll only keep this till she marries. Then she'll spend a tidy fortune on a hardwood suite that she fully expects will last forever." She paused and then added, "Or perhaps she merely bought what was available. In any case, everything on the bed is just a little off-kilter as well."

"So the room's been searched and restored," said Reggie.

"I would say so."

"What did you find in the loo?" he asked.

"Nigel may in fact have been here. Some man was, at any rate. He left the seat up."

"Anything else?"

"There are some essentials missing from the cabinet. And I found her travel set in the hallway closet. Five-piece, but the rucksack is missing. So she left intentionally, but in a hurry, I would guess. Which I might do as well if I came home and found my place tossed."

"Unless it was tossed after."

Laura went back into the living room and stood looking at the paintings that Mara had on easels by the window. Reggie joined her there.

"She must be in her domestic phase," said Laura. "And she's in a bit of a rut. She keeps painting a tree. This one's all made of rectangles, this one's less representational, and this one is background for a pretty yellow house—but they're all the same tree."

Reggie went to the mantel, picked up one of the photographs, and brought it back.

"This yellow house?" he said.

Laura looked from the photograph to the paintings.

"Oh, what idiots we are," she said. "We're looking in the wrong home, unless she grew up in this flat. She hid the map when she was eight, in the house where she lived then, and if they don't have accessible attics, then I bet she did the next best thing—she put it here."

Laura was pointing at a painting, at the ground beneath the pepper tree.

"She buried it?" said Reggie.

"And when she grew older and moved away, she forgot about it. Or maybe they moved when she was still a child, and she thought she would leave a box of treasures for the next child to find. And there would be all manner of wonderful things, not just silly papers. It's there. That's her safe place to put things, right there."

18

A short time later, Reggie and Laura stood on the brick red cement front porch of Mara's childhood home, waiting as a real estate agent struggled with the broker's access lock on the front door.

"I love your accents," she said as she tried again to get the numbers right. "This lawn will be green as Ireland if you give it a little water."

Finally the lock fell open. She eagerly shooed Laura and Reggie inside.

Laura stopped for a moment, just at the center of the front room, and Reggie watched her turn and appraise the structure as if she truly meant it.

Reggie just watched and said nothing. He had never seen a woman stand still—in a room or on a stage—as evocatively as Laura. Whether it was strength, or vulnerability, or designed seduction, or all of them together that she sought to convey, she did so with the slightest upward tilt of her jaw, or adjustment of her lower lip, or what seemed an almost willful summoning of a rosy blush to her cheekbones.

Of late Reggie had been seeing too little of that blush, whether willful or involuntary.

The agent began to explain that the gleaming hardwood floors had just been buffed.

"Yes, they certainly have," said Laura, and then, according to plan, she asked if they could see the backyard.

"Of course," said the agent.

"So important for the children," said Laura as the agent took them through the kitchen. The agent smiled knowingly and asked how many there were; Laura replied that there were none yet, but one never knows.

"There's a beautiful old pepper tree," said the agent. "You could attach a swing to it."

Laura walked out under the tree, admired the branches, and said that perhaps one could. Then she casually pushed some fallen leaves about with her foot and studied the ground.

"Don't worry about all these leaves," said the agent. "It just sheds seasonally—I think. They're really not a problem."

"I'm sure not," said Laura, smiling and looking up but still nudging the dirt casually with her toe.

"I think I'd like to see all that storage space now," said Reggie.

"Of course," said the agent.

Laura said she'd just stay and get the feel of the backyard for a few minutes more, and Reggie and the agent left her there as they went into the house.

Reggie examined the storage space in the garage, and the closets, and underneath the kitchen sink; he asked about the type of wood used in the new flooring and the number of sealing coats used on it; he said something random about the color scheme used for the bathroom tiles; finally, mercifully, as he stood in the kitchen and wondered aloud about the cost of re-doing the cabinets, Laura appeared in the doorway.

The agent was looking the other way, fortunately. Reggie gestured subtly, and Laura reached down and brushed the last remnants of dirt from her knees. Then she nodded at Reggie and entered the room.

"Yes, it's a lovely yard," Laura announced. "Great for caus-ing a ruckus."

"It's a fine house," Reggie said conclusively to the agent, "but we'll need to mull it over."

The agent sensed failure and suggested that she show them another.

"No need at all," said Laura. "It's a perfect house. It's us. Not the house. I mean, I'm just not sure the house is quite us. We need to toss it about a bit. Don't we, dear?"

"Yes," said Reggie. "That's what we'll do."

"Well, don't wait too long," said the agent. "I've already had a second call on it today."

The agent drove them back and dropped them at the Bev-erly Hilton.

Laura walked up close beside Reggie as soon as they got out of the car and whispered to him, "What a splendid little eight-year-old she was."

"No argument, but what makes you say so?"

"The things she chose to keep and protect."

"Such as?"

"I don't think I'm at liberty to say; she meant everything in there to be a secret, of course. And I put all of it carefully back. Except these."

Laura reached inside her blouse and carefully pulled out three thin paper sheets.

"I'm glad they used vellum for these," she said. "It would have been a bit scratchy otherwise. But I'm afraid they're a bit damp now."

She handed them to Reggie.

"Pleasantly scented, though," he said.

"I did try not to sweat," she said.

She was smiling in a satisfied but eager sort of way. Reggie recognized it as her victory blush; it was the way she would be when coming offstage on a particularly good night, and in his opinion, there was nothing better in the world.

"I have to take these to someone who can read them. But I can be back in two hours," he ventured hopefully.

For a moment, the look on Laura's face told him she would say yes to this proposition. But then her expression changed.

"I won't have time," she said after a moment. She hesitated again, looked away briefly, then looked Reggie in the eye. "I have work to do with Robert later—I mean, if we've done everything we can here for the moment."

"Robert?" said Reggie.

"Yes," said Laura. "When I told him I had to come out here, he said he'd come, too; insisted on it. Very sweet of him, really."

"You mean he's here?"

"Yes."

Reggie absorbed that. "I see," he said. "What . . . sort of work?"

"Why, script changes, of course. What else would it be?"

"Of course," said Reggie. "So much of Shakespeare is in need of a good polish."

Then Laura went up to her hotel room, and Reggie caught a cab.

19

Traffic was light, and Reggie got to the Pasadena Geological Institute in good time. He found the young woman working at her terminal, a bit too closely for the good of her eyesight.

Reggie sat down and put a vending machine cappuccino on the table next to her.

"Mine?" said Anne, accepting it gratefully. "How'd you know I needed that?"

"I was at university once," said Reggie.

"So what else did you bring me?" she said.

Reggie gave her the map that Laura had dug up from Mara's backyard.

"Can't say much for your filing system," she said, brushing residual backyard dirt from the papers Reggie presented to her. She paused for a moment, snuffled her nose, then looked at Reggie with a puzzled expression.

"Chanel?"

Reggie didn't answer.

She carefully unfolded one of the sheets and looked at it. After a short moment, she gave a soft whistle.

"This has got methane pockets everywhere, like a honeycomb," she said. "All of them eight percent and higher."

"Is that significant?"

"It is if you light a match. Whatever they were planning, this would have sunk it."

She turned back to the terminal and entered the site number from the map. A new screen display came up.

She stared at it, then gave Reggie a look, then stared in astonishment at the screen again.

"Holy shit," she said under her breath.

"What is it?"

"This is a live dig."

"It's what?"

"Your location is the North Lankershim terminal of the Silver Line—"

"Are you sure?"

"Of course I'm sure," she said. "Here, look. This circle here is the dig for the North Hollywood terminal of the Red Line at Chandler Avenue—their tunnel is running west of the Cahuenga Pass and under the Santa Monica Mountains, and geologically speaking, you can see that it's not prohibitive. Well, maybe you can't, but I can. They'll have their problems, but at least they're not going to blow themselves to kingdom come. But our dig—the Silver Line hub—follows a different route, tunneling on the east side of the pass, so that it can hook up with a line that will connect Glendale and downtown L.A. In the database, it looks like a cakewalk. But now look at your map—every one of those little triangles indicates a gas concentration way over the limits. I've seen that dig; and they aren't prepping for this. Damn, they may have already hit one of these. There was a guy killed in a fire there a month or two ago. They said it was the tunnel linings—just like that downtown fire yesterday. But that's because they trust the geological survey data. They believe what's in the database, so they look for another cause."

"You're saying they're digging into methane and they don't know it?"

"I'm not saying it, you're saying it. Your map says they're tunneling into a methane minefield. I mean, if this thing is for real."

She put down the sheet and swiveled in her lab chair to look Reggie in the eye.

"Okay," she said, "this is getting serious. You gotta level with me. How'd you get ahold of this thing?"

"A copy of it came in the post. And I know the copy is nearly twenty years old, because that's when it was sent."

"Why would someone send it to you?"

"It wasn't sent to me," said Reggie. "It was sent to . . . ."

"Yes?"

"Look," said Reggie, "I can't see that it matters how I got it, all that matters is—"

"Of course it matters how you got it. No one's going to believe this without some kind of provenance. If this is real, the Valley Transportation Authority needs to know about it, and the North Lankershim dig sure needs to know about it. But this is no easy thing, and if I'm going to get this in front of them, I've got to know—how'd you get it?"

"An eight-year-old girl sent it. Twenty years ago. To Sherlock Holmes."

Silence. She looked at Reggie with exactly the expression he'd expected.

"Excuse me?"

"She sent it to Sherlock Holmes."

"You mean with the funny hat, the pipe, and all that?"

"I know how it sounds. But hear me out." Reggie explained his business address, and the process of the letters, as rationally as he could.

"Uh-huh," said Anne.

"There's more," said Reggie. "I think my clerk at Baker Street may have been killed because of this."

"Yeah, right."

"You've said it yourself. Decisions are made on these things that affect money everywhere in the Valley. So suppose twenty years ago someone wanted the subway to be planned for one route rather than another . . ."

"They'd alter the data," she said, sounding as though she were beginning to believe it.

"Yes," said Reggie.

"And if they were smart," she added, "they'd destroy the original."

"Yes. But the original survived. An eight-year-old girl saw to that, trying to find her father. And when that sandhog was killed in the fire at Lankershim, the stakes were raised. If this surfaces now, whoever made those changes twenty years ago will be looking at homicide."

"Oh, now you are freaking me out."

"And myself as well. I shouldn't have involved you in this." Reggie stood. "I'll let the foreman at the Lankershim site know what we found."

"Whoa, hold on. No one's going to believe you. Let me see that thing again. What an idiot I am, it'll be right there— signatures. It'll have the signatures."

She eagerly picked up one of the sheets and looked in the right-hand corner.

She squinted and held it up.

"Twenty-year-old penciled, handwritten, Chanel-scented signatures." She gave the sheet back to Reggie. "Can you read it?" she said. "I've got contacts in, so you can't go by me."

Reggie looked. "It's not your contacts," he said. "I can't make them out, either. My guess is one of them should be a man named Ramirez—it was his daughter sent the map—but I can't tell anything from this."

"Well, okay," said Anne. "Tell you what. You go to the North Lankershim site and give 'em a heads-up if they'll let you. I'll get Professor Rogers into this. I can't just waltz this over to the Valley Transportation Authority and drop it on them, but he can. His office hours are probably done for the week, but I think I can track him down; I know where he does his afternoon jog. We'll have his attention now."

"Thank you for your help," said Reggie

"Fair trade for the cappuccino," she said, pushing back in her chair. "But one more thing."

"Yes?"

"Is this a hobby of yours or something? Is this how you Brits take vacations—you go someplace hot and dry and mess around with stuff? Like in . . . what was that old film—*Lawrence of Arabia*?"

"No," said Reggie as he got ready to leave. "For me, it's all been pretty much involuntary."

"Uh-huh. Well, hold still a second." She got a tube of something out of her backpack, put a dab on her finger, and applied it to the bridge of Reggie's nose.

"You've got just a little sunburn going there," she said.

Reggie left the institute and took a taxi back to the Valley.

It was past noon, and hot despite the hazy overcast, when Reggie got to the Lankershim site.

The same pleasant female security guard was there as before, but she was busy shooing away camera-toting tourists. Reggie walked through the gate and then toward the excavation pit, where Sanger, his back toward Reggie, was directing workers on scaffolding.

Reggie reached the edge of the excavation and looked down. He guessed it to be at least ten stories deep, probably more—the shadows at the depths made it hard to tell. It was a sheer vertical drop.

Sanger turned around now and saw Reggie.

"You again? How'd you get in here?" Sanger shouted toward the security guard at the gate. "Walker! Over here!"

"Don't blame her," said Reggie. "I snuck around. It's important. I couldn't take a chance on not seeing you personally."

"Tell it to security. Right now I'm due in the pit."

Sanger stepped onto a five-by-three metal platform that served as the lift into the multistory excavation. Reggie followed.

"You need to see this," he said.

"Don't have the time. And if you're still straddling the platform that way after I push the button, the half of you that stays up here can wave good-bye to the half of you that drops."

Reggie pushed the sheets of the survey map at Sanger.

"What the hell—," said Sanger.

"Look at it," said Reggie.

Sanger looked at it.

Reggie watched his eyes shift from the location label at the top to the data on the center of the page—and then to the date stamp at the bottom. Sanger stared at that.

A faintly quizzical expression turned to an overtly angry one. Then he turned the sheet over and looked at the back; and then at the data tables on the front again. His face turned redder than it already was from the sun.

"Shit!" said Sanger, and in what was apparently a reflex ac-

tion, he slammed his fist into the platform button control behind him.

The platform motor whirred.

Sanger, as tall as Reggie and forty pounds heavier, suddenly
grabbed Reggie by the collar and in one quick motion pulled
him fully onto the platform just as it began to drop.

With Reggie secure on the platform, Sanger immediately
let go. But then he hit the lift button again, and the platform
stopped.

He glared at Reggie. "It won't work," he said. "You won't
get a dime out of me."

"I don't want your dime."

"Let me tell you something. Every square inch of this route
was sampled and mapped by the best firm in the county.
There's less methane in that tunnel than in your gut."

"This map says otherwise."

"I don't care what your map says."

"I hear one of your men died in a fire here a month or so
ago. Do you care what killed him?"

"I know what killed him. He ignored the rules and lit up next
to the plastic liners. Just like those winos at the downtown site.
And the plastic liners here ignited the acetylene tanks, and that's
how you got the explosion. The investigation showed that."

"Investigations can be wrong. Especially when there are
vested interests. You can ignore this, but we both know what the
map shows. It shows you tunneling with perfect precision into a
disaster."

Reggie hit the button to start the lift upward. "You need to
stop drilling, take new samples, and prove it one way or the
other," he said.

"Right. I'm going to stop drilling at a penalty of two million
bucks a day. On your word."

"Before, you could have claimed ignorance. Now, you can't; you've been warned. You have to exercise due diligence and check it out."

"Geez. What are you, some kind of lawyer?"

"Some kind."

The platform reached level ground at the top of the pit.

"Figures," said Sanger. "Well, listen up. I've got lawyers of my own to throw at you, and everyone like you—so a bullshit nuisance suit doesn't scare me one damn bit."

Sanger thrust the map back into Reggie's hands. Then he turned and shouted across to the security gate.

"Walker, get this shyster off my site. And make sure he doesn't hurt himself in the process. You know what will happen if he does."

20

As he rode back to the Bonaventure, Reggie checked for messages from Nigel. But there was nothing. Not on his mobile, not at the Bonaventure, and not at the office. Not a word from him.

Reggie called the jail and learned that Nigel's bail from the night before had been posted—in cash—by the law firm of O'Malley and Associates.

"You're telling me someone sent a lawyer with one million in cash to post my brother's bail?"

"If you want to put it that way," she said. "That's what it says."

Reggie got out of the taxi at the Bonaventure. On his way through the lobby, he called O'Malley and Associates and used his barrister's credentials to talk his way through to the senior partner. He demanded the name of the client responsible for Nigel's bail.

O'Malley pushed back with a lecture about attorney-client

confidentiality, told Reggie nothing, and then hung up the phone.

But that was to be expected. Reggie got in the lift and, despite the hour in London, rang Ms. Brinks at her home. She didn't pick up, but he left a message for her to find out everything she could about the O'Malley and Associates client list. Confidentiality notwithstanding, many law firms liked to brag about their biggest names in advertisements and, especially, on Internet sites. Something about the novelty of the Web—or perhaps the implicit sense that it was in fact no more real than television—seemed to get their guard down. Reggie guessed an L.A. law firm should not be an exception.

And at the last moment, he added that she should do a search on Lord Robert Buxton while she was at it.

Now, finally, Reggie was back in his room. He checked his hotel phone again. There was one message, a short one from Wembley, asking that Reggie call him back.

Reggie decided to ignore that.

He rang Laura. He got an answering machine.

Some days you just can't reach anybody. Reggie hated days like that. He called room service. Thank God, they, at least, answered; he was hungry. He ordered prime rib and mashed potatoes.

Then the phone rang as soon as he put it down.

It might be Laura; he picked up.

It was Wembley.

"I have some news," said Wembley.

"You're working late, Wembley. Not on my account, I hope."

"Common sentiment," said Wembley, "among the people I investigate. But I have some good news, and I wanted to tell you directly. Forensics is back on the blow that killed Ocher. They think your brother is not a good fit for that."

"Glad you're coming around," Reggie said.

"From the relatively upward angle, and the position we think the perpetrator had to be standing, we think it was most likely a woman."

Reggie waited. "Is that all?"

"Yes."

"Thank you for the call."

"Before you go—I've been trying to reach Miss Rankin."

Reggie hesitated. "Because . . . ?"

"I'd guess her to be about five seven, correct?"

"About. Why?"

"That would be the right height," said Wembley, who then paused, apparently to let it sink in.

"You've got to be kidding," Reggie said after it did.

"The forensics—"

"Screw the forensics. How do you know it wasn't just a short man, or even a taller one crouching a bit to throw you off?"

"So you're saying your brother could have done it after all?"

"Of course not. But—"

"In any case, no one would have the foresight to perform such a ruse, especially in a crime of passion."

"Passion?" Reggie said incredulously. "Ocher and Laura?"

"Not that kind of passion. Her motive was anger at Ocher, on behalf of Nigel, because of the way she knew Ocher treated him."

"That's absurd," said Reggie.

"So she didn't hate him for that?"

Reggie hesitated. True, Laura had never liked Ocher. But if she had not so deliberately drawn attention to that fact in the first interview with Wembley in chambers, Wembley would not have gotten onto this tack at all. But Reggie could hardly tell Wembley now that Laura had simply been trying then to steer suspicion away from Nigel.

"You're a bloody idiot," he said, for lack of anything better.

"Anyway," said Wembley, "we found her fingerprints on the murder weapon."

"She picked it up after," said Reggie. "I was there."

"But you initially told the investigating officers that nothing had been touched."

"That was their misunderstanding. I said it was as we found it. It did not occur to me to immediately point out that Laura gently removed an object from Ocher's skull after the fact. Make obstruction of that if you can."

"Well, of course she could have done that to cover prints she knew she had left earlier."

"This is nonsense, and you're interrupting my meal."

"Fine," said Wembley. "But do let me speak with Miss Rankin. I presume she is with you?"

"No."

"We tried the number she left in New York. It forwarded to a hotel in Beverly Hills." Wembley paused, in his annoying way, for effect. "A man picked up. Would he be in a position to know?"

Reggie didn't answer; he slammed down the phone.

God, was he ever slipping. If he ever made it back to London, he'd be mincemeat in court.

A few moments later room service arrived, mercifully, and Reggie started in on the prime rib and mash.

Then the phone rang again.

It was Professor Rogers.

Rogers apologized for the brevity of their previous meeting. He'd had a very full calendar, and just hadn't been able to focus fully on what Reggie presented to him. He thought he should take a second look. Reggie should bring the document, it might be important, but Rogers had a limiting schedule, and they would need to meet halfway. He had a place in mind. At the lake. At the Hollywood Reservoir. Did Reggie know it?

Reggie said he could find it. But why there?

Rogers said something about his usual jog.

They agreed to meet—at five, at the south gate, over the dam.

Reggie picked up his raincoat, which might be a bit much for the weather, but he had no light windbreaker, and he was inclined to keep the map pages out of sight. He tucked them into the inside pocket.

Several minutes before five, Reggie got out of a taxi at the reservoir gate. It was still open; with probably an hour or so of daylight remaining.

The Lake Hollywood reservoir—situated just above the band of dirty amber haze that marked the city's smog level, with a public access road that ran around the perimeter and across the dam—was like a Scottish loch plunked down in the heart of a desert. Trees lined the edges of the road and the shoreline, the cobalt blue water shimmered in its angle from the setting sun, and the early evening air raised scents of sagebrush and pine.

A sign at the gate marked the reservoir road as a public trail, and it was clearly popular with the locals. Young women ran by in shorts and halter tops. Cyclists whirred past. The place was a match for Hyde Park on a spring day.

Reggie walked out onto the road that spanned the concrete dam. The dam was some 250 hundred yards in length and perhaps 20 feet across; the road across it was flanked on either side by a waist-high cement wall. On one side of that was the deep blue water of the reservoir. On the other was a rocky canyon.

Reggie leaned against the wall on the water side to wait for Rogers. Two middle-aged women jogged past, one of them eyeing Reggie and his raincoat suspiciously.

A cyclist passed from the opposite direction. Then a teenage girl being pulled by a red setter on a leash. A tanned, svelte woman in spandex shorts and halter top, gliding comfortably on in-line skates, diverted Reggie's attention for a moment. Then her boyfriend glided up beside her.

Nearly twenty minutes had passed. Reggie began to wonder if Rogers would show. He turned and looked back toward the gate to see if anyone else was arriving.

Suddenly there was impact. Reggie was thrown back against the wall—the spandex skater was in his arms, pressed full front against him, her arms encircling his waist. She apologized profusely and charmingly and disentangled herself amid considerable sweat and heat, and it would not have been an unpleasant collision—but as soon as she had disengaged fully, Reggie realized that she was clutching something that was his.

She had the map.

Reggie reached toward her, but at the same moment the lady's companion swooped in from the opposite direction and took the sheets from her outstretched hand without breaking stride.

The two were on skates, breaking in opposite directions, and Reggie was off balance; they would surely get away with it.

But no one had informed the red setter of the plan. The dog saw a game in progress and gamboled forward, turning its leash into a taut three-foot hurdle. The skater had no time to prepare. He stumbled and had to use one hand to catch himself, and although it wasn't much of an interruption, it was enough. Reggie closed the gap in an instant; before the skater could reestablish his momentum, Reggie had him by the arm.

He pulled the skater back and grabbed for the map. They struggled up against the low wall—and Reggie would have controlled the situation, or so he believed—but then there was an impact again, and this time in earnest: The female skater had returned, putting her full momentum into it, striking Reggie high in the chest with a surprisingly hard shoulder.

There was no chance to brace for it. Reggie fell backward over the wall behind him. He had the map pages in his hand, and he stuffed them into his raincoat pocket just as he fell.

The free fall was just long enough for him to realize the stupidity of that effort—for what good was the paper if he was on the hard side of the dam?

But he wasn't. He was on the water side.

It stung on impact and was shockingly cold. And he was much heavier in the water than he should have been. Reggie struggled out of his raincoat—what a brilliant precaution that had been—and got to the surface.

He broke out of the water with a gasp. Still breathing deep and fast, he got his bearings.

He looked up at the top of the dam. He saw passersby looking back at him over the wall—the girl with the setter, a tall, bald man whose sunglasses glinted down at Reggie—but he didn't see either of the skaters.

The water was much too cold to hang about, and he began to swim—with difficulty, on his back mostly, using his legs and one arm for momentum and the other arm dragging the bloody raincoat as if he were rescuing it.

It was only fifty yards or so, and that was a good thing.

Reggie slogged ashore, stood, and tried to shake off the cold.

He was at the shoreline just before the dam. Above him was the access road from which he had just fallen. Next to him was a steep slope, thick with undergrowth.

He began to climb the slope, finding a path between the rocks, manzanita, and low-growth pine.

He stopped. A glimpse of bright clothing caught his eye. He paused to look.

Below and to his right, lying between patches of sagebrush near the base of the dam, was Anne.

Reggie began to scramble quickly back down the slope. His feet dislodged clumps of dry earth and small rocks, sending them tumbling down the slope ahead of him; he immediately adjusted the angle of his approach, afraid that the tumbling rocks would strike her and cause more injury.

But when he came closer and saw the angle of her body—and the stillness of her eyes—he knew the tumbling rocks did not matter.

She was already dead. He knew it even before he knelt beside her.

Her body was broken. The ground around her head was saturated. She had no pulse.

For an unbearable moment, there was nothing but silence. There was nothing and no one else around, there were no surroundings, there was just Reggie. Reggie and a young woman who was dead because—he was sure of it—she had done him a favor.

Now Reggie looked up. She could not have just fallen; the wall was too high for that.

The in-line skaters were nowhere in sight. And the onlookers who had watched Reggie swim to shore were gone now as well. But at the near end of the dam—standing at the beginning of the access road, behind a clump of scrub oak, as if he thought it provided concealment—was a smallish, white-haired man in a jogging suit.

Reggie stood up, staring.

The two middle-aged women joggers he had seen earlier were paused now as well, on the road above the slope, and they were looking down at Reggie—but he was reckless of what they might be thinking.

He was too focused on the white-haired man standing at the edge of the dam at the access road.

Rogers?

The not-quite-concealed man stared back. Reggie had forgotten to be subtle, and now the man knew he had been seen.

The man bolted suddenly, like a rabbit from a hedge, running across the access road toward the opposite end of the dam.

Reggie sprinted up the rough slope after. He had staggered before, but not now. His shock and grief, and his initial anger at himself, had found a better target, and the adrenaline of it pushed him up to the road in short order. He began running.

Rogers—if indeed it was Rogers—was only halfway across the dam; he had a lead of no more than 150 yards. That meant the result was not in doubt—the man was probably headed for the gate at the opposite end of the reservoir. That gate was more than a mile away. Reggie was capable of a six-minute mile, and the man was doing nowhere near that pace. He knew he would catch him.

But now there was a shout from behind Reggie.

"That's him!"

It came from the two women.

But they weren't pointing at the man getting away at the opposite end of the dam.

They were standing at the edge of the roadway, above the slope where Reggie had found the young woman—and they were pointing at Reggie.

Several male runners in USC tank tops came up alongside the women, paused, and looked.

"There!" screamed the women, still pointing at Reggie. "He's over there!"

Reggie turned and looked back at them. He gestured to the women and the contingent from the USC track team and then pointed at Rogers—or the man who might be Rogers—but he could not make himself understood.

And now, the tall, bald man in sunglasses joined them, and he too was pointing at Reggie:

"That's him!"

The USC runners took off toward Reggie in a heroic sprint.

At the same time, two counterclockwise runners, coming from the opposite direction, crossed paths with the white-haired man, who urged them on in Reggie's direction.

And close on their heels were two private security guards on bicycles.

Joggers, cyclists, and runners of all shapes and sizes were now converging on Reggie from both directions of the road. For a brief moment, he wondered whether he should remain in place and just try to explain.

But the white-haired man had already rounded a bend and vanished from sight; there was no hope now of getting past the throng to catch him.

"There!" shouted the first two women, pointing at Reggie again. "He killed her!"

This would not work.

Reggie abandoned the dam and ran back down the road to the near gate with all the six-minute-mile speed he could muster. He approached the final bend in the road, the last one before the gate, and he looked over his shoulder.

Behind him, all the recreational enthusiasts from either side of the lake—runners, bikers, skaters, dog walkers, and combinations thereof—were in his hot pursuit.

Thank God; his taxi was still there, just outside the gate.

He climbed quickly through the gap in the chain-link fence. He knew he'd have just seconds before the posse appeared behind him, and if the cabdriver saw them, all bets were off.

Gasping, wheezing, and pouring sweat, Reggie jumped into the cab.

"You run in those shoes?" said the driver.

"My best time in a week," said Reggie. "You should try it."

"You'll stink up my cab," said the driver.

"Just drive, dammit," said Reggie, pulling money out of his wallet. "The Pasadena Institute. I'll buy you all the air fresheners you need."

The driver turned the cab around and headed down the hill, just an instant ahead of the pursuit.

It was night when Reggie arrived at the campus. In the foyer outside Rogers's office, the secretary was getting ready to lock up.

"Can I help you?"

"Rogers," Reggie said tightly.

"I'm afraid he's not in."

"Where is he?" said Reggie, walking past her. "Out for his evening run?"

"Sir, you can't—"

"Sorry," said Reggie. He entered Rogers's office and shut the door behind him.

She had told the truth: Rogers wasn't there. Reggie heard her pound on the door, then quickly leave, undoubtedly to get security.

On the walls were Rogers's many diplomas, and plaques of recognition, and photos of him accepting awards. One in particular caught Reggie's eye.

It was a smallish photo in a modest frame, easy to overlook and forget among all the others—unless you were specifically looking for something that went back a few years.

This one went back a score or more, judging from the clothes and Rogers's buoyant hair.

Reggie took a closer look. He saw Rogers and another man—who looked a lot like the man in the old photo in Mara's

flat—both smiling and standing in front of a car that bore the
name and logo of a surveying firm.

Reggie went to Rogers's desk and pushed papers about
until he found one that had Rogers's signature. He carefully
pulled a wet sheet of the map out of his pocket, unfolded it,
and compared the faded signature with Rogers's.

It matched. At least to the extent visible.

Through the office window now, Reggie could see Rogers's
secretary hurrying up the steps of the building with a uniformed
security guard.

Reggie left the office, found a side exit, and got to his cab.

There were flashing red lights and sirens on the ride back to
Los Angeles, but they were headed in the direction of the reservoir, not following Reggie.

Not yet.

He rang Laura at her hotel; she did not pick up.

He needed shelter. The Bonaventure was out of the question. Only one alternative came to mind.

"Take me to the Roosevelt Arms," Reggie told the driver.

It took a long drive through heavy traffic, but finally Reggie
reached the Roosevelt Arms. The clerk in the lobby of the Roosevelt Arms took a moment to look Reggie over. He seemed
pleased for some reason.

"Hard times?"

"Just give me a bloody room."

"You know, you just missed him," said the clerk, taking Reggie's money for a day in advance.

"What? Who?"

"The other guy. From before."

"Nigel?"

"I guess. That's what she called him."

"She who?"

"The girl he was with. Latina, very pretty."

"When did they leave?"

"A little over an hour ago. Just before those two guys showed up looking for 'em."

"What two guys?"

"I'm trying to remember."

Reggie put two twenties on the counter.

"Hell, I dunno," said the clerk, pocketing the money. "Looked like a couple suits on their casual day."

"Suits as in police?"

"Naaw, too stylish. Police suits are more like those guys over there."

The clerk was pointing one block up and across the street, where Mendoza and Reynolds were ordering at a take-away burger stand.

Their backs were turned. For the moment.

"Which room do you want?" said the clerk.

"Keep it," said Reggie.

His taxi was still at the curb. Reggie exited the Roosevelt Arms, got into the cab, and ducked down low.

"Beverly Hilton," he told the driver, and they pulled away just as the detectives turned with their sandwiches. In the mirror, it appeared that Mendoza gave the cab a second look, but it was hard to tell.

Reggie had the driver deliver him to the side entrance of the hotel; the lobby seemed a risk. He walked from there to the outdoor patio in back.

In places with weather like this, Laura preferred her evening meal outside. With luck, she was having a late dinner, and that would be why she was not answering the phone.

Reggie stood behind a palm tree next to the gate and looked in.

She was there, at a table just beyond the pool.

And, mercifully, she was alone.

Reggie came up behind her and put his hand lightly on her arm, and she turned.

"You don't look well at all," she said.

"I'm not. Is that coffee?"

"They say so."

Reggie took two quick gulps of Laura's coffee.

"The locals are looking for me; I need to get out of view."

"All right," she said.

"Sorry," said Reggie, "not the lift. I don't want to go through the lobby."

"Certainly," said Laura. "It's only four flights."

They found the stairs and Reggie told her about the lake as they climbed.

"I'm sorry," said Laura as they entered her room. "It's one thing when it's an obnoxious clerk. Something else when it's someone nice."

"We should close the drapes," said Reggie. "Anyone who has anything to do with that map is winding up dead. Nigel is at risk. So is Mara."

"What do we need to do?" she said.

"Rogers can't be in this alone. He had help at the dam. And someone behind this had enough resources to make Rogers want to sign that false report twenty years ago. And enough now to put up one million in cash to get Nigel out of jail and into the open."

"Who are the candidates?"

"Someone who was rich then, rich now, and getting richer still from the Silver Line taking the route they chose."

"That's a rather broad range, isn't it?"

"Yes. But there's another criterion. To bail him out, some-one had to know almost as soon as we did that Nigel was in jail.

That means that someone is getting inside knowledge of our activities. And that narrows the list."

"Considerably, I would think. Who is on it?"

Reggie hesitated. He knew what he was going to say next would get him in trouble.

But then his mobile rang.

"It's not for me," said Laura.

Reggie picked up.

The voice he heard on the phone was male, raspy, middle-aged plus, and weathered.

"You're the British guy," said the voice, "with the brother. Right?"

"Probably," said Reggie.

"You want to clear him for killing that bastard under the freeway—you bring it to me."

"Bring what?"

"The map, dammit. My map. You know what I'm talking about."

"Bring it where?"

"Bring it to the North Lankershim dig. Right now. The station platform in Tunnel 110-Left. Don't be seen."

"How—"

"Stay away from the main gate, that's where the security is. Go to the south gate, where they let the trucks in during the day. You'll know what to do when you get there."

"Who—"

"Just get there. Now."

The man hung up.

Laura was standing as close as possible to Reggie to listen.

"Where?" she said.

"I want you to get on the next plane back to New York. Or better, London."

"I can't do that."

"You can take Buxton with you if you like."

"Not bloody likely, not while this is going on. In fact, I'm sticking to you like glue until we're all out of here."

"You don't need to—"

"Of course I do. Nigel means as much to me as he does to you. Besides, clearly it's not being with you that's dangerous. It's being discovered by you. So I'll do the prudent thing. Where you go, I go."

Reggie saw that it was a settled issue.

"As you wish," he said.

"So where is the bloody thing?"

"In my coat pocket."

Laura picked up Reggie's coat. "I hope you don't mean this pocket," she said as she examined the coat.

"Why?"

Laura pulled out the contents of Reggie's waterlogged coat pocket. She laid the wet sheets of vellum on the glass coffee table and pressed out as much water as she could. Then she folded them carefully between the pages of a thick weekly *Variety* magazine, placed all of it together in a paper bag, and gave the whole package back to Reggie.

"I hope they survive long enough for our purposes," she said.

"I hope we do," said Reggie.

21

With all the old shops permanently closed, and no neon residuals to illuminate anything, there was probably not a darker place in the city than the Lankershim construction wasteland where the cab dropped Reggie and Laura. There was one weak amber streetlamp to cover three blocks. To the south, the Paradigm building was lit at the top. One block to the immediate north was a yellow light at the security gate for the dig.

"I'll go, you stay and call the police if I don't come back," said Reggie.

"Bloody hell I will. If you don't come back, me calling the police will be a bit late, won't it?"

"I—"

"We settled this issue. Now let's just do it."

"I hope you wore comfortable shoes."

They began walking toward the south end of the dig. Then Reggie put his hand on her arm and they paused.

There was one parked car, at what used to be curbside, just fifty yards from the south gate.

It was a powder blue 1960s Volkswagen Beetle.

"I know that car," said Reggie.

He approached it from one side, and Laura from the other.

In the dimly lit street, it was impossible to see anything through the rear window.

"Wait," said Reggie. "The driver's side is halfway down. Can't be right."

Reggie went to the driver's-side window. He started to lean inside for a better look.

There was a sudden explosion—of fur, slobber, and growling canine teeth—and Reggie jumped back.

"Bloody damn dog!"

Mara's Saint Bernard had half its body in the front seat now and half in the back, where it had compressed itself, like a huge coiled spring—until Reggie arrived.

"Don't be angry, just because he scared you."

"Knocked me down a full flight of stairs last time he did that."

"Doing his job," said Laura, approaching the animal. "Sweet baby. Not annoyed with me at all, are you?"

Reggie looked inside again, warily, as Laura stroked Mookie's head.

"Keys are in the ignition," he said. "Keys in the ignition, and window down. Do you suppose she'd walk away and leave her car like that, counting on the dog to protect it?"

"No," said Laura. "She wouldn't leave him here. He's her baby. Something's wrong."

Reggie stood back from the car and looked around. At the north end of the site, there was a small yellow lamp on at the security station booth; presumably there was still a guard there.

But the south edge of the site, just fifty yards or so away, was dark.

"We're almost there," said Reggie. "We need to move on."

"We can't leave him here," said Laura. "If the sun comes up in this heat, he could cook."

"If the sun comes up and we're not back, I doubt that I'll care whether he cooks."

"We can't just leave him," repeated Laura.

"All right, then," said Reggie. "If we let him out, can you tie him up?"

"Of course."

Reggie stepped back from the car, and Laura let the dog climb obediently out. She tied it by the end of its leash to the nearest pole.

"Sit!" she said firmly, and the dog did.

Reggie and Laura moved on to the south edge of the site.

The perimeter of the chain-link fence was topped with spirals of razor wire. But there was a gate.

The gate appeared at first to be chained shut. Reggie gave it a push.

The lock fell open, and the chain dropped to the ground with an interminable metal clatter. Reggie looked about furtively, but the security booth was apparently too far away for anyone to have heard, and he saw no one.

He opened the gate, and they entered the site.

To the left, a dirt-carrying conveyor belt angled ninety feet overhead, with a mountain of the day's diggings piled at its base. Directly ahead was the main excavation itself.

The tunnels had to be below, at the bottom of the 150-foot excavated pit.

They walked on, past stacks of concrete tunnel segments, toward the excavation.

As they drew closer, it became apparent that the pit itself was completely dark—there were amber lamps along the surface, but there was nothing but black in the depths. The lamps gave just enough light to locate the lift Reggie had seen when he spoke with Sanger earlier.

But the platform cage was locked. And as they moved cautiously closer to the edge, it was clear that the platform itself was, quite inconveniently, at the lower levels.

Reggie took a step closer to the edge of excavation and peered into the darkness below. At the far end a faint arc of light spilled out from some source, but it was too weak to illuminate more than a bit of damp ground.

"Now where do you suppose the tunnel is?" asked Laura.

"Further down than one would like," said Reggie.

"And was this our only mode of transportation?" asked Laura, looking at the vacant lift cage.

"I believe I saw a set of stairs somewhere along here—scaffolding, really, and it's a long way to the bottom. Can I persuade you to reconsider?"

"Nothing of the sort," she said.

They walked for several yards along the perimeter until Reggie found the metal spiraling steps to the excavation floor.

They both paused at the edge and looked down.

"It's even further than it looks," said Reggie.

"I'd say you're right about that, since we can't see past three steps in this dark."

"Are you sure you want to proceed?"

"Stop asking that," said Laura. Then she said, "You first."

Reggie went first. The metal steps clanged and echoed as they began the descent.

Within a few moments, the top of the rim from which they had descended was no longer distinguishable in the darkness;

below, everything was dark as well, except for the weak light at the far end.

Laura stopped and reached down to touch Reggie. "Did you hear that?" she asked.

"Hear what?" He turned toward her.

"I thought I heard something above."

"Something like what?"

"A click. Something hard on metal."

"I didn't hear it."

"All right, then, let's both hold very still."

Reggie did.

They were standing very close to each other—of necessity on the narrow stairs—she two steps and one-half turn above him. He could hear her breathing. He felt her body heat, and he could tell that at some point in the last twenty-four hours, she had put her perfume other places than just behind the ears. If they hadn't been standing with no guardrail over a pitch-black chasm on a mission of utmost urgency—

"What are you doing?" said Laura from above.

"I'm holding still."

"Not completely. And the position of your face is quite untimely. Kindly hold still in your own space."

"If I lean any more into my own space, I'll be in a ten-story free fall. What are you doing?"

Laura was reaching up and touching the edge of one of the metal steps above them with her fingertips. "If someone else is on the stairs," she whispered, "we should feel the vibrations."

"Do you feel vibrations?"

"Nothing from the steps," she said. "Let's shove on."

Reggie roused himself from his position, and they moved on. Several long moments later, they reached the end of the ladder and stepped off onto gravelly ground.

Somewhere water was dripping; there were thick scents of wet earth and fresh concrete and a sharp scent of diesel fuel.

Now they knew that the faint light they had seen from above was coming from the tunnel opening, fifty yards or so away. They approached tentatively, not speaking, walking past the high mounds of freshly dug earth and stacks of rebar and concrete tunnel linings.

Reggie looked hard into the shadows and saw no one. But it was too dark to really tell; anyone could have been in the excavation watching them, and there was no way to know.

They reached the entrance to the tunnels—two of them, each about fifteen feet in diameter—but only one of them had any source of light. Black lettering on the concrete face of that one identified it as 110-Left.

Reggie checked his watch again, then stepped to the opening and looked in as far as he could.

"Well, we're here. Tunnel 110-Left," said Laura.

"I think the idea was we go inside."

"No doubt," said Laura. "Cheery thought."

They entered the tunnel, walking between the steel rails.

In this part of the tunnel, concrete linings had already been set in place. Lamps attached to the upper portions of the walls glistened in shades of white, gray, and silver off the concrete, and reflected iridescent patterns on the steel rails and dark rainbows on oily substances that floated on the occasional pools of water.

But the electrical installations weren't complete, and there were gaps, with darkness and loose hanging wires, between the glow of each lamp, and there were dark recesses in the tunnel walls.

It was surprising how much their footsteps echoed on the damp sand and gravel.

In the far distance—or near distance; it was nearly impossible to judge, given the perfectly straight path of the tunnel and the reflecting light—was a dark obstruction of some kind, dead center in the tunnel, with a faint halo from residual light in the tunnel that continued behind it.

They were moving toward it rapidly, and as they got nearer, pieces of tunneling equipment and trailing carriers were distinguishable along the sides of the tunnel.

Reggie put his hand on Laura's arm to stop her from continuing forward.

Now the haloed obstruction in the center of the tunnel was distinguishable. It was the mole, a massive tunneling machine.

And on a recessed service shelf in the tunnel wall on the right was a dark object that Reggie had at first supposed was another piece of equipment.

But it wasn't. It was a man, sitting very still on the shelf, legs dangling over the edge, facing the farther end of the tunnel, in the direction of the mole.

Reggie and Laura took another few steps, then stopped.

The man turned his head; the features of his face were still indistinguishable.

"Closer," he said.

It was the same voice Reggie had heard on the phone, but now he was certain where he had heard it previously.

It was the angry man from the soup kitchen. It was Mara's father.

"Ramirez?" said Reggie.

"Move closer," the man said again. "I can't see your faces."

They moved closer. Cautiously.

Now the man stood up. He was wearing the oversize dirty overcoat Reggie had seen when he'd chased him in the alley.

Ramirez stared back at Reggie's face for a moment and seemed satisfied.

"Show me the map," he said.

Reggie pulled the *Variety* magazine out of his coat pocket and extracted a sheet of the map from it.

"Closer. Can't tell from here."

Reggie stepped closer, unfolded the map, and without letting go of it, displayed it for Ramirez.

"Okay," said Ramirez. "That's it. That's the one."

Reggie expected Ramirez to try to take the map now, but he didn't. He just stared at it intently, as if mesmerized, as Reggie held it out before him.

"Damn eyes. Can't see shit anymore. But see that mark at the bottom corner? That's me. That's my own mark. That one's the truth." He said this almost longingly. To Reggie, it seemed the man was beginning to lose focus.

"How will you clear my brother?" Reggie said quickly, bundling the map back into the newspaper.

"What?"

"My brother. You said you can clear him."

Ramirez paused and looked annoyed, as if Reggie were insisting on the trivial. "Yeah. They think he killed that jerk under the freeway, right? Well, he didn't. I did. I killed the little bastard."

"Why?" said Laura.

"The guy was lurking. I watched the place for days, so there was no doubt about it. Always seemed to be coming down the stairs when she got home. Always seemed to be coming down the stairs when she got her mail. Not shuffling around like he was shy and wanted to meet her or something like that, but lurking, dammit, for no good.

"Three nights ago I see him go into the alley. After midnight. There's no doors over there, just fire escapes, and windows, and one is Mara's, so I paid close attention. Then I see him start to climb her fire escape in the dead of night. I stopped him."

"One way to put it," said Reggie.

"Killing him was just good luck. I wasn't trying to hit him that hard. And I wasn't trying not to."

"For what it's worth," said Reggie, "I don't think he was actually after your daughter. I think he was after your surveys. I think he learned that what he had stolen from her earlier was just a copy. He was looking for these. The people who sent him needed the originals."

"Point is, no one sneaks into my little girl's window in the dead of night. Not him, and not you, either. Guess I didn't hit you as hard. But I knew she wasn't in at the time; must have made me soft. Anyway, I wheeled the guy's body away in a grocery cart. I figured I'd push him all the way down to the channel, but when I got to the overpass, I saw somebody running up from the warehouses on the other side of the road."

"I suppose that would be my brother," said Reggie.

"I didn't ask for introductions. I covered the body and took off."

"We'll need you to tell all this to the police."

"What? Oh, like a confession? No problem. I mean, if it actually comes to that. C'mon."

Ramirez jumped down from the service step and started to walk where the tunnel construction was still in its early stages, freshly dug and unsealed. He moved slowly into the portions where the concrete had not yet been poured.

There was one single lamp, just next to where the mole had stopped. The lamp sent out yellow light that glimmered off the steel of the mole and reflected in amber and blue streaks through plastic sheeting that covered the nearest tunnel walls, shimmering the way a fire flickers.

Laura looked into all that and then back at Reggie. Both of them stayed put.

Ramirez stopped and looked back at them. "C'mon, what are you waiting for?"

"The police will take your statement. We can all leave now."

"What? Oh, no. You don't get it. We can't leave yet. Don't worry," said Ramirez. "It's not far."

Reggie looked at Laura.

"I suppose we have to take him back with us, don't we?" she asked.

"Yes," said Reggie, "or we can't prove a thing."

"All right, then."

They both moved forward after Ramirez.

They walked on in the tunnel, fifty and then more than a hundred yards. Construction was less complete here, with bare earth and stacks of steel and wood braces along the sides of the tunnel.

And then they stopped.

Ramirez was behaving oddly, touching the freshly excavated walls as they walked, putting his face right up next to the dirt, and muttering something that sounded like "fools." He took several rapid steps farther into the tunnel, staring overhead as he went. Then he poked his nose up against the sides of the tunnel and began making sniffling sounds. Then he swiveled and came quickly back.

"What do you smell?" demanded Ramirez.

Reggie and Laura looked at each other.

"Nothing," said Reggie.

"Just the damp earth," added Laura.

"That's nothing," said Ramirez, "you smell that everywhere." Then he took two quick steps, and with a fierce grab, he pulled a handful of dirt and clay out of the wall behind them.

"Taste this," he said to Reggie, proffering the handful of dirt.

"Pardon me?"

"Taste it," repeated Ramirez. "My own buds are all shot to hell from the booze."

Ramirez seemed quite tense now. Reggie tasted the dirt.

"Well? What's it taste like?"

"Dirt?"

"Oh, hell," said Ramirez, turning from Reggie to Laura. "You try it."

Laura took a small portion of dirt and clay between two fingers and placed it on her tongue. She pressed her lips together and considered it.

"On the buttery side, with a bit of an aftertaste, but rather standard, I should think—except for a hint of something unpleasantly like rotten eggs."

Ramirez stared.

"You sure know how to taste," he said. He leaned on a spool of cable, rubbing his forehead and staring woefully at the solid earth before them. "It's just where I knew it would be."

"What is?" said Reggie.

"The gas," said Ramirez. "They've drilled within a foot of the highest hydrogen sulfide pocket in my entire survey. I know there's methane here, too, and it's worse, because you can't smell it. The sulfide, it gives you warning and will generally asphyxiate you before it explodes, so that's a plus. But the methane gives no warning. One spark, and instant hell. Everyone in the tunnel is cooked."

"Do you mean everyone," asked Laura, "as in us at this very moment right where we are—or everyone as in the people who will come in tomorrow and work here?"

"Both," said Ramirez. "They have no idea what they're

doing. They don't know about the gas, so they're drilling ahead, and they haven't even connected the fans. Look above you."

Reggie looked. Ramirez pointed at the ventilation fans, which were set at regular internals for the length of the tunnel—but which all hung limply, with loose wires dangling.

"They don't know what the fuck they're doing," he said.

"Tell us all about it," Laura said with an empathetic smile. "Let's all just sit down over here where it's nice and dry—it's so damp going further into the tunnel, don't you think? And you can tell us all about it. Perhaps we can help."

Reggie was familiar with this smile. And Ramirez was looking at Laura. That was probably a good thing.

"It was the ponies," Ramirez said, and he sat down.

Laura moved in and sat on the service shelf right next to Ramirez.

"Ponies?"

"I won at the track the first day I went. The horse was called Lucky Mara, so I had to bet on it, and it won big. You know how it goes. You keep trying to recapture that."

"Yes," said Laura.

"Santa Anita, then down to Del Mar. The exactas were killing me. And the trifectas. Hell, any long shot, and a whole bunch of sure things. Anyway, I was in debt to my eyeballs.

"Pretty soon there was nothing left. I'd mortgaged my house, hit up every friend I had at work. I was into the loan sharks deep. Everyone knew about it. And these were the real bad guys. They were beginning to lean.

"On the day it was all due, I couldn't pay. I was told to expect a call.

"We were sitting down to dinner. I'd tried to get my wife out of the house before the call came, but it didn't work, and all that happened is we had a huge fight. Mara ran upstairs to her room and cried. Then the call came."

Ramirez paused, as if still surprised by the whole thing. "It wasn't who I thought it would be. I thought it would be one of my loan sharks, or someone worse. But you know who it was?"

"No," said Reggie, getting just a little impatient. "We don't."

"Do tell us," said Laura.

"It was my surveying partner. Rogers. He said something about the job at Lankershim. Said we were in a position to do someone a favor. Wouldn't say who. But someone would take care of everything I owed, and I'd get a little besides, if I'd just change a few numbers in my report. That was it."

Ramirez looked away. "The unholy sonofabitch."

"But I did it," he continued after a moment, looking at the ground. "I falsified the readings. I made a tunnel through hell look like a walk in the park." Then he looked up again, and his face was as hard as the walls of the tunnel. "Unholy sonof-abitch," he repeated. "He's messed with my family for the last time."

"What sort of messing are we talking about?" asked Laura.

"Understand something," Ramirez said angrily. "Nobody was better at that work than me. I cataloged every foot of every core we drilled. Some guys will fudge a record every now and then if they forgot to make the note on the spot; some guys just get a little too general, and pretty soon you've got Core 62 reading just like Core 12, when really Core 62 is more toward sand, and Core 12 is more toward clay. I note those things, I see every detail, and I write them all down."

"Yes," said Laura, "we see that. Even how things taste."

"And I throw that all away," said Ramirez. "I falsify readings on flammable gas concentrations. And within two years, with what they paid him, Rogers ended up owning the surveying company we both worked for. But I couldn't live with myself after. Got permanently drunk, and one day I just left. Went to Alaska. Worked on the pipeline; sent money later on when I could, under another name. Sent a nice little puppy for Mara's fifteenth birthday."

"What made you return?"

"I heard about the first fire. The sandhog who was killed. I figured I had to do something before somebody else died. And then when I came back, I found that guy hanging around my little girl—"

Ramirez stood suddenly. He looked at his watch.

"Get going," he demanded. "We're due at the platform."

"What do you mean 'due'?" said Reggie.

"Just move," said Ramirez. "I'll tell you what you need to know when we get there. You already did enough damage by blowing my cover."

"What do you mean?"

"Rogers has always been afraid I'd come back, and I knew he'd have people on the lookout for me, especially after the fire. But he didn't know where I was until someone saw you chase me into the rescue mission. And then tonight a guy comes through the line at the soup kitchen, shoves a note across to me, and then runs like hell. I open it up and I see it's from my good buddy, my friend, my old partner, Rogers, and he's got my little girl. And your brother, too, not that I give a damn, cause I just have a sense that you guys showing up caused half of this. He's got them both."

"What do you mean, 'got them'?" said Reggie.

"Just follow me and shut up."

Ramirez turned his back to them and moved on.

Reggie and Laura paused.

"He was all sentiment and consideration early on," said Laura. "And now he's just demanding. Why is that always the case?"

"I have to follow him," said Reggie. "But you don't—"

"Oh, just be quiet and move on, would you? He's got that much of it right."

They continued on after Ramirez for several minutes more. Then the pale light reflecting from the lamps and concrete linings began to give way to a wide, dark area on the right-hand side, and they slowed their pace.

They were approaching an unfinished station terminal—a platform on their right that extended for fifty yards or so along the length of the tunnel before it ended. The platform was unlit except for two lamps at the tunnel's edge; it wasn't possible to see into its depths, but Reggie could make out the outlines of support columns and what were probably stairs leading to a second level and, presumably, to an exit.

They walked single file until they reached the edge of the platform. Then Ramirez ordered them to stop.

"Okay," he said, "here's how this thing is going to work. That sonofabitch Rogers is going to show up on the platform. He's going to want to see the map—the original. Once he's seen it, he's going to offer to take the map in exchange for my daughter. And your brother, if he's still alive. And then—"

Ramirez stopped in response to their stares.

"Well, how would I know?" he said half-apologetically. "Point is, he'll offer to trade her—him—them—for the map. He's probably going to even offer to let them step down from the platform and join us in the tunnel."

"No," said Reggie. "He won't do that. The fact is, we all know who he is now. He wants the map—or to see it destroyed so it can't be used against him—but he can't let any of us live."

"Who said he'd let us live? I didn't say he'd let us live. We all know too damn much. I just said he'd let us all be in the tunnel together. He made me bring you in this way for just that reason.

He's on the platform, where there's ventilation and it's safe. We're in the tunnel, where there's gas. He wants us all in the tunnel. Then all he has to do is toss a match. He's not fooling anybody."

"So what's your plan?"

"Plan is we make sure Mara stays up there. And your brother, too. I mean, if he's still—"

"Yes, we get it," said Reggie.

"And we make sure Rogers comes down here to see the map. That's the one thing he has to do, he has to know that no one has the original."

"But after he has seen it, he'll just go back up on the platform, and he'll toss that match," said Reggie.

"No," said Ramirez. "He won't get that far. I've got matches, too."

Everyone was silent for a moment. Then:

"Question," said Laura.

"Yeah?"

"You lighting the match while we are all in the tunnel . . ."

"Yeah?"

"I find a flaw in that."

"I made this mess," said Ramirez, "and I'm going to clean it up. I'm ready to die."

Reggie was about to respond that he and Laura were not.

But now there was a sound from deep on the platform.

"Daddy?"

This voice transformed Ramirez into a vehicle of perfectly focused intent. His back seemed to straighten, and he turned to face the direction of that voice as if guided by a laser.

He leaped toward the platform and started to climb it.

"Stop there!"

Now an exit light flickered at a back corner of the mezzanine, partially illuminating one end of the platform but leaving the other dark.

In fitful, strobelike bursts, it revealed Rogers, standing by a cement column at the south exit of the platform. He was holding Mara tightly, with one arm twisted behind her back. And he had some sort of implement—in the shadows it was impossible to discern just what—stuffed in his pocket.

Ramirez froze in place, his hands gripping the edge of the platform as he glared across at Rogers.

"Let her go," growled Ramirez.

"Not a problem," said Rogers. "I'll send her right down. Just show me the map."

"Don't move, baby!" shouted Ramirez. "Daddy will come get you."

"Stay where you are," said Rogers. "Or I throw her down there with you."

Ramirez hesitated. "Told you he'd play it this way," he whispered to Reggie.

"And you were right," said Reggie. "So what's your plan now?"

"My plan?" said Ramirez. "You're the fancy lawyer. You want out alive, you negotiate this. But my daughter stays up there no matter what—I'll light you and me and the whole damn tunnel up before I let him send her down here with us. Look up there."

Reggie looked up. The fans in the tunnel hung silently by their disconnected wires. But the fans in the platform ceiling were whirring madly.

"They only come on when there's gas," said Ramirez.

Reggie stepped forward and shouted up at Rogers. "He hasn't got the map. I do."

"Show me."

"We'll bring it to you," said Reggie, "when I see my brother."

"Done," said a voice.

At the opposite exit from Rogers, barely distinguishable in the shadows, a figure fell to the ground from behind the center support pillar.

"It's Nigel," whispered Laura. "And he's hurt."

He was. Nigel stirred slightly, lying on the floor of the platform, and reached a hand back to touch a blood-wet patch on the back of his head.

Now a tall, broadly built man with a bald head stepped out from behind the column. Reggie knew he had seen him before, his sweaty forehead flashing in the sun, as Reggie looked up from the chilly water of the Hollywood Reservoir. And somewhere else, too—without the cap it was obvious: The man had been on the flight from Heathrow.

But now the flickering light from a dying tunnel lamp caught the glints of a gun.

"Just toss the map up here," said the man.

"Do that, we fry," whispered Ramirez.

"Would do," said Reggie to the man with the gun, "but this is not the map."

"I don't believe you," said Rogers.

"All I brought is *Variety* in a bag," said Reggie. Then he pulled the newspaper—with the map still folded deep within it—out of the bag and held out both the empty bag and the *Variety* for viewing. "See?"

"You're lying," said Rogers to Reggie. "You did bring the map."

"The map proves two murders. Murders you committed. You really think I'd bring it with me?"

"Don't know what you're talking about," said Rogers.

"She was your own student, you bleeding wanker," said Laura.

"Your fault," said Rogers toward Reggie. "You shouldn't have gotten her involved."

"Stop talking," said the tall man to Rogers.

"And his clerk," said Laura.

"I didn't touch the clerk," said Rogers. He tightened his grip on Mara, and she winced noticeably. "You can look to your own for that."

"You are getting to be a very annoying little man," said Laura.

"Look to my own—," began Reggie.

"Shut up," said the man with the gun. "Keep your mouth shut, Rogers." And then to Laura, "Everybody shut up." The gun was leveled at Reggie. "I want the map, now."

"It's on its way to Reggie's secretary," Laura lied defiantly. "She knows everything, and she's surprisingly reliable."

The man at the platform stopped at that and looked over at Rogers, who looked back. But now Reggie saw Nigel—half standing—trying groggily to reach something behind the pillar.

"Here," Reggie called out, "see for yourself." He stuffed the newspaper and all of its contents back into the bag and tossed the bag onto the platform—but just out of reach of the man with the gun.

The man reacted and moved toward it.

Then there was a solitary click of a sound—and all the lamps in the dig flickered once and went out.

They were in pitch black.

"Oww," Mara said loudly.

And now from somewhere—it sounded far away, but it was impossible to tell in this environment—came a painful, mournful, deep-throated echoing sound that Reggie could not at first identify.

"What the hell is that?" he said under his breath.

"What the hell was that?" said Rogers.

"Let go of me, dammit!" cried Mara.

This time, as soon as she spoke, that deep-throated sound came again, but now it was reverberating from everywhere, as if the source were right in their midst.

And—in Reggie's judgment—it sounded annoyed.

"How solid a knot did you tie?" he said to Laura.

"Only what I thought would do."

"Get on the platform quick," said Ramirez. "Get on the platform if you don't want to get lit up."

Reggie grabbed Laura by the arm, and they stumbled forward in the blackness. He found the edge of the platform sharply with his right knee, cursed, and boosted Laura up. He followed after her, took two quick steps forward in the dark—and then slammed directly into what had to be the large bald man with the gun.

Reggie pushed forward as hard as he could, grabbing for the man's arms.

And then he heard—and half felt, it was so close—a heavy scuttling sound passing on the hard, smooth surface of the platform. From the cadence of it and his earlier encounters, he knew what it was.

Someone was in trouble, and who it was just depended on how well Mara's 150-pound dog could see in the dark.

But Reggie was losing his grip on the gunman. The man was larger than he was, stronger, and apparently equally good in a scrum. He got one arm free and gave a hard shove.

Reggie held on by the man's collar, and they both fell back into the tunnel.

Now there was a scream, in a man's voice, from the mezzanine.

And then the backup lights came on.

Reggie looked into the mezzanine and saw Rogers, in a torn

jacket with a bloodied arm, scrambling toward the lower portion of the platform to escape the dog.

With his other arm, Rogers held a road flare. It was lit.

Mookie, having protected his owner, now stopped his pursuit to look back at her for instruction.

Rogers raised his arm to throw the flare into the tunnel.

"Mookie! Fetch!"

The dog leaped from the mezzanine for what Rogers held in his hand.

But the animal had too much bulk to be that precise. His jaws seized on Rogers's arm, knocking the flare loose and causing Rogers to fall into the tunnel.

The flare slid across the platform, caromed off the side wall, and then, scattering sparks, continued rolling toward the tunnel edge of the platform.

For an instant, no one spoke or moved.

Mara, Nigel, and Laura were all on the mezzanine.

Reggie, Ramirez, the bald man, and now Rogers were all in the tunnel.

There was no hope of climbing out in time.

"Get back!" Reggie shouted up at the mezzanine.

"Run," said Ramirez, pushing Reggie ahead of him.

They both managed three or four running strides headlong down the tunnel.

And then there was the flash.

All sound, light, and sense was subsumed in a burst of wind and flame.

Reggie hit the ground with one knee and then with his face, and the gravel stung into his forehead, cheek, and chin. He felt the heat and light consume the air above him, and for a moment he wondered whether he was on fire.

Then the inferno subsided.

The air felt brittle, as though someone had left a pan on the stove too long. The skin on the back of Reggie's head and neck felt as though it would break with the slightest movement. He raised himself cautiously, painfully, an inch or so from the ground.

And then there was the second blast.

22

Reggie's mother was speaking to him. His father was at the table, too, the formal dark cherrywood dining table, and his brow was furrowed. This was evident, and Reggie knew of its importance, because his mother's voice was saying, "Your father's brow is furrowed."

Reggie couldn't actually see that himself; the entire room was filled with smoke, and the figures of his father and mother, seated with him at the table, would appear, then fade, and then reappear amid the haze.

Reggie's mother was saying something else, too, something Reggie could not make out, and as he struggled to make it clear, something still in contact with his conscious mind suggested that perhaps it was time to come out of this dream.

Reggie struggled with that, but consciousness brought pain and pressure on both sides of his temple, and he sank back in.

What was his mother saying? That part of his mind was

working past hours; she had to be saying something. It would fill in the blanks.

"What has your brother done now?"

That was what she was saying. Wasn't it? He tried again.

"What have you done to your brother now?"

Was that it? Reggie wasn't sure. He tried to define the words in his mind again, but he was interrupted. Someone else was in the dream room, at the table with them now.

It was Laura. Had she been there all along? How could he not have seen her?

She was saying something, too, but she was not sitting now, she was rising from the table; she was wearing a flowing white scarf, and she was gliding from the room.

Reggie woke.

He was in crisp white sheets. A hospital bed. He knew it immediately.

The left side of his face felt puffy. He touched it. It was bandaged. There was a light covering on the back of his neck.

His right leg was heavily taped and supported by a hanging sling. He tried moving the leg gently, side to side.

Well, at least there must be no nerve damage. That tiny movement hurt like hell.

Where was Laura?

Reggie tried to sit up, but too quickly. He became dizzy and fell back.

After a moment, a cool hand stroked his forehead; someone said something soothing and then was gone. Some time went by, and there was a scent that was familiar but out of place. Then the scent was gone. Reggie slept deeply.

Then he was awake again. Someone was standing by the bedside, demanding something, and not in a soothing voice.

"Give me a minute," mumbled Reggie.

"Take all the time you need," said Lieutenant Mendoza.

Disappointed with whom he was waking to, Reggie began to drift again—but then his mind fixed on something, a question, and it wouldn't let go.

"Why two?" he mumbled.

Mendoza said something unhelpful in response. Reggie sat up with a start—and then the pounding inside his head forced him back down.

Yes, bloody hell, he was awake, Laura was not there, and Mendoza was sitting across from him.

"Why two?" he said again.

"Two what?" said Mendoza.

"Explosions. First blast. Second blast. Why was there a second blast?"

"Oh," said Mendoza. "Fire marshal had an idea about that. First blast in the tunnel knocks out the power to the platform fans. With no fans, gas fills the platform area—and you get your second blast."

"Where is Laura?"

"Who?"

"The woman who was here. Before you came in."

"There was no one here," said Lieutenant Mendoza. "Just the nurse who let me in."

"Who got out?"

"From where?"

Reggie managed to raise himself up and grab Mendoza by the collar. "Don't be daft," he said hoarsely. "Who got out before the second explosion?"

Mendoza calmly pried Reggie's hand loose and spoke in his most condescendingly professional tone.

"Not quite sure yet," he said. "We found one scorched and deceased adult male in the tunnel. Or maybe two; a little difficult to tell at the very center of the blast. But we're not completely sure who got out, because we're not completely sure who went in. Why don't you tell me?"

Reggie said nothing. He knew the detective knew more than he was saying.

Mendoza shrugged. "My guess," he said, "is that it's all a sibling competition of some kind. And at the moment, you're in a dead heat, if you'll pardon the expression. I still like your brother for the body-in-a-basket thing under the overpass."

"My brother is in the clear. Ramirez confessed to it, as I'm sure you know by now."

"Ramirez has been unconscious since we pulled him from the tunnel. He hasn't confessed to anything, so far as I know."

"He confessed to me prior to the explosion."

"Uh-huh. And I guess I have your word for that."

"If you poke around a bit, I think you'll figure it out for yourself."

"I expect I will resolve it, one way or the other. But we've also got a young woman thrown off the dam at the reservoir. She was just twenty-four, you know. I like you for that one."

"I shouldn't have got her involved," Reggie replied at first. But then he bristled, glared at Mendoza, and said, "If authorities here had paid better attention to things, it wouldn't have come down to just me and her figuring the bloody mess out for you. It was Rogers that killed her. He realized he had a problem after I first went to see him. He had an ambush set up to take the map from me at the lake. But she tracked him down there first, thinking the wanker was actually going to help—and he panicked when she told him what we knew about the map."

"And now Rogers is dead. Convenient."

"There was a second man. At the reservoir, and in the tunnel."

"So I hear."

"You haven't found him?"

"No."

"I'm sure you will in time. If he was at the center of the blast, he might be a bit dispersed at the moment."

"Uh-huh. What's the fellow's name? I'll check with missing persons."

"I don't know his name. A white male, fifties, something above six feet, one ninety or thereabouts."

"Narrows it down to a million or so local suspects."

"Rogers forced Ramirez to alter the map, and this man paid Rogers to do it. His involvement stems from that."

"Ahh, yes, the map. Well, you may have something there. Motive, anyway, for someone, if you can prove this wasn't just some colossal screwup."

"Exactly."

"Brilliant. Where is the map?"

"On the tunnel platform, last I saw," Reggie said reluctantly.

"It was in the tunnel. With the great big fire."

"Yes."

"Uh-huh. Good luck with that one," said Mendoza, and he stood. "I'd ask you not to go too far—but I don't think that's going to be a problem."

Mendoza exited.

Reggie sat up and made an assessment.

The head pounding recurred only when he moved; when he was still, it receded to a generalized ache.

So that was a plus.

He knew he'd have to lift his leg to get it out of the sling. He tried that tentatively, and his right knee responded with swollen, radiating pain.

He was about to try again—but then the bedside phone rang.

It was a single room; the call couldn't be for anyone else.

Reggie picked up.

"Hello, Heath," came Wembley's voice, annoyingly and, Reggie presumed, deliberately cheery. "Are you well?"

"Quite," said Reggie. "Yourself?"

"In the pink."

"Glad to hear it. How can I help you?"

"I'd like to see the three of you back here for a little chat, Heath. Miss Rankin. You. Your brother."

"Not a good time," said Reggie.

"They tell me Miss Rankin is more than able to travel, and you and your brother can be moved in a day or two. From what I understand, you're making rather a mess over there anyway. I'll get extradition if I need to," said Wembley.

"Give us two days then," said Reggie. "I doubt they'll let Nigel out before that. I'll see you myself day after tomorrow. If you still need to talk to Laura or Nigel after, you'll know where to find them."

"Fair enough," said Wembley, now sounding a bit suspicious. "Just be here."

"Thank you," said Reggie, and he hung up the phone.

He took a breath, clenched his teeth, and readied himself again to try to get out of bed.

This time he managed it. He raised his leg cleanly up and out of the sling.

And then his foot came down with a little more force on the floor than he would have preferred. He choked back a scream. He stood and waited for a wave of nausea to subside before finding his clothes.

Reggie stepped into the corridor, then was dizzy again, and he leaned for a moment against the wall and tried to think.

Wembley had revealed more than Mendoza had about the state of things. Laura must have gotten out cleanly, but Nigel must be injured.

Reggie looked to his right, toward the nurses' station. The attending nurse was busy on the phone, looking the other way. It was just as well. There was no telling what instructions Mendoza might have left.

Reggie straightened, tried to ignore the pain in his knees, and began a stroll, or something like it, down the corridor. He pushed open the door of the first room. There was an elderly woman, sleeping, and an empty bed.

He went on to the next room, where a balding, sixtyish man announced personal surgical details of which Reggie would just as soon have remained ignorant.

He moved on to the next room.

And there was Nigel.

He was lying flat out in the bed, unconscious. A nurse was tending to him.

"What's his condition?" Reggie asked.

"A concussion."

"When will he come out of it?"

"You should ask the doctor that. But I've seen worse."

"He's had one before," said Reggie.

"Sure, honey," she said helpfully. "Who hasn't?"

"Was there a woman visitor here earlier?" asked Reggie.

"Yes, he seems to be a popular guy."

"Tallish redhead, highly freckled?"

"The first one. The second was medium, Hispanic, also very pretty. She said she had to go see her father. In the burn wing."

The nurse exited.

Reggie sat on the plastic hospital guest chair. He stared at Nigel and tried to push back a memory of thirty years ago—when he'd waited outside a surgery while his distraught mother and a doctor peered into Nigel's eyes, assessing the results of a concussion that Reggie had caused.

In relating that incident years later, their mother, unable to deal with the knowledge of one son hurting the other that way, had transferred that guilt onto one of Nigel's chums, and in family legend, that's where it had remained.

Making it all the more awkward for Reggie, hearing the story again and again at family events.

This one isn't my fault, he reminded himself. Nigel came out here against his instructions.

But perhaps because of his lawyer's training—or perhaps in spite of it—Reggie looked back one step in the trail of proximate cause.

He had given Nigel the menial position that, as it turned out, included the job of answering the letters.

Yes, but there was no way he could have known Nigel would do such an extraordinary thing with them. So Reggie was not the cause.

He looked yet another step back—Nigel had taken the job because of his troubles with the Law Society.

But those troubles were of Nigel's own making, so Reggie was not the cause there, either, and it was time, he knew, to be done with that.

But then Reggie looked back one more step, to what had preceded Nigel's gloriously successful—and then completely disastrous—first trial.

And what had preceded that was Laura's breakup with Nigel.

And the lover she had dumped him for was Reggie.

That was not proximate cause, either; no court on either continent would say so, there were too many intervening events and too much exercise—and often foolish exercise—of Nigel's free will in between.

But Reggie's mind was not a court of law, and as he sat by his brother's bedside, there was no jury to provide exoneration.

Mercifully, now his mobile rang.

It was Ms. Brinks.

"I have your list," she said.

"Which list is that?" said Reggie.

"Clients of O'Malley and Associates," she said. "Remember, you asked for—"

"Yes, I remember," said Reggie. "What did you find?"

Ms. Brinks began to rattle off a long list of people and corporations known to be clients of that law firm.

Reggie dismissed each in turn; he could see no possible connection for any of them.

"Perhaps it would help," said Ms. Brinks, "if I knew what sort of connection you are looking for."

"Someone, or some thing, with some likelihood of communication, however indirect, with me, Nigel, or Laura."

"Oh," said Ms. Brinks. Then, after just a short pause, "Well, there is one more thing, then."

"Yes?"

"I . . . just don't know whether I should say."

"If you've got something, Ms. Brinks, you'd better spit it out."

"You asked me to look into Lord Buxton. So I did. And you were right, there's a connection. I mean, indirectly."

"Say that again?"

"He owns one of the companies represented by O'Malley and Associates. And . . . I just don't think it's my place to say—"

"Ms. Brinks—"

"Well, in the *Star* a few days ago, there was an item about him in the company of Miss Rankin. In New York City, some premiere or another. Now, I don't want to be presumptuous, sir, but the indirect connection I'm referring to is—"

"Thank you, Ms. Brinks. I will connect the dots."

"You're welcome, sir."

Reggie hung up the phone.

Buxton.

Could it really be? Could Buxton be behind any of it at all?

That would be perfect. Laura would drop the man like a stone.

Reggie sat alone in the room for several moments more, contemplating the possibilities. And then the door opened, and he looked up with a start.

It was Laura.

She entered the small hospital room, her dark red hair spilling down over her neck and exposed shoulders, making her seem unusually vulnerable. She looked across first at Nigel, unconscious in the bed, and then she appraised Reggie.

"Where does it hurt most?" she asked.

"My head and neck and arms and knees," said Reggie. "Nothing more. What about you?"

"Not a scratch," she said. "Nigel saved the Saint Bernard, you know. It seems the blast put it airborne, and Nigel cushioned its fall, so to speak. Heaths are apparently excellent buffers."

"Bloody hell," said Reggie.

"And then it cushioned mine. I'll be sneezing now for a month, but fair trade."

For a moment they both sat in silence, looking at Nigel. Reggie thought he caught Laura glancing surreptitiously over at Reggie watching Nigel, but she looked away again and said nothing.

Reggie spoke first.

"Wembley is getting ready to drag us all back to London about Ocher," he said, "with you first on the list. And Mendoza still wants to hang something on Nigel here if he can. We need to establish a connection between Ocher and what happened here and make everyone see it."

"Sorry," said Laura. "I was wandering. Don't know quite why. How do we do that?"

Reggie hesitated. He had avoided this earlier. He couldn't avoid it now.

"We need to identify the inside source," he said. "The person who put up Nigel's bail."

"Yes, I recall you mentioned that. But who is it?"

"You might not like this."

"I can't imagine why. Tell me."

"Your friend Buxton," said Reggie.

For a brief moment, Laura just stared. "You can't be serious," she said.

"He has the funds to have done it."

"Reggie, what possible motive would he have?"

"I don't know, exactly. Not yet."

"Then why are we even discussing him?"

"Laura, he owns the majority interest in a company that is represented by the same law firm that posted Nigel's bail."

Laura looked away, puzzled over that for a moment, then looked back.

"That's it?" she said.

"Sorry," said Reggie. "Didn't want to present bad news about your friend, but there it is."

"Reggie—if you draw lines from all of Robert's acquisitions to all their subsidiaries, the amazing thing will be if you discover a major law firm that does not represent one of his interests somewhere. And you know this, you know it perfectly well. Why are you even bringing this up? And why do you keep saying 'friend' as if in quotation marks?"

"It's just beyond credibility," said Reggie, "that he would fly out here just to get rid of all the thees and thous in *The Taming of the Shrew*."

"It's not just 'thees' and 'thous,' if you must know. He's decided to go ahead with the movie spinoff, and he came to set that up. There will be a quick promotional shoot at the studio in Century City before I go back to rehearsals."

"I see," said Reggie, with as little inflection as he could manage.

"Usually when you say it that way, you don't," said Laura. "But just tell me this—how is Robert supposed to have known that Nigel even was in jail, or about any of what we've been doing at all?"

Reggie didn't answer at first. He was digging a hole for himself, and he knew it. He was well past the clay and about to drill into bedrock, and his better sense told him to stop—but he didn't.

"Well, bloody hell, Laura, you've been spending your evenings with the man, what in blazes am I supposed to think?"

"If you can even imagine that I would be so foolish and untrustworthy as to confide—"

"No, I don't, I don't think that at all."

"But you thought it, you did think it, you said it just now! If I didn't think it would break some stitches somewhere, I'd slap you so hard your teeth would rattle into the next millennium!"

She stood and turned toward the door.

"Laura—"

"Reggie—for all this time you've waffled and I've waited. Now you think you see a threat come on the scene and suddenly you think it's me that might have a shag on the side?"

She went to the door without waiting for an answer. But then she paused and looked back.

"You can call me," she said, "when your brother wakes up. Or when you do."

And then she was gone.

Reggie remained there beside Nigel's hospital bed and wondered if Laura had meant it literally.

Then something occurred to him, something so obvious that he realized that something other than rational logic must have been running him of late.

If the inside source was not Buxton, who was it?

He took out his mobile and rang Ms. Brinks in London.

She asked how everything was.

Reggie lied. He told her he now had what he needed to put an end to the whole mess—including the original survey map and the evidence to tie it to who had altered it. He would deliver both to the transit construction authority and to Mendoza. Between that and Mara's testimony, he would see Nigel clear of the mess—on both sides of the Atlantic.

Ms. Brinks asked if she could do anything more to help; Reggie told her nothing else remained to be done and hung up the phone.

Then he got up and went into the corridor.

He began looking into rooms again until he found a man who lay bandaged head to toe in light gauze, with catheters and intravenous tubes extending uncomfortably from his arms and groin. The man's forehead and one entire side of his face was covered, and Reggie wouldn't have been sure who it was.

But he saw Mara sitting at his bedside.

Her face showed a bruise on her right cheek and a deep sense of worry, but she seemed otherwise undamaged.

Reggie found a chair and sat down next to her.

"I suspected he had come back," she said when she looked up. "Just a week after Lance Slaughter moved into the building, I began to notice this older man at the shelter—he'd just stand outside and stare across at my building all the time. At first it creeped me out. But he wasn't staring in the same way that some guys will—he was just sort of . . . watching. And not so much watching me, as . . . well, watching out for me, it seemed like. Watching over my place. And once I began to suspect it was my father . . . well, I had to be real careful what I told anyone. I couldn't even go over to the shelter to try to talk to him; I was sure that would put him at risk. I had to watch out for him as well."

Now Ramirez moved slightly in his bed.

"Hi, baby."

"Hi, Daddy."

Ramirez shifted his eyes to the side, noticing Reggie.

"You were lucky," he said. "A few yards made all the difference."

"Who was it?" said Reggie. "Who did all this?"

"It was Rogers," said Ramirez. "You saw."

"But who paid Rogers off?" said Reggie. "Who was the other man on the platform?"

"Never saw him. Rogers knew him, I didn't. Never saw him." Now Ramirez became agitated and moved as if to sit up. "Anyway, I fixed it! I came back and fixed it!"

"Daddy—"

Ramirez slumped back into the bed, and his eyes closed.

"You can't talk to him anymore," said Mara at his side.

"Your father killed Lance Slaughter. Did you know that?"

"Not for sure. I mean, not right away. But . . . well, yes. I suspected it."

"Mendoza will still charge Nigel with it if he doesn't hear otherwise."

Reggie saw her hesitate.

"I know," she said. "When he comes to again, I'll . . . I'll ask him to tell me."

It was only a moment's hesitation, between conflicting loyalties, and in Reggie's view it meant something that she gave Nigel such weight.

"Will that be enough?" she said. "I mean . . . to get Nigel free of this?"

"Your father can clear Nigel," said Reggie. "If Mendoza hears his statement. But someone behind this—the money behind all this—will escape because we don't have the map."

"I want whoever made this happen to pay," said Mara.

She picked up her backpack from behind the chair and opened it. "I kept this safe for twenty years," she said. "You think I would let it burn?"

She pulled out three rolled-up sheets of singed paper. Then she just held on to them for a moment.

"You better make good use of this," she said to Reggie.

"I intend to," he said.

She gave him the map.

Reggie left Mara with her father and returned to Nigel's room. He walked over to the bedside and looked.

Nothing had changed. Nigel was still unconscious.

Reggie turned and went back to his chair and was about to sit down. Then he heard Nigel speak.

"Bloody hell," said Nigel. "How long was I out?"

Reggie returned to the side of the bed.

"Where is she?" said Nigel.

"She left a bit ago," said Reggie. "Annoyed with me, I think."

"Oh, I see. You meant Laura. I meant, where is Mara?"

"With her father."

"She's all right?"

"Yes."

"And Laura is all right?"

"Yes."

"I hope everyone else is dead. The bloody dog, too. God, my head is pounding."

"Join the club."

"Don't tell Mara what I said about the dog."

"Why in bloody hell didn't you contact me when you got out of jail?"

"I've made you either a suspect or an accomplice in two murders on two continents. I would think that would be enough contact. So when they let me out, I just went directly to Mara's."

There was something possessive in the way he said her name this time, and there was not much room for misinterpretation.

"You mean you just showed up at her door, said, Here I am, take me in, and she said yes?"

"Pretty much," Nigel said in an overly self-satisfied tone. "Isn't that how it always works for you with a beautiful woman?"

"No," said Reggie, looking doubtfully at Nigel. "Not exactly."

"Well," said Nigel, retreating a bit, "perhaps it wasn't exactly that way. But something changed between the time you first spoke to her and the time I got out of jail. I think because she learned that her father had returned and was in trouble. She was looking for help, and I was there.

"We stayed at her place at first, but I had a sense the wrong people would know we were there. So I took her to the Roosevelt Arms. I know it's not the Bonaventure, but it's safe. Or at least I thought it was. And they accept pets."

"Who posted your bail?" said Reggie.

"I wondered that, too, and I still don't know. I realized at the time that someone must be getting me out just so they could round me up and, they hoped, get the map. But just knowing that doesn't help. And apparently the clerk at the Roosevelt will tell anybody anything for a fee. Mara and I went to the Lankershim dig, looking for her father. They followed us there. Rogers and the other wanker had both me and Mara at once; they had the gun, and I couldn't risk doing anything."

"Who was he—the other wanker?"

"I don't know. But I've seen his face before. I'm pretty sure his photo was hanging in the café across the street. And Mara's attentive neighbor—keep forgetting his name . . ."

"Lance Slaughter."

"He had a photo hanging there as well. Don't know if that means a connection between the two. You should ask Laura to take a look. She can tell a producer from a director from an actor at a glance."

"Yes," said Reggie. "I will when I see her."

Nigel sat halfway up and peered at Reggie. "Have I been missing something?" he asked. "Is there a problem between you two?"

"There may be a problem."

"Well, you've been a fool to let her ride for so long," said Nigel. "I mean, Buxton, for God's sake." He started to shake his head in amazement but immediately stopped. "Oww," he said. "Bloody hell. I hope they have real drugs here and not some bloody holistic—"

"Have you ever considered," Reggie interrupted, "how things might have gone between you and Laura if you had not invited me that time to see her at the Adelphi?"

Nigel stopped whining and stared at Reggie. "No," he said. "Why should I?"

"No reason," said Reggie.

"You remember what I was like," said Nigel. "The state my career was in. Do you think I had the vanity to believe that a woman like Laura would marry someone with prospects like mine? I mean, yes, good looks count, but—"

"I'm sure she would have seen possibilities," said Reggie.

"What? Since when do you regard my career as acceptable? And you know my work habits; I've been a poster child for attention deficit disorder since the day I was born."

"Seems to me your prospects weren't so bad until . . . until after."

"Until after . . . ?"

"You know," said Reggie, waving his hand vaguely. "Until after . . . Laura and me."

Nigel sat all the way up and looked at Reggie with a whole new kind of stare.

"How I botch my career is my responsibility, and my fun. And if I want to throw it away, that's my choice. What happened, did they transplant your cerebellum or something here?"

"No," said Reggie. "At least not that I'm aware."

"Dear God," Nigel said, "please don't tell me you've been delaying Laura all this time just because you think you stole her from me."

"Of course not. Especially if you put it that way," said Reggie. "I've been delaying because I'm a fool. Idiocy is idiocy, Nigel, it doesn't have to have a deep-rooted psychological cause."

"Exactly my point earlier," said Nigel.

Reggie's mobile rang. He picked up.

He listened for a moment.

"I'll be there," he said.

He shut off the phone. "That was Paradigm," he told Nigel. "But not the production lot, where we wasted so much time. The real business end, in the tower next door."

"And they called you because . . . ?" said Nigel.

"Because Ms. Brinks has been working overtime, I expect," said Reggie. "Although there's still one piece that . . ." He thought for a moment, then said, "When you found that first letter in the archives—the one that came twenty years ago from Mara—you said it was misfiled in some way?"

"Yes," said Nigel. "In its own folder, and out of sequence—not where you would expect it to be."

"But Ocher said Parsons kept things in excellent order."

"Not this one."

"Out of sequence so that no one else would find it," said Reggie, "and in its own folder so that the person who misfiled it could retrieve it quickly?"

"Possibly," said Nigel.

"I'll let you know," said Reggie.

23

Reggie left the hospital.

He wanted to go directly to see Laura. Not just wanted, he knew in his bones he needed to. But between problems he thought he knew how to solve and problems that he was afraid he couldn't, his choice of which to take on first was always the same.

And he needed two pieces of information before going to Paradigm.

One was something any estate agent should be able to find for him. He rang the woman who had showed Mara's house. She told him to come right on over to the office.

Reggie took a cab, and along the way he called Mrs. Spencer in Theydon-Bois and asked her a question about Parsons.

"Why, yes, I was full-time, and he was a prospective temp. So I did indeed interview him before he was hired," she said.

Reggie got from her the details of that interview and made a mental note to send her a thank-you basket if he ever got back to London.

Then he reached the estate agent's office, and the woman there greeted him happily. Apparently business was slow.

"You talked it over, didn't you? You like the house? I knew you would."

"Well, no," said Reggie. "Not quite. I'm actually here about something else."

"Oh." She recovered from her disappointment almost instantly. "What else can I help you with? I know of a really nice three-bedroom that would be perfect—"

"Five-fifty North Lankershim," said Reggie.

She paused. "That's the Paradigm Towers."

"Yes."

"You're not really interested in buying a house at all, are you?"

"No. Sorry. Not at this time. But if you can help, I promise that if I ever come back to this—this—place—and buy a house—I will buy it from you."

She paused for a moment, and Reggie thought he might have lost her. But then she laughed.

"What is it you need to know?" she said.

"Comparable values in the area now—and the price the land sold for before they built."

She nodded, and began typing into a keyboard. After a few minutes she stopped and wrote some numbers on a slip of pastel notepaper.

"There you are." She gave the paper to Reggie.

"You and your wife are such a lovely couple," she said. "Come back as soon as you are ready."

"Duly noted," said Reggie. "Thank you."

Reggie left the estate agent's office as prepared as he could be under the circumstances. Which was to say not fully prepared at all.

But he had gone into court many times with less.

He took a taxi north, over the Cahuenga Pass, headed for Paradigm.

The air had changed from the day before. He could feel it in his sinuses and in eyes dry as sandpaper.

The high gray haze had swept away to the ocean, where it was condensing on the horizon in a distinct amber layer, like the top of a custard pudding. Above that layer was a sky so clear and blue that it was startling.

Palm fronds were blowing hard toward the west, advertising flyers and sheets of newspaper kited along the street and plastered themselves against utility poles, and the air was more hot and dry than at any time since he had touched down.

As they entered the Valley, Reggie knew before the driver said it that this was a Santa Ana.

It was Saturday, and the car park at the Paradigm business tower was nearly empty.

Reggie saw his reflection in the obsidian-toned glass doors of the main entrance as he approached. The doors were locked and there was no lobby attendant in sight. He pressed a buzzer, and after a moment the doors opened.

He rode the lift to the last floor before the top, then walked down the corridor to the corner office of J. T. Krendall, Vice President for Corporate Affairs.

The door was open; he was expected. Reggie walked through the reception area to the interior office, where the nameplate on the door had apparently just been put up; the screws weren't even in yet, it was affixed for the moment with masking tape.

A man under forty, dressed in expensively casual clothes, was looking out the window as Reggie entered.

"I'm Krendall," the man said cheerfully as he turned to face Reggie. "Are you carrying any sort of recording device?"

"No," said Reggie.

"It's illegal in California unless both parties consent. I do not consent."

"Understood."

"Fine, come right in."

Reggie did so.

"My predecessor died just recently," said Krendall. "I get his office, my own nameplate, and the view. And now I set the rules. It's a nice gig. The king is dead, long live the king."

"To what king are you referring?"

"You hadn't heard? Died in a fire. Something underground, just down the street. Funny, I thought you knew. I mean, there he is, on the wall right up there."

Reggie looked. There was a photo of the tall, bald man, just like the one he'd seen in Joe's Deli, but a number of years older. The same man had been in the tunnel, and on the reservoir bridge, and on the flight from London.

"Thing is," said Krendall, "in addition to all the perks, I also inherit his mess. You're part of that. Part of that mess, I mean; no offense, of course. But no one likes that, right? It's a very uncomfortable position to be in. So how about we see if you can be part of the solution instead?"

Krendall seated himself with a show of ease behind the desk, but he was full of tense energy. He leaned back in his chair, but he kept his feet on the floor and jittered one leg like an anticipatory teenager.

As if it just occurred to him, he said, "You can sit down if you want."

Reggie declined; Krendall shrugged.

"So," said Krendall, like a talk show host, "tell me, who is Reggie Heath?"

"You've got to be kidding," said Reggie.

The smile vanished, the back of the chair came forward, and the hands got planted solidly on the edge of the desk.

"Fine," said Krendall. "Word is you have a document you plan to convey to the police, and the transit board, and hell, maybe the chamber of commerce for all I know. Thought we should talk first."

"Word from whom?"

"Excuse me?"

"Who tells you I have such information?"

Krendall ignored that question.

"We want to avoid some unfair publicity," he said. "That's all you need to know. So here's the deal: If you provide to us the document in your possession, we—and I mean that only in the corporate sense—we will in return pull some subtle strings with the DA to make sure you are allowed to go on your merry way back home, and—to just sort of help you on your way—we will make a contribution to your favorite charity, or offshore account, whichever you prefer, to the tune of . . . shall we say two million?"

"Pounds?" said Reggie. He just couldn't help asking.

Krendall frowned for a moment, then said, "Don't get greedy on me."

"Perhaps I'm wasting your time," said Reggie, and he made a pretense of turning to leave.

Krendall stood and called after him.

"Quite frankly, it's all just not as important as you think it is, Mr. Heath. You won't get a better offer anywhere else. We're the only ones interested, and our interest is only slight."

Reggie turned back and said, "Somewhat more than slight. I looked it up. A rather straightforward bit of research, when it came to it. Would you like to know what I found?"

"Do I have a choice?"

"No. You bought this land in 1974, in a speculative, inflation-driven market, with the intent, I'm sure, of leasing out the extra space to cover the cost and make a profit to boot. But when the price of commercial property in the Valley dropped, this venture began to look like a huge and foolish loss, and it was obvious to everyone that the decision-maker had paid too much. This put you on your back foot, and looking over your shoulder to see who they would get to replace you."

"Wasn't me," said Krendall, "I was still chasing tail at Encino High School."

But Reggie continued.

"Then a miracle happens. A new underground gets funded, and of two possible routes, the favored one would have cut right through your land. And everybody knew that if they built in your direction, not only would the transportation agency buy all that extra land, but the right kind of businesses located next to the terminal would make a ton."

"All common knowledge. If that's all you've got, I don't know why I even asked you here."

"I'm wondering that, too. But there's more. Just when your board of directors starts counting its bonuses again, the geological surveying firm hired by the transportation authority— Rogers's firm, with Ramirez doing the fieldwork—discovers that tunneling into your little piece of the Valley would be like trying to mine the La Brea tar pits. Methane everywhere. The subway would have to be rerouted, and no one would want your land. You couldn't allow that. So you bought Rogers off. And Ramirez, too."

"That's just speculation."

"No, the original unaltered map, and bank records that the DA's office can subpoena, will pretty much prove it."

"Maybe. But stop saying 'you.' It wasn't me; I wasn't even here then. And twenty years ago, it was all just plans on paper—no one really thought they'd ever actually build the stupid thing. Then they do it, the tunnel runs into a methane pocket, and someone gets killed. Go figure."

"Indeed. Bad luck, that."

Krendall looked suspiciously across at Reggie for some clear sign of sarcasm, but Reggie didn't acknowledge it.

"That's when you heard from Parsons," said Reggie.

Krendall studied Reggie. "I don't know what you're talking about," he said after a moment.

"Parsons liked to follow the international cable news," said Reggie. "He saw a headline about the subway fire at the same time that he happened to be doing an inventory of these annoying letters that now get delivered to my chambers. In one of them, some twenty years ago, an eight-year-old girl sent a copy of a geological survey map. When Parsons stumbled on it in his inventory, he had just enough science background to understand what the map meant. He put two and two together and decided it should equal enough for him to buy a small island somewhere. He made copies of the letter and the map and hopped across the pond to show them to Rogers and demand a fortune for their return. Then he came back to London while Rogers was supposed to be gathering the money.

"But Rogers decides he needs a more permanent solution. He agrees to meet Parsons in London and make the exchange—but then he lies in wait and does the blackmailer-in-front-of-a-bus thing. Whether he managed to take the documents off Parsons before or after the push, I don't know—but I'm sure he was disappointed when he discovered that they were only copies."

Krendall studied Reggie for a moment. "You've got no proof for any of that."

"If you were involved in none of it, Mr. Krendall, you wouldn't know one way or the other what proof I have," said Reggie, "unless of course someone filled you in after your predecessor died. Someone who rang you this morning, and that's the reason you and I are having this conversation. Either that is true, or you in fact do have prior involvement. Which is it?"

Reggie looked at Krendall, and Krendall glowered back.

"Like I said before, it was all my predecessor."

"Good to know. As to what is in fact provable—the police had no reason to expect foul play in their first investigation. But now they will. Airline records will show Parsons coming here and then Rogers going to London after. The curb in London where Rogers did his push is directly in front of a café that is populated by regulars, and now that they know to look, the police should have no difficulty finding someone who saw Rogers in the immediate vicinity at the time. That will be enough to start a circumstantial case. The rest will be standard fieldwork."

"Rogers was a guy who really needed to learn to think outside the box," Krendall said finally. "But I've never met the man myself. And anyway, you're talking about prosecuting a dead man—so what's the point?"

"It didn't end there. It might have, if Rogers had just managed to get the map. But of course he didn't. That's why you sent the follow-up letters to 221b Baker Street."

"No," Krendall said quickly. "I didn't send them. It was . . ."

"Yes?"

"Fine," said Krendall. "Like I said, it wasn't me. It was like this: Rogers comes back from London, waving copies of this damn letter and the survey map, and tells my predecessor that there's another version of the map in some dusty office on Baker Street that can send everyone involved—again, I was not—to jail. And on top of that, he's worried that the nice grown-up daughter of the guy who did the unaltered survey might start to think about just what it was that she sent twenty years ago— or worse, that the guy himself might hear about the fire, get all guilt-ridden, and come back. And then where would we—in the corporate sense—be?"

"Rather screwed, in the corporate sense."

"Exactly. So my predecessor takes a couple precautions. He writes to get the stuff back. Easy enough. He forges the signature from Rogers's copy of the letter. He knows Dorset National is a financial institution, and financial institutions verify address changes, so he doesn't use his return address—he uses the real one, where the girl actually is, and he just stations this lousy actor there to keep an eye out—for the map when it comes back in the mail, and for Ramirez if he decides to show up. It was all just a precaution, nothing dramatic, and it might have been— should have been—just fine.

"But a couple weeks go by, and there's no response to his letter. So he goes out to London himself to do a little careful reconaissance and see what's going on.

"He learns that you have just taken over the premises. That it's your brother who is answering the letters now, and maybe he just hasn't opened that letter yet, and my predecessor's best chance is to finesse it—send another request, and hope that you guys will just routinely dig it out and send it back.

"But in case that doesn't happen, he wants a backup plan. He needs someone on the inside to make certain the map gets returned. And he needs some leverage on the person in control of those premises in case things go wrong."

"The person in control of my chambers is me," said Reggie.

"Of course." Krendall nodded.

"No one has leverage on me."

Krendall shrugged very slightly, then continued. "My predecessor does his due diligence and learns that there's no point in approaching your brother—apparently he's not the type to be induced by money to do something that is technically legal anyway. Kind of weird for a lawyer, if you ask me. But no matter. Where one person isn't willing to make fast money, there's always someone who is. My predecessor took money where it needed to go."

"To someone inside my chambers."

Krendall ignored that, and continued. "If you brother had just sent the thing back, everything would have been fine. But noooo, that wouldn't do. He tried to contact the girl. So now there was a problem: a meddling Brit with a document that could send us—some of us, in the corporate sense—to jail.

"Yes," said Reggie. "Too bad about the meddling."

"But why talk about the past?" said Krendall. "Let's talk about now. Right now, although I think they're being paranoid, someone over in Legal has some slight concerns about civil liability. So while no one here was involved in any way—especially me—we do have an interest. And we can make this worth your while. Pounds, even, if you insist."

Reggie stood. "I think not," he said. "I just came here to confirm the London contact. And I think I have that now."

He turned to go. He was at the door when Krendall called calmly to him.

"Let me phrase this another way, Mr. Heath."

Reggie paused.

"I understand you are a Registered Name in Lloyd's."

"I am," said Reggie.

"It's a very special thing, isn't? Wonderful the way it works; we would never do it that way here. When you are a Registered Name, you are personally liable—and I stress personally—for any shortfalls that might occur in the industry you cover. You invest a large amount of money into the fund just to join, of course, but if that gets tapped out—the insured can come after your personal assets. Correct?"

"Roughly."

Krendall shakes his head. "It just astonishes me. I mean, I know you get a great return—just as long as the world operates the way it's supposed to—but if something truly spectacular and out of the ordinary comes along, your personal fortune can be on the hook. Right?"

Reggie said nothing.

"It's the most amazing thing that you do it that way. Like I said, we would never open ourselves to something like that here. Corporate is corporate, and personal is personal, and if you're going to take a risk, you'd better do it in corporate." He paused, then: "You're heavily into the Blackthorne Syndicate, I'm told."

"Told by whom?" said Reggie. Krendall had his attention now.

"Doesn't matter who," said Krendall. "But before you start telling the authorities what you think you know, I suggest you ask about your holdings."

Krendall smiled in an irritatingly confident sort of way. "It's one thing to turn down a whole bunch of money when you have a stash of your own," he said. "Perhaps it's something else to lose what you already have. Take care, Mr. Heath, and have a really great day."

Krendall pressed a button on his desk, and Reggie heard the door lock unlatch.

"Oh, wait, just one more thing. Do you guys really eat a dessert called spotted Dick? Just curious."

Reggie hated to leave on such a dismissal—but no adequate response came to mind.

24

Reggie sat in the penthouse lounge of the Bonaventure, slowly turning a glass of gin and tonic.

The lounge was turning, too—it was known for that, locally. It rotated so that one could watch through the windows and see all aspects of the city, appearing, disappearing, and then coming round again.

Or one could have if the Santa Anas were still blowing. But they had stopped. Now the air was still, the gray haze was getting thicker and dirtier by the minute, and no matter where you were in the rotation, it was just more haze.

Reggie checked his watch impatiently. The Lloyd's agent was due any moment.

From Paradigm Pictures, Reggie had returned to his hotel room and phoned London, in an attempt to speak to the broker who headed his Name syndicate at Lloyd's.

Reggie's broker was unavailable owing to an impending hernia operation; that was the bad news.

The good news was that Lloyd's did have a representative in the area; Mr. John Wellingham was seeing to a major client in Los Angeles, and he could speak for the syndicate. Reggie's documents would be faxed there, and Wellingham would meet Reggie at the Bonaventure late that afternoon.

So Reggie waited.

He could have had someone verify the details over the phone, but he wanted to see this for himself.

He had always been so bloody careful about his investments. He hadn't been one of those so enamored by the prestige or profit of being a Name in Lloyd's that he would jump into just any syndicate. He'd chosen his carefully.

Surely Krendall was bluffing.

Reggie watched through the revolving window as the Hollywood sign slowly passed by.

Now the lift doors opened, and a man stepped out who Reggie guessed had to be the Lloyd's agent—no tan whatsoever on his face, wearing a traditionally tailored Gieves & Hawkes suit, a dark narrow tie, and a Turnbull & Asser shirt that looked as if it were finally getting a bit tight in the collar, having been in use, probably, for the past ten or fifteen years.

This had to be Wellingham.

The man paused and looked about—and then walked directly to Reggie's table and introduced himself.

"I understand you have some questions about your portfolio, Mr. Heath?"

"I do," said Reggie, motioning impatiently for Wellingham to sit down. The man was much too upbeat.

"I trust I'll be able to answer them for you," Wellingham said with an ingratiating smile. He opened his briefcase and took out a folder.

"Ah yes," he said, looking inside. "I believe I do have it all here."

"Enlighten me."

"Your returns so far this year are very slightly lower—less than a single percentage point in difference—from last year in this quarter. And I apologize for that, but I'm sure you realize that the proper way to view this is over the long term, and—"

"I'm not concerned about the rate of return."

"Oh. Well, that certainly is taking a very long-term view, then."

"I want you to confirm for me exactly where my allocations are placed."

"Where your allocations are placed?"

"Tell me," said Reggie, leaning forward on the table, "just exactly which risks have I bought into?"

"Oh. I had assumed you were quite familiar with that."

"And so had I also assumed, but let's just check it now, shall we?"

"Of course," said Wellingham, his professional cheeriness giving way to a professional officiousness reserved for trouble-some clients. He pulled another folder from the briefcase.

"We opened your account in 1991, with instructions from you not to accept any risks in certain specified areas, among them new medical devices, especially those related to cosmetic enhancements—well, you dodged the whole silicone implant bullet on that one, didn't you? Also, no pesticide manufactur-ing, no asbestos-related products—now that was a truly bril-liant exclusion, Mr. Heath, are you using some sort of crystal ball?"

"Was that rhetorical?"

"Yes, of course. But I must say, these were very wise exclu-sions on your part, as it would turn out. Some of those syndi-cates have had a rough go."

"Just tell me this: Am I in any way on the hook for damages connected with the blasted tube they're building here?"

Wellingham raised an eyebrow. "An underground? In this city? Really?"

"Yes," Reggie said impatiently. "Please have a look."

Wellingham looked. He studied the papers for a moment, shaking his head, then nodding, then shaking his head again.

"Well?"

"No," Wellingham said finally, looking up from the brief. "I don't see anything at all like that."

"What about the Blackthorne Syndicate?"

"Interesting you should ask. That's why you find me in Los Angeles at the moment; one of our larger corporate clients for Blackthorne called just yesterday, needing some very specific details on his company policy. Now, let's see . . . yes, you do have a substantial portion there. But it has no involvement with construction risks. It's quite conservative stuff, really, as you insisted. Only the safest of industries. Entertainment. I'm surprised you don't remember it. You signed into it just last week, after we responded to your initial inquiry."

"I made no inquiry."

"Yes, I believe you did," said Wellingham, consulting his notes. "Your Ms. Brinks phoned in the request. Our representative sent the details over, and you signed the forms the next day."

"Ms. Brinks made the inquiry."

"Well, yes. But of course, making the inquiry wasn't binding. No one could do that on your behalf. What was binding, of course, was your signature on this form. It is your signature, isn't it?"

Reggie knew it was. He remembered signing in the lift. He didn't really want to ask the next question, but there was no avoiding it.

"Do I cover Paradigm Pictures?" he asked.

"Now there's a coincidence; they are precisely the client I

was visiting. Ahh, let me see . . . yes, you do cover them. But only for the most egregious and unlikely of possible events. To invoke your responsibilities would take something along the order of maliciously negligent or criminal acts by their board of directors, or a member thereof, or a highly placed manager with power to . . ." Wellingham paused and sat back in his chair. "My word, those are precisely the sorts of acts their representative was asking about."

Reggie looked away for a moment, then drew a tight, shallow breath.

"At what level is my financial interest in this syndicate?"

"Well, of course, at the standard level for Names."

"By 'standard level,'" said Reggie, "you mean there is no limit on the amount for which I am liable?"

"Ahh . . . theoretically, yes."

"So I am liable for a bloody one hundred percent of my assets."

"If the damages are larger than the combined value of the syndicate's Names . . . well, yes. That is quite so. But after all, what is the likelihood of something like that? Oh, look—is that the Hollywood sign I see over there? Why, in a few moments, I think we will have come full circle."

25

It was Monday morning in London, and Reggie knew he must be coming down with something.

After the conversation with Wellingham, he had sat in the rotating lounge for several minutes, absorbing what the Lloyd's agent had said, and watching the setting Los Angeles sun flash repeatedly before his eyes.

Then he had roused himself and delivered the original map to Lieutenant Mendoza. He took a copy of them to Sanger—whom he found on the platform above the scorched tunnels at Lankershim. Sanger stood watching at nightfall as inspectors with flashlights and clipboards continued to crawl about the pit, and all the machines at his disposal sat idle. He accepted the map from Reggie without a word, and just looked away.

Then, finally, Reggie had returned to his hotel and collapsed into an exhausted sleep, barely waking in time the next morning to catch his flight to London.

As Reggie drove now from Heathrow to Baker Street, the morning air felt unusually chilly, tickling the back of his throat.

Or maybe it just seemed that way after the dry Los Angeles heat.

Reggie checked his watch as he drove. He had asked Wembley to meet him at Ms. Brinks's secretarial bay. If everything was on schedule, Ms. Brinks was just now arriving, and Wembley was already there, and not in a good mood.

Reggie himself was running late for the meeting, and this was by design. The best way to convince Wembley of anything was to let him discover it for himself.

When Reggie reached the lobby on Baker Street, he was almost thirty minutes late for the appointment.

With luck, that would be just enough.

But perhaps that would be a good thing.

As Reggie got in the lift, he was joined by a man in his fifties—smallish, in impeccably conservative attire—whom Reggie did not immediately recognize.

The doors closed, and then the smaller man spoke.

"Heath, isn't it?" he said, extending his hand.

"Yes," said Reggie.

"Alan Rafferty. Dorset National Internal Leasing Division. I believe we met once."

"Yes," said Reggie. "At the lease signing."

"Stop by for a chat, won't you? I'm on the top floor."

"Certainly," said Reggie. "I'll pop in first chance."

The lift doors had opened, and Reggie stepped out.

"Hear you're doing a bang-up job with the letters," said Rafferty.

Then the lift doors closed. Reggie wondered what Rafferty meant—but it would have to wait.

He walked quickly down the corridor and approached the secretarial bay outside Nigel's office.

He paused at Ms. Brinks's desk.

She wasn't there. The lamp was out; no flowers in the vase; even her porcelain cow pencil-holder was empty.

There was no light coming from Nigel's office, either, and the door was closed. But Reggie saw the blinds move. Someone inside had bumped the window.

And then someone bumped it again.

Reggie opened the door.

And there was Wembley.

"Take your feet off the desk, please," said Reggie. Wembley was not so casual as to naturally prop his legs on anyone's desk, and Reggie knew he had done so for effect.

"You might have made an effort to be on time, Heath," said Wembley. "Rather than count on me breaking her down without even trying."

"Seemed unnecessary," said Reggie. "If I find you frightening, you can imagine how poor Ms. Brinks must feel."

"Poor Ms. Brinks indeed. She must do her jog with hand weights, to have done that to Ocher with just one blow."

"I believe she does. Did she go quietly?"

"No, she made rather a scene. She wasn't pleased at all with your Mr. Ocher. He was getting between her and two hundred thousand pounds. Apparently the American entertainment executive offered her that much to find that document everyone was so worried about it. She was to verify that Nigel was sending the thing back as requested—or to pilfer it if he wasn't cooperating, which he wasn't. But Ocher caught her in the act of stealing it from your brother's files—good soldier, that Ocher."

"Yes," said Reggie.

"Your brother might have caught her, too, if he'd taken the time to look around. Apparently she was still here—hiding behind the tall file cabinet, with the documents in hand, when your brother came in and rushed out that morning. But then

Ocher came in right after, and did catch her—and she bashed him as soon as he turned his back to call it in. She delivered the documents to the American, who'd flown out for that purpose. I expect he wouldn't have paid so much if he'd known this wasn't the original."

"Very American approach," said Reggie. "Just buy your way out."

"She was none too happy with you, either, you know."

"Me?"

"She thought it was due time you made her an office manager."

"To manage who, herself? She was the only staff."

Wembley shrugged. "Employee morale, you know. I suppose you're lucky she didn't just go postal, as the Americans call it—interesting phrase in the circumstances—and bash you instead."

"My brother will appreciate the bronze back when you're done."

"Of course."

"I'll send you an address."

"Oh? Not coming back, then, is he?"

"I don't think soon."

"Hmm. Your clerk dead. Your brother in America. Your secretary in the nick. I expect you'll be needing some office help."

"I'll manage."

"Too bad about the Lloyd's thing."

"What?"

"Ms. Brinks said a few things on the way out. She said you could lose everything. She said you will no longer be able to pay your hires."

"I'll manage," Reggie said again. "Was there anything else? I have a plane to catch."

"The post appears to be piling up," said Wembley, getting up, finally, from the desk.

Reggie looked at the letters stacked in Nigel's in-basket. "Yes," he said.

Wembley stopped. He picked up a couple of letters off the top.

"Heath, I take it you know who these are addressed to?"

"Yes," said Reggie.

"Bloody hell," said Wembley.

"My sentiments exactly," said Reggie. "Now put them down, please."

26

The fire smoke rising from the lot in Century City might or might not have been part of a shoot, but Reggie could see the flames, and they were real, regardless of the cause.

He walked toward them.

Against the backdrop of the fire, Laura was in the embrace of a popular American action hero, whom Reggie recognized but did not consider to be competition. Laura did not take actors seriously.

The director called a break; Laura saw Reggie from the set, and she crossed toward him on the sidelines. She stopped several feet away and just appraised him for a moment.

"That's the look I want," said the director, passing by.

"Can we talk?" asked Reggie.

They walked away from the shooting set to a side street on the lot. They were alone.

"Did you identify your mysterious snitch?" said Laura.

"Ms. Brinks."

"Ahh. Of course."

"She's been building a pot of resentment for years. I should have seen it."

"Yes," said Laura. "But the gradual things are so hard to recognize."

"My apologies for supposing it was your friend," he said.

"You're still referring to him that way, as if he were especially significant."

"Is he?"

"Probably not in the way you suppose." Then Laura smiled slightly and added, "It isn't someone else, Reggie. It's just that it's been a long while on a roller coaster."

"If you were looking for a steadier ride," said Reggie, taking that in, "I don't know why you didn't choose Nigel at the time."

Laura looked surprised at that remark. "There are those moments when a woman wants to be nurtured, Reggie," she said, considering it, "and those moments when she wants to be . . . well, trifled with, I suppose. There's a certain freedom in that, and when one is very young, freedom can be more important than comfort." She paused. "You both presented yourselves to me with bright feathers flashing in the sun; I had to choose. And God help me, I chose you. I chose the trifler."

Reggie stepped toward her on that, but he paused when he heard what she said next.

"I suppose I've lived with that kind of insecurity long enough that I've gotten used to it," she said. "That's an odd thing, isn't it? But it might be true."

"It doesn't need to be—," began Reggie, but she stopped him.

"In any case—I've been offered another role. I mean, literally. After New York, I can have two months' work in the South

Seas. It will be a shameful amount of money, and for just a few shoots and languishing in the sun."

Laura paused. Reggie had the sense that she was waiting for a very specific response from him.

But he couldn't shake the feeling that at this moment she was waiting out of mere curiosity.

"I don't see how I can top that," he said.

She seemed annoyed by this, and she looked away for a moment. Then she said, "Have you ever noticed, Reggie—how your brother will take the chance even when he's sure he's got none?"

"I'm not sure what you mean."

"Think about it," she said. "Ring me when you've got a clue."

"How do they say it in this town? We'll do lunch?"

"A shame if just that," said Laura as she turned away, or, at least, it sounded like it. The director was calling places.

Laura walked back onto the set.

Reggie walked back to his taxi.

He paused as he opened the door, and he looked back. He could still see Laura on the set.

She put a hand to her face for a moment, and Reggie thought he heard her say something to the director about the damn bloody smoke.

A NEW LETTER AWAITS THE BROTHERS—
THIS TIME, FROM SOMEONE WITH A TIE TO
HOLMES'S ARCHENEMY PROFESSOR JAMES MORIARTY

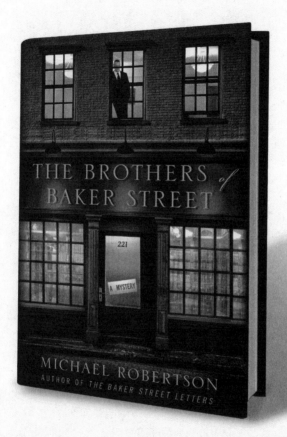

Reggie's life is in shambles—to earn it all back, he takes on a new client—a black cab driver accused of murdering two American tourists. But while Reggie is working on that case, the letters to Sherlock Holmes are piling up—including one from someone who claims to be the descendant of Professor James Moriarty.

MINOTAUR BOOKS

A THOMAS DUNNE BOOK